SHADOWS
IN THE CAVE

SHADOWS
IN THE
CAVE

Caleb Fox

A Tom Doherty Associates Book *New York*

SHADOWS IN THE CAVE

Copyright © 2010 by Winfred Blevins and Meredith Blevins

A Tor Book
Published by Tom Doherty Associates, LLC
175 Fifth Avenue
New York, NY 10010

www.tor-forge.com

Tor® is a registered trademark of Tom Doherty Associates, LLC.

Library of Congress Cataloging-in-Publication Data

Fox, Caleb.
    Shadows in the cave / Caleb Fox. — 1st ed.
        p. cm.
    "A Tom Doherty Associates book."
    Sequel to: Zadayi Red.
    ISBN 978-0-7653-1993-7
    1. Cherokee mythology—Fiction.   2. Fathers and sons—Fiction.
3. Gods—Fiction.   I. Title.
    PS3606.O89S53 2010
    813'.6—dc22

                                                        2009040695

First Edition: March 2010

Printed in the United States of America

0 9 8 7 6 5 4 3 2 1

To Meredith. You know.
Besides, I tell you with
my eyes every morning.

ACKNOWLEDGMENTS

Hundreds of hands and minds go into the making of a book, more than I could ever mention. For this book, I am especially grateful for the frequent consultations, abundant information, and educated judgment from my friend Vincent Wilcox, retired curator of Museum of the American Indian, Heye Foundation. The Honorable Clyde Hall of the Shoshone-Bannock Tribe has been my guide along the red road and cherished friend for a quarter century. My brainstorming partner, my source of inspiration, and my wellspring of joy every moment is my wife, Meredith. A deep bow of thanks to you all.

The demon that you can swallow gives you its power, and the greater life's pain, the greater life's reply.

—Joseph Campbell

1

A ku looked back and forth at his parents. He was bending a sapling to tie into a hoop, and he could feel it about to break. His twin sister looked away from their parents and held her breath. His grandmother, who seldom stopped talking to herself in low tones, kept mum. Aku never knew whether she was talking to her dead husband, to spirits only she saw, or to herself. Because his parents almost never argued, the silence rang like a gong.

"Go to the river and get water," their father snapped at the twins, "both of you."

Aku stopped to grab a gourd, so his sister beat him out the door. Outside, Salya announced, "I have to pee," and strode off.

That meant Aku had to meander to the creek alone, stick his hands in the cold water, and shiver as he walked back to his family's hut with a full gourd. He looked around the town where he'd been born and raised. Tusca was a circle of over a hundred huts opening in the direction of the rising sun, and dominated on the west side by the usual arbor serving as a council house. Tusca was the leading war village of the Galayi tribe, and his father was the Red Chief, the war leader. The tribe's two peace villages made the people what they were, those who walked in the wisdom of the Immortals.

The five war villages were their acknowledgment of the realities of life.

Salya came prancing back. She was wrapped in her hide robe, and shared it with Aku. After the all-night rain, the morning air was cool and moist. Both of them wanted to creep into their family's house, near the warm center fire. Still, they obeyed their father. The chief made sure his children listened to him.

Inside, Meli handed her husband a buffalo horn filled with warm sassafras tea. If she was going to gentle him, she needed to gentle herself first. She took her horn of tea and retreated to a corner of her own hut. Big sheaves of tobacco were stacked on deer hides against the walls. Her husband smoked this tobacco to call the spirits and ask for their help. Medicinal herbs hung from the ceiling, each with its distinctive smell. Now she went to them and drew the aroma of several into her chest—Indian pinkroot, wild plantain, spigelia, lobelia, and others.

She was an herbalist, expert in treating snakebite, worms, curing infection, easing bowel troubles, and many other maladies. She loved the hut's rich aroma from the sacred tobacco and all her herbs. Now she held three separate herbs and inhaled the scent of each deeply, thinking of its healing power. She took a sip of her tea and touched the dulled flowers of the pinkroot. Still she couldn't settle her mind.

She barely flicked her eyes toward her mother, who was back to murmuring to herself. Meli heard a whisper outside and guessed that the twins were near the door, eavesdropping.

She sat down beside her husband, and he started in again, more gently. "Now is the time to go." By habit Shonan spoke in tones of authority. Because Meli loved him, she would let him trot out his argument again. Early summer was a convenient time to travel. The rainy moon was past, the corn was planted but not yet up, and the time to gather seeds, berries, and nuts against winter's hunger was several moons away.

Outside, Salya rolled her eyes at hearing her father's whole thing again. As a child she'd been a natural imp. Now, at twelve, she was turning into a rebel.

Meli swigged her sassafras tea and held her tongue. The truth was, she didn't have enough reasons to counter her husband's, and he paid attention only to reasons. She had a bad feeling about this trip, which Shonan wouldn't accept as a reason. Still, she was glad Shonan was the way he was, big and strapping and sure of himself, all so much the opposite of her. She had to be clever to stand up to him, but she wouldn't have wanted less of a man. He mentioned two of his comrades who also wanted to take their families. A war chief would always think of security.

Finally, she lowered her voice and ventured her two objections, which even she only half-believed. "Salya's not strong yet," she said. The girl was getting over a coughing sickness. The trip to Adani's village, Equani, was a long walk over mountain ridges and through rivers.

Now Meli whispered. Outside the twins leaned closer to the door, but missed their mother's words.

"Besides, Crani needs us." She kept her back to her mother, though when three generations shared one hut, as the Galayi people usually did, there were no secrets.

"Salya is fine," said Shonan. "And the neighbors will see to your mother." He spoke loud enough for everyone to hear, inside and outside. Crani was as important as anyone to a man of the Galayi tribe, his wife's mother. When you married, you moved in with her family, not the other way around. Shonan had never been easy with the deference due his mother-in-law.

Meli thought about what to say. Her husband didn't

believe anyone was weak. He could do anything, and thought others didn't expect enough of themselves, even twelve-year-old girls or aged parents. His confidence was the reason the village warriors elected him their leader. It was also why he'd been able to intimidate the tribe's enemies thoroughly, so that a trip from one Galayi village to another was safe now, even for a small group. He had changed the lives of the people of all seven villages. After all, he was the grandson of Zeya, the hero who had saved the people by bringing them a new eagle-feather cape.

Meli loved him for all of that and much more. But he listened only to head reasons, and usually only to those in his own head. Sometimes Meli had feelings, or a kind of second sight, and couldn't express her perceptions in a way her husband would listen to. She got the talent for second sight from her mother's grandmother, Tsola.

Outside, Salya said, "Enough of this." She took Aku's hand, pulled him back into the hut, and immediately said, "I want to go see Adani."

"We all need to see him," said Shonan, "and he needs to see us."

Every spring the Galayi people planted corn and then made the journey to the peace village named Cheowa, the principal of all Galayi towns. Here they sang, drummed, and danced for a quarter moon, celebrating the return of the season when all things grow and asking for the blessings of Grandmother Sun on their crops. Some also made pilgrimages up the mountain to cure their bodies in the Healing Pond, outside the entrance to the Emerald Cave. That was where Meli's great-grandmother lived, Tsola, the Wounded Healer of the tribe and the prophetess empowered to wear the eagle-feather cape and see the future. The Dance of the

Planting Moon was one of the tribe's three big annual ceremonies.

This spring Adani—the word meant the grandfather who was your father's father—hadn't made the trip from his own town, well to the southwest. The family said he was too feeble. Shonan, Meli, the twins—all of them knew that meant Adani wouldn't survive another winter. If they were going to see him again before he went to the Darkening Land, this was the time.

"Shonan, I want to see Adani, too," Aku said. For some reason the boy never called his father "Father."

"You kids be quiet!" said Shonan. "Your mother and I are talking."

"Shonan," said Meli, "you promised Yim some help. Why don't you and Aku do that, and we can talk later?"

Shonan looked into his wife's eyes and understood. She was wise. He led his son out of the hut.

❖

"Red Chief," said Yim, "Aku. Just in time." Yim and his son Fuyl were already at work rebuilding a corner of their hut. They were opposites, the father squat and sturdy, the son handsome and slender.

The hut was made of walls of slender limbs plastered and held up by posts, and the roof thatched. One of Yim's corner posts tilted off-kilter, threatening to open his home to the weather. Yim wanted to go along to Equani to visit his own family, and he wanted his home snug while was gone.

Yim was the quietest man Aku had ever known, so he knew better than to chatter with his friend Fuyl.

Shonan and Aku shoved the post upright, lifting the corner of the roof, while Yim and Fuyl braced it with dirt and stones. Aku pushed, but he was reed-slender and did little good. His father's thick, powerful legs and strong back did the work. Aku wished he had the kind of strength his father respected men for.

All four stamped the dirt firm.

Yim nodded without a word to the big pile of muck a few feet away. It was a mix of dirt, straw, and animal dung. They would smear the goop onto the thin limbs, and when it dried, the plaster would keep the inside warm and dry.

While we're gone, thought Aku.

❖

As soon her husband's legs disappeared out the door flap, Meli felt Crani's light touch on her shoulder. Her mother gave Meli a toothless smile and handed her an awl and a piece of deer hide. Salya joined them. The three generations of women often sewed together in silence, communicating without words. Now they began to stitch moccasins. "I will be fine," Crani said. "And the children do need to see Adani again."

"Shonan, too," admitted Meli.

The women concentrated on punching the sharp awls through the tough hides and lashing them with thongs. Crani's fingers were discolored now, and puffed up like sausages, but she had the strength to push the awl needle through the hide.

Meli pondered her husband, always bluff, hearty, and practical. He might have a little regret about marrying into her family, with their gifts as shamans and shape-shifters. Regardless of his vigor and self-confidence, he had his needs, including the blessing of his father.

If ever she wished he was different, she needed no effort to remember why she wanted to spend her days with him. He was passionate about her.

Most Galayi men did not have passion for their wives.

They chose a mate as an antlered deer chose a doe, because their bodies felt the need, and then they looked for another doe. For a sits-beside-him woman they chose companionship rather than passion. Sometimes, yes, an adolescent's heart was taken with a girl. That generally went the way a creek tumbled swiftly through rapids. Youthful feelings soon eddied out.

In their case, though, Shonan was devoted to Meli and her only from the time they met at fourteen winters. He felt to her like a big boulder heated to the core by a thousand suns for a thousand days, warm all the way through, an unending source of comfort. If she lay close beside this man's love, she knew, it would last a lifetime. She and her children and grandchildren could make a family around it.

When he asked her to marry him, she made a request— that when her younger sisters were offered to him as wives, as they inevitably would be, he would decline. The radiance of his love was a gift to be treasured. She wanted it for herself and their children alone.

He said that those words made him love her more.

Meli looked toward the door flap. Shonan and Aku would be back eventually.

"I'm a lucky wife," she said to her mother.

"That's true. And you gave up some things."

Crani seldom said even that much. Meli had hidden part of herself for the sake of the marriage. She had only a little of her great-grandmother's gift of seeing the future, and none of the ability to travel from this ordinary land to the world of the spirits and back. She did have the other gift that ran in her family, but Shonan forbade her to use it.

Before the two were wed, Crani warned Meli gently. The spirits gave human beings abilities, some courage, some fleetness, some quickness of mind, and some a kind of magic. If you scorned your talent, the powers would scorn you.

Meli chose to put her marriage first. But all these years, protected by her sister, her mother, and other women, Meli had practiced her particular gift in secret.

Shonan lectured the children about such magic stuff. Like every Galayi, he knew that spirit powers lived in the Land Beyond the Sky Arch and sometimes roamed this world below. He knew they let some people see them and showed some what the Immortals knew. But he thought such powers were fading into the past. "No Immortal taught us how to dam creeks and flood our crops with water," he told them. "No Immortal taught us how to make a blow gun. No spirit showed us how to throw a spear with a handle." Learning to throw atlatls with levers, in fact, had changed the lives of the Galayi.

"The spirits brought us here to Mother Earth a long time ago," Shonan often said. Everyone knew the story of how crowding forced all the animals, including human beings, to come to Turtle Island. "More and more they are leaving us alone. A man has to make his own way, relying on his own brain and the strength of his own hands and legs."

He said these words especially to Aku. Meli was afraid that, of the twins, Aku was the one who inherited her special ability. Shonan with that kind of son—it was a bad combination.

"Do it for your family," said Crani.

Meli thought a moment—*It's silly to be afraid*—and put away her sewing things. When Shonan and Aku came back, they saw her packing the family's belongings in big rawhide containers.

Adani, Shonan, and Aku, the heart bond of grandfather, father, and son—that was what mattered most.

2

The walk to Adani's village took six days. The country was rugged—high mountains and swift rivers—but it was safe. Since Shonan had become war chief, few enemies ventured into Galayi territory anymore. Then on the fifth day's walk from their home, it happened.

Shonan thought at first he was dreaming. Then he went stiff in the elk hides. Meli's body was still soft, her breathing deep and slow. She hadn't heard anything. Shonan sat up, wide awake, and looked around. This campsite could be defended—that was why he chose it. Though the boulders were nearly invisible, shadows blacker than darkness, he knew where everything was, where everyone was.

Two more calls propelled him into soundless motion. Owl hoots in the forest, or rather the voices of enemies imitating owls. They wouldn't attack in the dark. A man who died in the forest at night might never find his way to the Darkening Land. First light would be when they'd strike. Shonan looked at the stars, judged how long he had, and knew that it was enough. His foes had started too early.

No thoughts: he reached for the war club, spear, and knife laid out next to his pallet. He crawled to where Yim slept and laid fingertips on the man's cheek. Decades as a warrior served Yim well. Instantly, without sound, he was wide awake and arming himself, Fuyl behind him.

A touch startled Shonan. It was old Feyano, ready to go. Age made no difference to Feyano. Shonan liked to travel with comrades of years' standing. Getting up, the war chief bumped Feyano's son. Shonan nodded at him. The more weapons the better.

Shonan looked around in darkness that was almost absolute. The moon was down, luckily. He made motions, and his companions understood. Swiftly and in absolute silence each one rousted out his family, got them hidden behind a big boulder, or on top of one, or squatted behind the huge downed log. They bunched up the empty bedding to fool the enemy. If they were lucky, the attackers would come creeping in, hoping to catch the Galayis in their beds. And then the hunters would become the prey.

Heads stuck up, bodies crouched, people crawled to their hiding places. No sounds. Even Galayi babies were trained to silence. When they cried, their mothers held their mouths shut and pinched their nostrils closed. After enough repetitions the child stopped crying. Basic safety.

Meli led the twins under a big overhang. They shivered with cold and would goose-bump until . . . until what? Meli shivered with uncertainty. Her husband defeated every enemy, but she felt it again now, not just the fear of human warfare, but that odd feeling she'd had since she and her husband talked about it the morning of their argument, that hint, that sense of something else wrong, something worse. If only she'd paid more attention to what her grandmother said and developed her second sight, the eye of the spirit.

To the devil with Shonan. At least she could take a look at the dangerous present, could use the other gift, the one she'd never given up, regardless of what he said—this was the time to defy him. The sky was beginning to shade from black to gray, so she would have to act fast.

She padded, one slow step and one gentle shift of weight at a time, to the back of the boulder. She crawled up toward Shonan, deliberately making a little noise. He turned around with brows furrowed, concentration broken.

She pointed to herself, made a flying motion with her arms, drew a big circle around her head, and pointed to her eyes.

Shonan shook his head vigorously—*No!* He understood well enough. But he didn't want a spy in the sky, not if it was magical. He didn't want women to do men's fighting. Most of all, he didn't want his wife at risk.

Meli backed away from him on all fours. When she felt grass beneath her feet, she raised to her full height and began. She was pleased to see how he fixed his eyes on her. Did he object to what she was doing? She didn't care.

The twins crept close to her and watched intently. She was glad of that. Salya had been the one who guarded her secret. Meli turned her attention to Aku. *Look,* she thought, *behold this power that also belongs to you.*

She shifted the shape of flesh to feather. Nose became beak. Feet turned into claws. Arms became wings. Blood and brain, eyes and instincts became an owl's. She raised her wings, took two quick steps, and launched into the air.

She loved flying. As a child she dreamed of nothing else, not that she could remember. Her first flight as an owl, when she was twelve, had been the most marvelous experience of her life. Her heart shot higher than her wings. She jiggle-jaggled in the air. She dived, just to feel the exhalation. She soared.

She turned her head back toward the twins and her husband and let out a single hoot. It was a pretend bit of playfulness to relieve her fear. Of tonight's owl hoots, only hers were genuine.

She turned her disc of face to business. Owls saw well in the dark, and in the half-dark around her now. She would spot their enemies, count the number, note their positions, and signal the news to her husband. Her gift would protect her family.

Aku watched from below. His mind didn't believe or disbelieve—it flamed in amazement. His mother an owl. The mother he loved, a hoot owl. By her will. By her power. Awe lifted him higher than her flight. Salya smiled and squeezed his hand.

Meli arced to the left and sailed a graceful line across a sky the color of dove feathers. When she got to a gully, she made three quick dips of her head.

Three enemies in that gully, no doubt creeping downward.

Aku looked at his father. Shonan was glaring at his airborne wife. He certainly didn't mind knowing where the attackers were, but . . .

Meli turned and flew straight down the trail the party had walked. Two dips—two enemies right on the trail.

She circled behind the boulder where Aku and Salya were hiding. One dip there.

In a flash the enemies ended the game. A voice barked a sputter of ugly, guttural words, like axe blows. A gang of voices erupted with the same sounds, a war cry. Men— Brown Leaves, Shonan saw—dashed into camp and swung weapons at empty bedding. Finding nothing, they looked at each other in mystification. Shonan decided they should die puzzled.

He sucked in oceans of air and howled them out in the Galayi war cry—*Woh-WHO-O-O-ey! Woh-WHO-O-O-ey!*

AI-AI-AI-AI! His comrades joined in at horrific volume. At the same time they bounded down from boulders, out from behind trees, and from rocky crevices. The enemy closest to Shonan was squatting next to the hides he and Meli had slept under. Shonan kicked him in the head so hard he heard the man's neck crack.

He whirled, his stone club cocked. A Brown Leaf was foolish enough to charge and thrust with the point of a spear. Shonan swept it aside with one hand, spun, and clubbed the man fiercely in the back of the head. He loved the clamor of battle.

Shonan's comrades shouted, roared, swung, slashed, stabbed—they roused themselves into an orgy of slaughter. He himself jumped across several empty beds, grabbed a Brown Leaf from behind, and slit his throat. Then he said to Yim, who was winding up with his own club, "Sorry to interfere, you get the feather." Galayi warriors were awarded eagle feathers for brave deeds like killing enemies.

Shonan, Yim, Fuyl, Feyano, and his son looked around. It was over.

Shonan corrected himself. It might be over. Six enemies, Meli's count had been right, but maybe she hadn't seen them all. His eyes found her in the skies.

Aku spied her, too. She slowly glided around the camp, still checking. Then she wingflapped her way upward, so that she could see further.

At that moment Aku noticed far above his owl mother the dark shape of a high-flier, wings fixed, body sailing imperiously above all. Though the light was barely enough, he saw it was a hawk. Yes, a red-tail hunting in the predawn light.

Horror strangled him. He tried to cry out loudly, but his voice clotted in his throat.

The hawk hurtled down. At the last instant, points jutted out below its belly. Talons and the hurling weight of the predator hit his mother at full ferocity. Aku thought maybe he heard a sound like a hiccough, or the first squeak of a hoot.

Several owl feathers spurted into the air.

The hawk winged off, feet clutching a dark lump.

Aku, Salya, and Shonan looked at each other, eyes glassy with agony. No words were possible.

Dead enemies were strewn around the camp, but Aku's eyes were fixed on the real enemy winging away. He sent Meli a thought—*Change back into a human being and you'll be too heavy for him.* But he knew the talons had pierced her heart in the first instant. The lump got smaller, to him a mother, to the hawk a meal.

Aku and Salya held each other and wept.

When that was over, the brother and sister walked out onto the hillside and spent endless time meandering around. At last they found three of their mother's feathers.

"Do you want these?" Aku asked Salya.

"No," she said, "but I ask you to wear them in your hair."

Aku gave her a wild look.

"Aku, say out loud why you must honor our mother." Her brother was kind and sensitive, but he often needed coaching.

"She died to save her children."

"And her husband," said Salya. "And because?"

He looked at her foolishly.

"Mother gave you the gift she had, the gift to change shape, like she did. Now you will wear these as a sign that you know she was an owl as well as a human being. To honor that."

She tied them into his long hair in back, tail feathers properly pointing down.

When they got back to the group, ready to go, Shonan stared at the feathers. Aku and Salya stared back.

Finally, their father said in a raspy voice, "We don't have a body to bury."

He meant that they could hold no proper ceremony for their mother, give her no food or water or even moccasins for her trip to the Darkening Land. They could do no proper mourning. She was gone without a farewell.

Shonan grabbed Aku roughly by the shoulders. "Remember what got her killed. It was that damn magic." The father glared at his son. Aku said nothing.

"I see you're wearing her feathers. Take them off."

Salya spoke first. "No."

"This is how I honor her," said Aku.

Shonan's face contorted. "I know, she used to say you have it, too, you could be a shape-shifter. I made her promise she wouldn't teach you. Look! Now you know where that so-called gift took her."

His father's eyes held Aku harder than his hands. "Promise me now. Promise you'll never do it."

Salya spoke with defiance in her voice. "Aku, promise me and our mother that you will do it."

Father and daughter glared at each other. At the same moment both of them repeated, "Promise."

Aku started to stammer something out, but he was tongue-tied. Finally, he said, "I am my mother's son."

3

Y ou have to eat by yourselves," Shonan told the twins.
"I won't be here."

"Even tonight?" Aku said. Salya wanted to say something
about "your great mission," but she knew it would sound
sarcastic.

Salya thrust Shonan a strip of dried meat and waved him
away. She and Aku never liked it when their father skipped
eating with them. Their mother dead six years, their grandparents gone, they were already a family of only three, the
smallest in the Tusca village.

"I'm sorry," said Shonan. "I have to be alone." To think,
to plan, to anticipate, to revel in his success.

In the last of the day's light Shonan the war chief slipped
invisibly from the village, made use of every bit of cover
to glide around through the woods, climbed high, and then
crept downhill. He padded one careful step at a time toward
the boulder. "As silently as a leaf falls," he always taught his
young men. Finally Kumu was within an easy toss. Shonan
underhanded a pebble and plinked him on the shoulder.

The young man whirled, spear cocked.

"Easy," said the Red Chief, both hands up and palms forward.

Kumu let out a burst of breath. "You caught me again."

"It's my job," said Shonan. "And you're dead."

They both laughed. Kumu was silly-looking because one of his two front teeth was turned a quarter sideways. The dark gap on each edge made the enamel look whiter. And he liked to joke with everyone. His name meant "clown." Though he had been on a vision quest and surely had been given a grown-up name, he preferred to stick with Clown.

Tonight, though, was serious business. As war leader, Shonan chose the village sentries for each day, assigned them their places, and taught them the double-faced skill, patience combined with alertness. At least once every quarter moon he sneaked up on one of them, as a lesson. He always fooled them, and they never caught him.

"Well," said Kumu, scrambling down the boulder to join Shonan, "at least this will be the last time you kill me in this village."

"It will," said Shonan. "Get along. Enjoy the evening." Whenever he caught a sentry like that, Shonan did the fellow the service of taking the rest of his watch.

The war chief settled down atop the boulder, leaning back against part of it, so he wouldn't make a human silhouette in the dark. He had mixed feelings about the watch from sundown to the middle of the night. Along with keeping his eyes out for enemies, he half-liked seeing the village settle down to sleep. On such a warm summer evening no plumes of smoke streamed from the tops of the dome-shaped huts of sticks and mud—the women cooked outside. The men ambled back from wherever they had been, making weapons or telling stories or hunting, and squatted down to share supper with their big families. A while after dark the women put out their fires and gathered the children inside. The dogs curled up against the outer walls. The men slipped in to join their wives on the hide pallets.

For Shonan the scene struck a poignant chord. His heart and his bed had been empty since his wife was killed six years ago. He would never stop missing Meli. Lying down at night would be hard for as long as he lived. Even the twins strummed sorrow in his chest. Aku probably was heir to the gift for shape-shifting, which had gotten Meli killed. And Salya had exactly her mother's form and movements. True, mother and daughter had opposite temperaments, Meli water and Salya fire, but Salya had the same way of twirling a finger in a hank of hair while she thought. She had her mother's long, delicate neck. The shape of Salya's shoulder blades and the gentle arc of her spine sometimes gave Shonan a pang.

He had no intention of marrying again. For him there was only Meli. When his body ached for touch, he let it ache.

His answer to all this sorrow was ready: tomorrow he would launch his mission.

He'd been dreaming of it from last spring's Planting Moon dance to the one just past. It was ambitious. It would accomplish something big for the Galayi tribe. It gave him a satisfaction that would mean something in the coming winters of age. He would be an important leader. He would probably be elected a member of the Great Council, Red Chief of the entire tribe. Until now he'd been a fighter. Time to become a governing elder.

It had been his idea—he might have used the word "vision." The Galayi were a growing tribe. When his grandfather Zeya was born, it was the opposite. The people had broken their covenant with the spirits, committing the sin of killing other members of the tribe. As a result the villages were dwindling.

Zeya rescued the tribe. He made a great journey to the Land Beyond the Sky Arch to set things right and get a new eagle-feather cape. When Tsola listened to the music of the cape and got its wisdom, the band came together in peace. Soon the Galayi filled the mountains and valleys of their native land, and expanded into the foothills.

Now everything was different. They needed more hunting grounds, more fertile plots to plant, more wombs to bear Galayi warriors-to-be and Galayi mothers-to-be. It was Shonan who had seen the logical next step—to expand from their native mountains to the eastern sea.

He went with armed men to visit the Amaso people at their village, a small cluster of huts on the coast. They were a weakening people. He proposed to them that the Galayi send fifty families to join them, more citizens than they already numbered. The fighting men of those Galayi families would offer protection against enemies. The newcomers would teach the sea-dwellers the Galayi language, which was the one spoken by the Immortals themselves. In turn the Amaso people would show the Galayi how to take food from the water-everywhere, where the supply was infinite. The Galayi would have easy access to the shells of the sea, which all tribes prized in trade. And the Galayi would gain more land for planting. A good bargain all around.

The Amaso people came from their village to the Planting Moon Ceremony just past, and the two tribes had made the agreement formal. Tomorrow Shonan would lead the colonizing party to the ocean. It would be the great achievement of his life.

Now he let his eyes go for a moment to a place where no enemy would ever be spotted, the rose-colored twilight lingering on the tops of the western mountains. Governor. Hero. That would feel good. He missed Meli.

In the middle of the night he eased through the door flap into his own home. Though he could see nothing, he found his pallet easily, empty as ever.

In the darkness he didn't see that his daughter's pallet was also empty.

❖

"Where the devil is she?"

Aku told his father, "Salya never came home last night."

Shonan looked Aku straight in the eyes. "You're calm. That means you know where she is." Otherwise he'd have sounded the alarm.

Aku started tying the owl feathers into his hair.

"What's going on?"

"She's mad at you for taking her away from her friends. And her suitors."

Shonan swallowed bile. He was doing something great for his people, but his own daughter didn't see that.

"Stop that and go find your sister," said Shonan.

Aku kept on tying the feathers. Every day of the last six winters he'd made this statement, in his mind a tribute to his dead mother. He didn't care if it irked Shonan.

Aku pulled the last knot tight, rose, and ducked out the door flap. Shonan followed him.

"First, we have to make sure she hasn't been kidnapped," said Shonan. He thought like a military man. Unmarried women didn't disappear for the night, not ever. Though they might well violate the custom of waiting for marriage before sex, they always came home. "Is she with Fuyl or Kumu?"

These two young men had been courting Salya for the last few months. Ever herself, Salya put off choosing between them, and put it off, and put it off, until . . .

Her father's great plan had fouled up her love life.

"She's just trying to annoy me," said Shonan.

He looked around Tusca village. "I'll organize some men to go out into the forest to look for her."

"What do you want me to do?" said Aku.

"Go from house to house and ask if anyone knows anything. Start with Fuyl's house, then Kumu's."

Aku smiled to himself. If he wanted to, he could tease the hell out of his father. He could suggest that he transform himself into an owl—assuming he really did have the ability—and wingflap over the woods, looking for Salya. If she was out there, or there were signs of her, he'd find her a lot faster than any search parties. But he didn't mention it. First of all, Shonan was already too roiled up to cope with. Second, Aku had never practiced shape-shifting. He didn't know if he could do it. He might turn himself into something with one wing and four fins.

Fuyl's family knew nothing, and the young man was right there, taking his morning tea. His name meant "beautiful," and his face, caught in the firelight, looked just that.

When Aku scratched on the door flap of the hut of Kumu's family, his father Zinna immediately cried out, "Kumu?" The man never had any idea how loudly he spoke. The mother intervened at half volume. A moment's conversation told Aku that Clown had been missing all night, and they were worried.

Aku said, "I think he's with Salya."

Aku inquired in half a dozen more huts—no one knew anything—before Shonan reappeared.

"Kumu didn't come home last night either," said Aku.

His father cursed. After pondering for a moment, he said, "Where did they go?"

Aku shrugged.

"Where would you go?"

Another shrug.

"We'll ask the other families."

"I'm sure they're together," said Aku.

"Assume nothing," said Shonan in a grim tone.

After an interminable time, Aku saw several men coming down the river trail.

"Father!"

At the front of the band came Salya, sashaying like an innocent. Kumu trod behind her with a half-sure step.

"I'm sorry to be late, Father," said Salya. Her sassy eyes said she wasn't sorry.

Shonan saw immediately that Kumu's grin would have stretched across a river, and his crooked tooth made him look wild with glee.

"Who fooled who?" Shonan said to the young sentry.

"For the first time," said Kumu.

Salya giggled. The clown had tricked her formidable father.

Shonan glared at her. She didn't want to go to the sea coast. Kumu's family wasn't going, nor Fuyl's, so she was losing both her suitors.

"Well," he said, "I guess you finally chose."

"I knew all along," she said. The play in her eyes was very much her mother, which touched his heart, but her audacity was infuriating.

"Shonan, Red Chief of the Tuscas"—Kumu's word "Tusca" had a tease in it—"I ask permission to marry your daughter."

"How dare you—" Shonan began.

"Who dares what?" That blast of sound was Kumu's father Zinna, walking up. More accurately, staggering toward them and keeping himself upright with his war club. Shonan stiffened. Zinna reeked of fermented corn liquor. The Galayi people drank it at ceremonies. Maybe Zinna had saved some back. Or maybe Kumu had, to make sure his father was out of the way. Shonan seethed.

"Now calm down, Red Chief," blared Zinna. This burly, middle-aged man had been through a score of battles with the war leader. He was a whirlwind with that club, and Shonan counted on him. He'd earned the right to talk familiarly, but not to have trouble staying on his feet, and not to go into a giggling fit.

When the fit subsided, Zinna roared on, "You wouldn't want us to think you're better'n us."

Shonan relaxed his face. Airs of superiority weren't accepted among the Galayi.

"It's true, now, my boy has filled your daughter with his juice. He's been wanting to for a long time. Just think how great that is—the first child born in your new village may be a full-blooded Galayi. And I think he's got something to say."

Kumu repeated, "Shonan, Red Chief of the Tuscas"—no tease this time, but the formality of a serious man—"I ask permission to marry your daughter."

Shonan glared at them all. It ran straight against his plans. Zinna's family wasn't supposed to go to the Amaso village. Salya wasn't supposed to go with a husband, a new member of Shonan's family. Shonan wanted to present her to the village as marriageable. He had planned to give her to the son of the Amaso chief, a symbol of the joining of the two peoples. What better gesture?

Besides, though he liked Kumu, who wanted a clown for a son-in-law?

He looked his daughter in the eye. "No."

"I say yes."

"And I say no."

"How do you think you'll find me? When you're ready to go, where will Kumu and I be?"

"You'll be tied to a drag." The Galayi moved their belongings tied to poles pulled along behind their dogs.

"And Kumu will be walking alongside. My husband stays with me."

Shonan considered. Salya had chosen the one time she could get away with saying something like that. He couldn't delay the great journey.

Still, the word "husband" was foolish. Marriage was an important ceremony. The man's family made substantial gifts to the woman's. The village joined in singing songs of blessing for the new couple. A pair who got married without the families' permission would be ostracized, would probably have to leave the village and beg another to take them in.

"Get out of my sight," said Shonan.

The war chief had bigger things on his mind than his daughter's boyfriend. He also didn't care what his son thought. They'd lost half a day. Since he still intended to get started today, there was work to do. He walked around Tusca organizing everything. He encouraged people. He reassured them. He painted pictures of Amaso as an adventure, a new life. The families who were going stopped moping and set to lashing their clothing, their kitchen utensils, their clothes onto the drags. Their spirits rose.

Shonan was achieving the great task the top chiefs had set for him. He gathered young men—families were picked which had lots of young men—and organized them into groups that would scout ahead and behind for enemies, and walk the ridges to the sides. He helped women lash the poles to their dogs. He helped young men gather river cane for blow guns, for such cane didn't grow near the sea. He was helpful, encouraging, firm—a good leader.

He looked at the sky. Not enough time before dusk, but he thought it was important to get moving.

When the great congregation was organized, his daughter was standing at the front, between his son and the man she intended to marry.

4

Shonan walked observant. The mountains of his native country were a wild country, steep, rugged, heavily wooded. His migrants followed a twisting creek eastward, toward the sea. At will, though, it snaked around to point northwest or southwest, turned by the shapes of the great ridges. The rhododendrons and mountain laurel were thick as fur on the hillsides, blocking vision. Scouts walked ahead and behind. Others flanked themselves to each side and followed trails that led to observation points. Spotting enemies in this country was almost impossible, but Shonan and his soldiers had driven all enemies back to distant borders. He might have felt safe if he did not remember, every day of his life, that his wife was taken from him in an enemy attack in country just like this.

His duty now was to pay attention, but his daughter was making it hard.

"What?!" she said. "What do you expect? You're making us leave everything we love. Our friends? Most of them we leave at home. Our uncles, aunts, and cousins?" She spread her arms toward the forested mountainsides. "Why don't I see them? Every place I played as a kid, every place I stooped to get water, every place we gathered onions or seeds—where is it all?"

Shonan walked silently. Aku said, "Lots of our relatives and friends are here with us." A third of the village, in fact.

"Yes, being tortured. Walk three quarter moons to a place we've never seen and don't give a damn about, and then stay there forever."

Only Shonan and a score of soldiers had visited Amaso.

"Salya," said her twin, "you have your lover." *Unlike me.* "You will have a husband, children, your family."

Shonan and Kumu glanced at each other, but neither even whispered.

Salya plunged on. Sometimes she was like the drummers at a ceremony—carried away with their own rhythms and then wilder and crazier until dancers fell on the ground laughing, unable to move to such a beat. And the drummers loved it. They banged on until . . . who knew what made them stop? Who knew what would make Salya stop?

Shonan strode along on one side of her, her clown lover and twin brother on the other side. None of them cared if she banged out her mood. It was half anger and half play, and would wear down. Shonan's mind was on the country. He couldn't see far to the rear, high ridges shutting out half the sky. He couldn't see past the forest to the next region they would reach, the piedmont, the foothills of the mountains. He knew it, though. It was a good country, full of oaks, chestnuts, silver maples, sweet gum and black gum, and lots of game. They would spend a night in a Galayi village in the piedmont, Equani, where three narrow streams joined into one broad river. Everyone had relatives there. It was the last time they would sleep inside for the three quarter moons of their walk.

"When we're happy where we are, you ask us to start all over in a village of strangers! Why? So you can be important? You want to be a hero like your grandfather?"

Shonan gave her a sharp glance. Smart remarks about the hero Zeya were out of order.

Salya stopped as if she was out of breath, but she always had enough breath to start a fire. She could have gone on about all their neighbors, the babbling and shouting of the children they knew, the roughhousing of the boys, and her girlfriends and their chance to smile slyly and gossip about boys their own age.

Shonan and Aku knew Salya's barbs well, and in their way they were friendly. She liked to stir the pot. But she didn't often run the wolf of her anger this long.

"Kumu," said Shonan, "would you run ahead and speak to Yim and make sure things are all right? Wait for us there."

It was a gesture accepting Kumu as part of the party. The clown trotted off.

"You done?" said Shonan to Salya, knowing he shouldn't ask.

Those words pricked her into rambling on. No one listened.

Aku, especially, had other things on his mind. His father had indicated that things would work out with Salya and Kumu.

Aku was silent because his mind was far away. He was the twin who was glad to go to Amaso. Salya thought he wanted to get away from a gang of teenage boys who didn't like him. They were preoccupied with being manly and muscular, devoted to the ball game and to weapons and learning to fight. They thought Aku was strange because he was built like willow limbs lashed together at the joints, and had about the same strength. Worse, there were the owl feathers in his hair—when people saw owls they thought of death. "You hate this village," Salya had said yesterday, "but I love it."

She was wrong about him. He was elated to move to the sea. He dreamed of smells, embraces, and caresses at the eastern village nestled against the great waters. Though he had told no one, his lover waited there.

❖

That night Shonan slipped out of camp and went hunting for fresh meat. On a long trip, carrying parched corn and ground seeds and dried flesh, people longed for fresh meat. Shonan would get a deer—he always did—and then say the prayers for forgiveness that kept the deer people from getting angry. When he brought it back, he would give most of the meat to other families, saving only a few scraps for his own. That was the way of a good leader.

"Poor Father," Salya said, "does he think he's fooling us?"

"He's a good man," said Kumu.

"The last six years have been hard," said Aku.

"Hard for him," said Salya, "and he makes it worse for himself."

"He's a good man," Kumu repeated.

Salya squeezed his hand.

Everyone had seen what Shonan had done since their mother died. He led war parties at every season, even when the snows should have kept every sensible man at home by his fire. He beat all their enemies back from the edges of Galayi territory. He claimed new hunting grounds for the Galayi. He won every battle and lost none. Sometimes, as soon as men of other tribes merely heard the Galayi war cry—*Woh-WHO-O-O-ey! Woh-WHO-O-O-ey! AI-AI-AI-AI!*—they ran for their lives.

Now he was going to be the war leader and surely the most influential man of Amaso, turned into a new Galayi village.

The Amaso people seemed likable enough, though they were touched by the spirit of beggars. They needed Shonan.

Which brought everyone to this day. Salya was playful with her lover and twin, but with her father it was different. Kumu stayed silly. And Aku . . . He liked walking alongside his father and learning things. He like ambling along with Salya and Kumu, because they were all laughter, as long as Shonan wasn't close by. But half the time he avoided his father and sister and dreamt his dreams. Shonan was carrying his ambitions, which crackled like lightning. Salya was preoccupied with the man she wanted.

In the half-blue, half-gray of the evening he watched Salya and Kumu shoulder their elk robes and head off into the twilight. Salya glanced back furtively.

Aku studied his father. He'd known all along. "You wanted to build a bridge by giving Salya to the chief's son," he said.

"Grandson," Shonan corrected.

Silence. "He's good-looking. I thought he was a catch, but . . ." Shonan looked in the direction of the lovers, who had disappeared.

"I have an idea," said Aku. He hesitated. "Let me be the bridge. My . . . She's the daughter of the seer, Oghi. Her name is Iona. She's . . ." He made a point of talking about things other than her smells and caresses, and emphasizing that she was the daughter of the second chief.

When Aku finished, Shonan said, "All right. You want her."

Aku stopped himself from saying "Wildly" and only said, "Yes."

"She wants you."

"Yes."

"I'm happy for the two of you. Let's think about it," said his father. "Meanwhile, we'll keep it to ourselves."

❖

In the middle of the third night the waters flooded camp. "Put it higher, in the crotch of the tree," someone yelled. People were trying to protect their dried food. When it got soaked, it was useless. The campground clattered with curses at the river. Clothes were wet, bedding was wet, firewood was wet—the rest of the night would be miserable, and a couple of days would be lost.

Shonan glanced up at the stars and saw that dawn wasn't far away. A little good luck to take the edge off a lot of bad luck. It happened sometimes. A hard rain would pound the mountains several ridges over, where you couldn't see the clouds. The river would rise in its narrow canyon, and the few wide camping spots would get flooded.

A hand touched his elbow. Salya. "I'm sorry, Father, it's my fault."

True enough. If Salya hadn't pulled her trick, if they'd started on time, they would be in a fine campground downstream, where the mountains opened into foothills, and the riverbed was wide enough to stand some flooding.

Shonan said to his daughter, "Just help take care of things."

❖

In the early morning light the men scrounged up enough tinder to get fires started. People stripped out of some clothes— nudity was no issue among the Galayi—and got into others. They ate the mushy corn which had once been parched, because it wouldn't last anyway. The grass seed they'd ground into flour they threw away. They laid their soggy meat strips across branches—in a couple of days the meat would dry out fine, unless it rained again.

Spirits were as soggy as the ground, emotions muddy. Salya made tea, and Shonan's little family gathered around to warm up from inside. Aku stuffed his belly with corn mush. Kumu munched idly, looking distracted, and then addressed Shonan.

"War Chief, let me run back to Tusca and get us food."

Salya caught her breath. Clearly, she hadn't been warned.

As he spoke, the early sun caught Kumu's twisted tooth and he looked silly. But Aku knew this clown was serious. He had watched Kumu play the ball game. He was a natural athlete. More important, he played like a demon of determination.

Shonan looked at the man who wanted to marry his daughter. Kumu had a good idea. The party could walk slowly, underfed, to the Equani village and ask for food. Any Galayi village would help out. But Shonan didn't want to come into Equani as a beggar. He wanted this journey to be a triumphal march, a procession led by a strong leader to benefit the nation. And Kumu wanted to be the hero of the moment.

"I can be up there tomorrow before the sun sets, back here by the end of the next day."

That was a stretch—the first half of the journey was uphill, and on the return trip he'd have a load. Still, Kumu might do it. "I will send six other young men along," said Shonan. "You will lead."

Kumu resisted smiling.

"But this is a trade."

Both Salya and Kumu frowned.

"You go home." That word struck Aku as odd. "Tell

people what happened. They'll see to it that you get food. Then, when the party returns, six men come back and you stay in Tusca."

"Father!" snapped Salya.

Shonan held up a placating hand.

"If you will grant me this favor, I will give permission for the two of you to be married at the Harvest Ceremony."

Salya still looked mad, but Kumu's eyes lit up. The three great annual ceremonies, the Planting Moon, the Harvest Dance, and Sun-Low Dance, those were the traditional occasions for weddings, with all the Galayi people there to celebrate.

Before Salya could object again, Shonan said, "Aku and I have a surprise for you."

Aku told his twin sister and Kumu about his lover, Iona, daughter of Oghi, seer of the Amaso people. "When I saw her the first time at the Planting Ceremony," Aku said, "we . . ." Salya put her hand on her brother's and squeezed it.

Shonan said to Salya, "I had intended to give you to the grandson of the chief. But I am willing, instead, to give Aku to Iona, the daughter of the seer."

Salya covered her face with her hands.

Shonan turned to his son. "But you can't be like these two, and spend every night together before the ceremony."

Aku grinned and nodded. He thought, *The afternoons will do fine.*

"Let's do it like this. We'll have two marriages, twin brother and twin sister, at the Harvest Ceremony, marrying two good partners, Kumu and Iona."

Salya peered at Kumu between her fingers.

Taking her gently by the shoulders, Kumu said, "Let's do this," he said.

Salya crumpled into his arms, which was daring in front

of her father. "I guess so. I'll miss you too much. I guess so." She broke into big sobs.

Kumu held her until she stopped crying.

Shonan said, "You're my daughter. I want you to be happy."

Kumu's eyes hinted of challenge. "War Chief, you mean this truly."

Shonan smiled broadly. "Yes."

Kumu lifted Salya's face to his own. "We'll join together with all the Galayi people singing for us."

Her eyes and her voice said, "Yes."

5

In her family hut at the Amaso village, beside the river that curved into the sea, Iona woke when the first hint of light lit the smoke hole. She sat up wildly, feeling like all the hairs would fly off her head and then her head would sail away from her neck. She groped inside for . . . what? The feeling of being herself? What she found was craziness. In a quarter moon, or perhaps a half, her lover would come to her. Until then, craziness.

She pulled on a doeskin dress, slipped out the door flap, walked up and down the ocean sands, searching for something, but she didn't know what. The village where she'd lived all her life, the sands stretching to the north, the cliffs rising to the south, the great water blasted with the light of the rising sun—she cared nothing for this familiar world. She felt like she couldn't breathe, like the air had been sucked off the planet.

Yes, she knew Aku was on the way. She knew he felt the same passion, bigger than anything she had ever thought people could feel, a force rough and crazy, like the white-frothed waves that racked the sea. She knew that when he came to Amaso, she would give him all they both wanted, they would fulfill the promise. But she felt empty *now*. She wanted something *now*.

She got an idea. She saw her father, Oghi, walking away from the hut they shared—only the two of them lived there. He was headed for the tide pools and soon would come back with his hands full of shells. He was the village seer, and he used shells as tools of divination to get glimpses of the future. She didn't understand how it worked. Now she ran after him.

Though she called him "father," he was no more than a dozen winters older than she, and he was the brother of her first father. Two winters ago her mother died giving birth, and last winter her father died of the coughing sickness. Oghi had never married and lived alone in a small hut about a hundred paces from the village. Though he declined to move into the village—the closeness made him uncomfortable—she moved in with him. Neither of them had any other family left.

"Father," she called, "what are the tides today?"

Oghi meant "sea turtle" in the Amaso language, and her father knew more about the ocean than anyone else in the tribe. In a vision he'd seen himself as an ocean-going turtle. Then he learned to shape-shift into the common turtle with the smooth red-brown back and the fine-tasting green fat. Though he was a monster as a turtle, the weight of two men, as a man Oghi was slight and looked boyish, except for his ancient eyes. His hair, oddly, had been red-brown from birth. He kept track of the weather and everything about the sea for the village.

"The tides will be big," he said. Sometimes the incoming tide pushed halfway to the village and deepened the separate fingers of the river until no one could walk across them, or the outgoing tide exposed long stretches of sand and rock, and sucked the river almost dry.

"Really big. Flood tide way upriver tonight. Go get some water. We'll cook these mussels."

"What about the ebb tide?"

"Biggest one in a moon tomorrow at midday. Bring back plenty of water. You'll want to stay away from the river in the morning."

Will I, now?

❖

At dawn she was ready. She shoved the log off the sand into the river, stood in the water naked, and held it back against the current. The outgoing tide shooshed around her thighs. If she didn't launch on the log, the force would take both dead tree and passenger, ready or not.

She looked at the sun, gathering itself on the eastern horizon far, far out to sea. She felt the river running out to . . . no one knew where, not even her father. It was against all wisdom, yes, it was. Of all Amaso people she, daughter of Oghi the sea turtle, knew that best. It was what she wanted— to be swept away by an immense force, to be *taken*.

She pushed the log and flopped onto it. The current seized both of them and for a moment snatched her breath away. Once, several years ago, she'd felt loss of control like this. She'd dared some other girls to climb an oak tree that stood on the edge of the high river bank, roots peeping out below. Taunting them, Iona crept further and further out on a thick limb. She was agile as a squirrel and as sure-footed. Her best friend scooted out onto the branch and—

It snapped off. The friend fell the height of two men to the flat ground and hollered like she'd been wounded mortally. Iona fell onto the sloping bank and tumbled head over heels all the way to the river sand. Her friends shrieked in fear. Iona stood up and roared like a bear, beating her chest. Not because she'd survived unhurt, but because of a feeling.

During the moment of the fall—the moment that lasted half a lifetime—she had felt absolutely out of control. She exulted in it.

Now—*Let it come!*—she lost control again. She rushed between the banks and swept out along the tidal flats. Where sweet river met salt ocean, the log spun in the churning sea. She whirled past the last point of land and into infinity. She felt triumphant. Let fate come—she wanted whatever it brought, she wanted an enormous blast of something, she wanted to throw away her daily wisp of a life, she wanted experience, real and strong. She wanted to feel alive *today*.

She saw it now—the ocean was as big as the sky. She wasn't a bird, she wasn't a fish. She couldn't swim in the one, couldn't breathe in the other. She was going wherever the tide took her, and it was running toward the end of the world, wherever that might be. She was possessed wholly—she lived in immensity. She wanted to feel owned, lips, arms, breasts, legs, crotch, the heart that drove the blood, the blood itself, the place her feelings lived—she wanted to be usurped and melded into this sea, this world, this power.

She stood up on the log, wobbly.

It rolled.

She plunged deep, took two strokes deeper, held herself underwater for a delicious moment, turned, and surged upward to the light. Her head popped into the air. At that moment the log banged her shoulder. She cried out in pain. With her other arm she grabbed a stud sticking out from the log and held on hard. She rotated her sore shoulder in several directions. It sort of worked. She clambered back onto the log and straddled it.

She looked around. Grandmother Sun was well up from her watery bed, bright and strong—a strong woman like Iona.

The girl looked straight up and saw an osprey cruising overhead, hunting. It wanted fish for its belly. It had the swiftness, strength, and skill to get what it wanted.

Iona wanted a belly full of life, and she would take what she wanted.

And she wanted to stay out here all day and play and ride the tide back.

❖

"It doesn't look like much to me," said Salya.

She and Aku looked from the top of a low hill across sand flats toward Amaso. The huts were few and shabby and the sands barren. The wide river split into a lot of stringy braids. She wasn't enticed by the horizon-to-horizon immensity of water to the east. It was just somewhere she would never be able to go. The sun, straight overhead, didn't make the place look better. She was dispirited, missing Kumu. The six men came back with the food, but, true to his agreement with her father, Kumu would wait in Tusca until he and Salya were married.

Aku said, "It'll be fine."

Salya humphed. She was back to wondering why her twin let their father push them to this odd place without protest. Didn't he love the mountains where they grew up? She liked the foothills full of canopied hardwood trees, too. She was bored by what her father called the coastal plains stretching eastward from the foothills, much too flat, and boasting none of the rich herds of game of the foothills. At least the traveling party had taken a lot of meat in the foothills.

"What do you think fish and crabs taste like?" she said. "I hear they're too salty."

"You'll like them as soon as you're here living with

Kumu," Shonan said. They hadn't heard him walking up. He gave Salya a hug. "And until then you can slow down on the grumping."

She sort of smiled.

The three walked close to the village, the traveling party trailing. The Amaso gathered. Aku's eyes searched for Iona.

"We better teach them to build stouter huts," Shonan said. The homes were just brush huts, spread fingers of flexible limbs bent into the shape of cupped hands, turned upside down and covered with hides.

"They say it's warmer here," Shonan said, "never snows. Maybe that's why the houses are flimsy."

Aku said, "Or maybe it's because the good hardwoods are eight or nine days walk back toward the mountains."

Salya nudged her brother and grinned. She liked talk like that.

They approached the council lodge at the west edge of the village. "I didn't want to tell you about this," said Shonan. It was a shabby thing, as though nothing important could happen there.

"I'm glad our weddings will be at the Cheowa village," said Salya.

Aku still couldn't spot Iona.

"There aren't enough people here," said Salya, "to make a real blessing."

"I told you I picked these people because they're weak and will be glad of the safety of becoming Galayis."

They'd heard it before.

An old man came walking toward them, bearing a pipe. A short, slight, boyish man walked next to him, Oghi the seer.

"Chalu," said Shonan, "the chief. They don't even have a war chief."

When the chief came close, he made the signs for wanting a ceremony.

Aku was proficient in the sign language. "Signal him yes," Shonan told his son.

Aku did, but his mind was on something else.

"As soon as we get our camp set up," said Shonan.

Aku signed it.

Chalu turned and made his doddering way to the council lodge.

Oghi signed to Aku, "She's waiting for you. You see the flat-topped rise over there?" He nodded toward it. "In the dunes right beyond it."

Aku started running.

"Where are you going?" called Salya.

Aku turned, ran backward, grinned big, waved, turned again, and sprinted toward Iona.

❖

Salya and her father set up their own camp and looked around. They had the same thought, but didn't share it. *We're at our new village, but we still don't have a home.* Salya shrugged. "Hey, we're used to it."

Oghi walked up. He and Shonan had a short, quiet conversation off to one side. Salya saw that several digital repetitions were necessary. Then each man nodded and smiled a lot.

People were gathering in the arbor used as a council lodge.

"Go find your brother and this Iona," said Shonan.

❖

Near the center fire stood Chalu, holding the sacred pipe, on one side of him Oghi and on the other Shonan.

Chalu picked up an ember from the fire with two twigs

and dropped it onto the sacred tobacco. Then he drew the smoke in deeply and offered it to the four directions. Shonan couldn't understand what he was saying. He watched carefully how Oghi handled the pipe and again couldn't understand. When his turn came, he performed the ceremony in the Galayi style. He thought, *We're not going to learn to be them. They're going to learn to be us.*

Chalu addressed the assembly, and Aku fingered his words to all the people of both groups. Shonan paid enough attention to see that it was a welcome to the visitors. "Except they're not visitors," said Chalu. "They will become our relatives, our children, even our fathers and mothers." Other words followed. Shonan gathered that it was a diplomatic speech.

When Chalu handed him the pipe, Shonan smoked ceremonially and repeated some of what the Amaso chief had said. "This is a great moment," he said. "Let us no longer call each other Galayi and Amaso. We are one people, and we will be known as the Amaso village of the Galayi tribe."

It was well done, a good acknowledgement for both groups.

Now Shonan raised his voice. "And I have something special to add."

Iona stood up beside Aku, who was still translating with his fingers.

"Proudly Oghi the seer and I announce to all the first blood joining between our two peoples. At the Harvest Ceremony in three moons my son Aku"—here Aku pointed to himself with both index fingers—"will be married to Oghi's daughter, Iona."

Aku held Iona's hand high in triumph.

6

Chalu said, "Let me show you a good place to build your houses."

Oghi signed the words, and Aku told them to his father.

The crowd was filtering out of the arbor, back to their huts or their temporary camp. Chalu asked Iona to stay behind while he led Shonan, Oghi, and Aku up a little hill to the north. He pivoted back, gestured to his people's circle of huts, and said, "You see there's no room in between."

There wasn't. The Amaso circle was tight, with the traditional opening to the east, and in this case to the sun rising from the sea. He turned to the north and spread his arms. "But this is a good spot."

Shonan was on guard.

The place Chalu had picked out for the Galayi circle was fine, a wide space of dirt mostly free of trees and brush. It was bigger than the Amaso circle. The only disadvantage was being further from the river, making a long walk to get water.

Aku was surprised when his father said, "No. No, no, no."

Chalu looked like his face had been slapped. "It's a beautiful place," he said. Oghi watched the war chief curiously.

"I want our peoples to live right together," Shonan said. "We should mingle constantly. I want your people to have a chance to learn the Galayi language fast. We shouldn't be two villages side by side. This is where we make a choice to be one people."

"But there's no room," said Chalu.

"We will make room." Shonan turned back to the Amaso circle. "I think we should build another circle just outside yours. The ground is not quite as even, but we'll make do. And in a couple of years it will all solve itself."

Chalu looked at Shonan, puzzled. "We'll teach you to build bigger houses out of posts and limbs."

Chalu said, "War Chief, we use these little huts because the weather is mild, and they're warm enough."

Oghi hesitated before he spoke. "Besides, sometimes a big storm comes in from the ocean and blows our homes to little pieces. If we build bigger ones, it will just be more work to rebuild them."

"We're going to have big families and lots of people," Shonan said. "We'll need bigger houses. If there are storms, we'll just build them stouter."

Aku thought of dragging posts from the stands of timber several miles back. He also thought of his father's will.

Apparently, Chalu felt that will, too. "All right," he said, "War Chief."

Aku thought, *My father will be principal chief soon.*

A hard time started for Shonan's group. He drove them to get their brush huts built in a couple of days. The huts were easy. What was hard was learning when the river was sweet and when it was salt, according to the tide. When people forgot to get water at the right time, they went thirsty.

But the days were sweet for Aku and Iona.

❖

Iona looked at Aku's sleeping face. He was worn out from loving her.

She put a hand on his cheek. She teased a wisp of his black hair with her little finger. She loved Aku. It was simple, it was powerful, but mostly it was enormous, bigger in every dimension than she'd ever imagined such a feeling could be.

Late this afternoon when they slipped to this sandy pocket behind a pine tree, which they did every chance they got, they lay down side by side and faced each other. Before touching her in the way that led to loving, he spoke to her from his heart. It was a small ritual they had, trading whatever words came tumbling out at that moment, even though they spoke different languages. She listened to his voice as she would to soft soughings of the wind, because she knew his intent without knowing what all his words meant. She felt like she understood the tones and shapes of his utterance.

It was awkward, and sometimes funny, not being able to talk to each other in a clear way. They could communicate about practical things through the sign language shared by the tribes. *Is this your sister or your aunt? The roasted chestnuts are over there. Why does the river look deeper today than it did yesterday?* With the sign language and gestures, they could fumble through speaking about such things. They also taught each other short phrases. Sometimes they tossed words into the air and shrugged. After being together for one moon and a few days, they understood sentences about half the time. All they really needed was to touch, and kiss, and embrace, and touch more intimately.

After he finished talking, their ritual was that she should take her turn speaking words he didn't understand. But she hadn't, not this time. The moon was rising out over the sea that she knew and he did not. She felt like the white globe was floating up into her throat, and no mere words could squeeze past it. She tried to say something and only felt a terrific pressure in her chest. She pulled him on top of her and urged him with her legs and her belly.

❖

Iona and Aku rolled onto their sides, still clasped together but spent. She looked at the last of the day's sunlight on his face, and the glow it gave his brown eyes.

Now was the time. She knew. She was content with the reality. At the Planting Moon Ceremony she and Aku had made love for the first time. Now they had been promised that they would be married during the Harvest Moon Ceremony. They hated to wait two more moons, but that was the tradition. Among the Galayi and Amaso peoples, marriages were agreed on as much by families as the couple, because it was not just a meshing of two people, but of generations of two families.

Now was the time to tell him. Still she hesitated. *Now.* "Aku, I have your child inside me."

There, simple words, singing in the air between them.

He looked deep into her eyes and saw play.

Quickly, he rolled her to his other side. The last of the sun was in her eyes. She was warmth, endless warmth. And honesty. And a hint of laughter.

He whooped. He whooped louder. The shushing of the waters, here where the river flowed into the sea, tossed his words away, made them no more than a gull's cry.

He bellowed. "I love you!"

And louder, longer, "I love you!"

In answer a bellow tapped at their ears.

At first they weren't sure what it was. They looked at

each other in question. They got up on their knees, crawled to the top of the low dune, and looked toward the village.

Oghi was running as fast as any man-turtle could run. He was also shouting something.

"What did he say?" asked Aku.

"Don't know! Shhh!"

This time they both heard it.

"She's gone!" Aku wasn't sure what he heard. He wasn't that confident in the Amaso language.

Oghi shouted again.

"She's gone," said Iona, her voice pulled tight by strain. She made the hand signs so Aku would be sure.

"Who's gone?"

"Your sister Salya."

"She's gone?"

"Get dressed!" whispered Iona fiercely.

Aku stood up to get his breechcloth on. About sundown a gust of rain had driven them tighter into their robes and each others' arms. Now a drop of cold water fell off the tip of a pine needle onto the part in his hair, right on the top center. He rubbed the cold spot with a stiff finger.

"Your shirt!" said Iona.

She was standing, smoothing her skirt down. Their clothes were made of deer hide.

Aku pulled the shirt over his head and double-checked his owl feathers to make sure they were tight. The Amaso people thought the feathers were daft. Owls were thought to be witches, and their night cries made people hurry inside. But the memory of his mother was enough for Aku.

Sea turtle man pulled up beside them and heaved out a half comprehensible mix of words and big breaths at Aku. Iona signed it.

"Your sister has disappeared!"

Oghi got his breath and spoke slowly so that Aku would understand. He was an odd young man, because his nick-name was Old Man.

"What do you know about it?" Aku asked.

Oghi looked at the sand and fidgeted on his feet. These two had circled each other warily for a reason—Oghi sensed the seer power in Aku, and Aku knew it. "You better hear what the moon women say first."

Iona signed those words.

"Let's go," Aku said.

Aku and Iona ran, outdistancing Oghi, who was short-legged and out of breath. Like raindrops splashing off a boul-der, the awful news couldn't get into Aku's head. *My sister. My twin. Taken? Dead?*

They sprinted into the circle of huts and across the village green. A new friend of Salya's staggered around making a sound somewhere between moaning and singing. Aku and Iona dashed right by her and out of the circle of houses to the isolated brush hut where women on their moon slept. A ring of men stood at a distance from three moon women, talking.

"She went out to pee just after the sun went down," one of the Galayi women told Chalu, signing to be sure to get the facts across.

"She said she'd be right back," said one of the other moon women. "We were about to eat."

"But she didn't come back."

"We went and checked."

"She's nowhere."

Shonan called out, "All right, everyone, have any of you seen Salya since sunset?" Anger licked his tongue.

No one answered.

"I'll ask all around the village," said Iona. Her tone was despair.

"Let's go check the signs," Shonan said to Aku. They both took burning chunks of wood from the cooking fire.

The women's pee place was beyond some scrub and behind a dune, a spot washed by the tides. One look and Shonan said, "Damn, damn, damn."

They barely needed the torches to read the signs, which were obvious in the light of the moon. Someone had been dragged away, heel tracks lining the sand.

"Why didn't she yell?" said Shonan.

Aku had never felt so dumb making words in his life. "Maybe they hit her over the head."

"Or maybe the sound of the damn surf was louder than her cries." His father missed the hills and mountains, disliked the roaring ocean.

The lines of the dragging heels and the footprints led to a place littered with moccasin tracks. In the middle of all the tracks was a smooth, back-shaped depression in the sand. Aku's mind felt as disheveled as the tossed grains.

"They laid her down here," Shonan said, "lifted her up again, and walked that way." The two followed the moccasin tracks straight toward the trail away from the town. Anyone could read the distinctive moccasin stitch of the Brown Leaf people, who lived on the far side of a big bay to the north, at one destination of the trail.

"I can't tell if some of these tracks are deeper than others," Shonan said, "but I think they carried her on a litter."

His voice was half growl. A scar flashed away from the corner of his left eye, the mark of a spear point. When his eyes became embers of anger, the scar turned white and Aku got nervous.

Shonan said, "Let's go get her."

Aku tried to order his thoughts. "Too tricky at night."

"Which is why they picked it," said Shonan. "All right, at dawn." He had always wanted to teach Aku the path of the warrior, and often teased his lanky son about learning. Aku didn't refuse, but he avoided.

Aku nodded his head yes. He had other thoughts he couldn't sort out.

Iona appeared at the top of the sand hill. "This is where it happened?"

"Right back there," said Shonan.

They all stared down at the print of Salya's back.

Two words raged in Shonan's mind. *My daughter.*

My twin, thought Aku.

"They're going to kill her," said Shonan.

Aku hesitated for a long moment. His twin, a part of himself. Though their faces were not the same, their mother always said they had the same eyes. "It's uncanny."

Finally, Aku said, "They could have killed her right here. They want something else."

"We're going after her."

Iona said, "Let's go to the council lodge." The three walked back toward the village, the younger two hurrying to keep up with the Red Chief. Shonan said, "These Amasos are supposed to be one people with us, but they're holding out."

As they walked, Aku's mind leapt back to when he stood at the edge of the river tying his breechcloth on. From one pine needle a single raindrop had fallen, and pinged him. Now he felt like it seeped through his skull and trickled down his veins to his heart.

7

Red Chief Shonan, Amaso chief Chalu, and the seer Oghi sat at the center of the run-down council house and smoked the pipe. Until now, the Amaso had never had a red chief for war, as Galayi towns did. Aku wondered how they felt about this change, and about listening to a governor who was still in truth an outsider. Aku watched the sea turtle man checking the rising smoke for omens.

Aku and Iona stood next to Chalu to sign to both peoples. "This happened three years ago," said Chalu.

"The Brown Leaf people have stolen your women before?" Shonan's thick eyebrows bristled.

Chalu stared into space. Beside him the sea turtle man drew his head almost down to his knees.

"And two years before that," said Chalu.

Now the white scar blazed against Shonan's red skin. "How long has this been going on?"

Aku wanted to apologize to Iona for his father, but he said nothing.

"Three times altogether," said the sea turtle man.

"So that's why you wanted to join villages with us."

People stirred.

Pride flickered in Chalu's eyes. "We have something to give in return."

Shonan's comment was hypocritical. Everyone knew the bargain was fair, and protection was Shonan's job.

"Always in midsummer?" said Shonan. Meaning, *This moon, when you suggested we arrive?*

"Yes."

Shonan said something under his breath. To Aku it looked like, "Bastards." He didn't sign it.

"You never saw any of the women again?"

"No."

Iona looked into Aku's eyes. She wanted to slip her arm around Aku's waist, but resisted. He took a deep breath and felt his mind get less jangly. For a moment he took her hand in his.

Shonan turned to Oghi.

"What do you think?"

Oghi tore grasses out of the ground, bunched them up, and dropped them. Then he glanced slyly at Shonan. "There are old stories. The mountain peoples used to raid their neighbors and steal one unmarried woman every summer. Stories said . . . they sacrificed the woman to the Uktena."

Every Galayi and every Amaso man, woman, and child knew about the Uktena, though few had seen him and none lived to tell about it. This creature was a horned dragon with the girth of a tree trunk. Its fish scales, spotted with great daubs of color, were thick as slate. Its one eye was a blazing diamond, which blinded anyone who dared to attack the monster.

The tales came down from long ago. All the people of the western mountains told similar stories. The Uktena had many names, bedded down in many places, haunted many mountain passes, plagued many villages. It was said that the Uktena, or Uktenas, lived in caves in the mountains and left the nearby tribes alone on one condition—that the tribes bring human sacrifices.

"Those are children's stories," said Shonan. "My people live in the mountains, and we have seen no sign of any dragon."

Oghi shrugged. "The stories died out before the memories of the grandfathers of the oldest men but . . ." Suddenly, he looked directly into Aku's eyes. "Maybe the Uktena has come back. Maybe he lives by the sea now, not in the mountains."

"You'd be losing an unmarried woman every year," said Shonan.

Aku squeezed Iona's hand.

Oghi seemed to draw his head back into his body. "Maybe the Brown Leaf people steal women each year from different neighbors."

"If it is the Uktena, what will happen?"

Oghi shuffled his feet in the sand. Aku noticed for the first time how odd they were, short and wide, with big toenails. "They won't kill her right away," he said. "It's a ceremony, it takes a couple of days. Then the Uktena doesn't eat her body—he sucks out her spirit. He uses her life force to make himself stronger."

"Her body goes to the Darkening Land?"

"Without a spirit."

Shonan turned to Chalu and let his disgust curl his words. "This is childish talk."

The Amaso chief glared back. He had thoughts, but he didn't speak them.

"A chief who is a true ally would warn us before inviting us to live here."

Chalu had nothing to say. Aku knew he held himself back out of sympathy for Shonan's grief.

"What do you think we should do?"

Chalu pieced words out. "You can send a runner to your nearest village and get enough men to go against the Brown Leaves."

"My daughter would be dead before they started."

No one had anything to say.

Shonan turned back to Aku. "My son and I will leave at first light. We need to know where to go."

"Come eat at my hut," Oghi said, "and our men will tell you what we know."

Aku saw a flicker in his eyes, the eyes that were old and young at once, serious and funny at once. He wondered what this meant.

Outside the council lodge Iona wrapped both her arms around Aku and looked at him with love. "I'll miss you to-morrow evening." At every sunset they slipped away and took pleasure in each others' bodies.

"Every evening," he mumbled.

"I better kiss you good-bye now."

❖

Oghi gave everyone roasted chestnuts and tea. His uncles and cousins had to crowd into the small hut.

Aku nibbled at his chestnuts. Shonan waited hardly longer than he could have held his breath, while the Amaso men spoke of where the Brown Leaf village was, how many people the Brown Leaves had, and how many fighters. At the first pause Shonan asked in the Galayi language, "What way will they go?"

Feeling embarrassed for his father, who resisted learning the Amaso tongue, Aku signed the words haltingly. Though Oghi understood some Galayi, a host had a right to use his own language.

Taking his time, Oghi got a hairless deer hide from a pile at the back of the round hut and took a half-burnt stick from the fire. He sketched a very irregular first line and said, signing his own words, "This is the shoreline." He drew lines to show two streams flowing to the sea. "Two wide rivers. There's a trail here that warriors use sometimes," he said. "It's shorter, but you'd get lost. There are big stretches to swim. For sure they won't take a captive on a litter this way."

He kept drawing until he made a third stream. "This is Big River," he said. "Along it a path runs back inland to the main trail."

Now he changed burned sticks and made a thick, weaving line that led from the Amaso village away from the coastline. He sketched in bumps to show where it went through the hills, long lines to show creeks. "This is the main trail. The streams are not too deep or wide," he said. "Women and children can use this trail."

He brought the main trail to Big River. "The two trails meet here."

Then he extended the thick line much further north and drew a huge inlet protected by an arc of land. "Brown Leaf Bay," said.

He fishhooked the trail line toward the sea and drew a circle. "The Brown Leaf village, near the shore." He ran his finger along the thick line. "This trail is easy to see, easy to walk. They'll take it."

"You're sure they won't worry about us following them?"

Oghi shrugged. "They've never been afraid of us before."

"Can we catch them?" asked Shonan.

"No doubt," said the sea turtle man. "Carrying a litter, it's more than a quarter moon's journey. We can run."

"Damn right," said Shonan.

They all studied the map, thinking separate thoughts.

"We have two days after they get back?" said Aku.

"The stories say the sacrifice is made like that, yes, in a ceremonial way."

"That ceremony will never start," said Shonan.

His eyes on Aku's felt like a strong grip. *How?* Aku wondered. How, with two men against a dozen or a score? Shonan the Red Chief was sure of everything. Aku was sure of nothing.

Oghi said, "Why not get ahead of them? Use the coastal route and beat them to the junction of the two trails?"

They looked at him. His eyes were jumping and hallooing now.

"I like surprises," said the sea turtle man.

"You said we'd get lost," said Shonan.

"Not if you have a very good guide. Such as me."

8

Salya was gone, gone, gone. Shonan let that single word be the mark of his rhythm as he loped along the sand behind Oghi. As far as he was concerned, the sea turtle man didn't run hard enough. On the other hand, Oghi was small, and at least he never stopped. He trotted step after step over the dunes, through the marshes, and across the creeks. He waded into the river without even slowing down. Their dog Tagu, with elk blankets and deer hides wrapped around dried meat, stayed at Oghi's heels, as if following a new master. At the rear Aku kept up, relieved that they didn't have to go faster.

When they came to the first creek, the turtle and dog swam the same way, head up and legs waggling below. The father and son swam like most Galayi men, on their sides. Oghi got to the other bank first.

The sea turtle man called a food break, brooking no disagreement. While the warriors munched their deer meat, he waded into the tide pools, popped shelled creatures off the rocks, and scooped out the meat. When he sat back down with them, he smiled and said, "Mother sea."

When they came to a big river marked on their map, they faced a high palisade on the far bank. "We can't land over there," Oghi pointed out.

"Let's swim upstream," said Shonan. He was leery of the sea.

"Can't," said Oghi. "The tide's going out. Formidable current." Aku was tickled by the formal way the sea turtle man talked. "The only way is the ocean," Oghi said cheerfully.

Without waiting for a response, Oghi plunged into the salt water and led them, swimming, parallel to the shore. Gradually, the palisade became a hill, a slope, then just some dunes. The sea was calm and glassy. The sea turtle angled toward the beach.

Just then he rocked in the water and called out, "Riptide!" Bizarrely, he started sailing out to sea.

In a moment Tagu was bobbing along behind Oghi, Shonan behind both of them, and Aku last. It was an odd sensation. Aku felt like he was flying above the sea floor, riding some sort of water-air to a destination.

What the hell was happening? He turned and swam as hard as he could toward the shore.

"Keep . . . ! Don't . . . . !" Oghi yelled, but his words were garbled.

Aku yelled, "What?!"

"*Swim,*" yelled Shonan. He waited for a moment while the sea sloshed over his head. "Don't . . ."

Aku stopped swimming for a moment. He felt as if he were sailing as fast as an eagle that launches off a rocky point and soars on firm wings. Except that he was soaring out to sea, and to death.

He aimed straight toward the shore and kicked hard again. After a furious effort, he stopped, turned, and saw that he was much further from the beach than anyone else, and not as far past the mouth of the river. Tagu issued one ferocious bark. Aku felt himself flying backward into the infinite ocean.

He looked down. The water was clear, and probably only

two or three times as deep as Aku was tall. He thought for a moment about stretching out on the bottom and not being able to breathe. He felt panicky. The more he looked, the more panicky he felt. And he could see that, all along, he was floating further and further into the ocean that went on forever.

In a flurry he set himself for one more charge toward the land. He kicked his legs and flailed his arms and kicked his legs and flailed his arms. Then he took a careful look down and saw that he was still sailing out to sea, as a cloud sails the skies at the mercy of the winds.

He stopped. He looked back toward the familiar land, where a person could walk, talk, find something to eat, and never come to a single place completely without air. The land was getting farther and farther away, and the palisade looked lower, much lower, and vague. He realized that he could float so far out onto the everywhere-is-water that he wouldn't be able to see the land. As the sky was everything above, the water would be everything below.

He looked down and saw the no-air-at-the-bottom place drifting along beneath him. He let himself imagine, just for a moment, how much of the no-air place there must be. Some people thought the ocean went all the way around the Earth, to the far side of the rolling country that was on the other side of the mountains where the Galayi people made their home. Some people said that, if you could walk on water, it would be a hundred days' walk all the way around to that rolling country. Other people said a thousand days. And probably the everywhere-water was as big up and down as it was across. The no-air part of Earth might be as big as Turtle Island herself was. Or bigger. At the very beginning, when all the plants and animals, including human beings, were ready to come down and live on Earth, the entire planet was water. Then Water Beetle started diving down and bringing up dirt, making places to walk and build houses and live. No one knew how much of the everywhere-water Water Beetle had covered with dirt.

Aku decided he couldn't swim anymore. He was far too tired in his muscles and he felt woozy in his head, too. He would sail like a cloud. Why not? He didn't have any choice, and it felt good. He would wag his legs gently and sail and sail and sail until the water was as big as the sky and then . . . He guessed he would slide down and lie on the bottom.

❖

"We've got to do something!" Shonan said.

"There's nothing to do," said Oghi, looking out to sea. He couldn't see Aku. "He's in the riptide. He can't swim straight against it, but he kept trying, and going the wrong way."

Both men were mixing in words of the Galayi and Amaso languages, hoping the other would figure it out.

"Where will he end up?"

Oghi shrugged. "Nobody who swam against one ever came back. We learned to swim across them."

"I'm going to do something."

Oghi looked at Shonan with questions in his young-old eyes.

"He's my son," Shonan said.

Tagu let out three soft barks.

Shonan could see that Oghi was pondering something, but he had no idea what.

"We could ride the tide out, just like he did."

Oghi stared into space.

"We could take something . . ." Shonan looked around and saw various pieces of flotsam, but they were all spindly.

He wasn't sure they'd hold him and Aku. Then he spotted a big piece of driftwood no more than twenty steps into the water. It was taller than a human being and thicker than a man's thigh.

"How far out does the riptide go?"

Oghi shrugged.

"I'm taking that log and going after my boy."

The sea turtle man let a beat go by, gave a truly odd smile, and said, "Me, too." He broke into a grin. "Tie Tagu to a tree, will you?" No question they couldn't make the dog stay, not when his master was out there.

Shonan waded into the water, climbed onto the log, and straddled it. He looked back and in amazement beheld . . .

The sea turtle man's fingers and toes turned to claws. His arms and legs were rough, bumpy, like a turtle's.

Oghi wore a scrunchy look of deepest concentration on his face. He fell onto all fours. His back metamorphosed into a carapace. His neck developed a wattle. His nose and mouth joined into a beak. His body doubled in size.

The turtle four-footed his way to the edge of the water. Only his young-old eyes stayed the same. Shonan would have sworn that he grinned, except that a turtle couldn't do that.

"A small person," said the sea turtle man, "but a giant turtle."

Oghi pointed. "Right over there's where the riptide starts." He launched into the water, swam with extraordinary grace to the log, and started pushing it toward the rip.

Shonan joined in. He didn't intend to say anything, certainly not ask for anything, not for a long time. The two of them got behind one end of the log and chugged it into the rip, and away they went.

❖

The sea was cool, and he was becoming cool as the sea. Aku waited. He daydreamed. He scudded pictures of Iona through his mind, and not only pictures but smells, tastes, the touch of her warm flesh, the music of her moans. Slowly, slowly, he scissored his legs, barely moving. All they had left was the strength of leaf stems.

Ocean slurped up his nose, and his legs wiggled faster. He sneezed it out. Nasty stuff.

He glanced up at the sun. Fine old Grandmother Sun, he liked her. He noodled his legs around. Yes, fine old Grandmother Sun. He looked at her through eyelids nearly shut, making the bright star into a bright haze. He wondered if she'd look like that from the bottom of the sloshing sea.

He looked down. He could still see the bottom, though it seemed further away. He supposed that if he lay on the bottom and looked up at Grandmother Sun, he would see a sheet of light, a glaze on the surface of the water, and Grandmother Sun's weightless beauty, lighter even than a breath of breeze on a hot summer's night.

It wouldn't be hot on the bottom, would be cold. Here he was cool, too cool. Bodies cool when people die. Down there cold, all the way cold. Wouldn't be a breeze, or any air at all at all at all. Maybe he would suck air in and slide gracefully to the bottom, the way a yellow leaf slides off the branch of an oak tree and floats to the frosty grass. And there on the bottom he would shudder with cold, shudder and shudder. For a little while he would hold onto that marvelous air and look up at Grandmother Sun's glaze of light and hold on some more and hold on, until the air evaporated, all of it, evaporated, and then he would close his eyes.

Now he let his eyes shut and turned his head up to the sun and bathed his face in her gift of light. He nudged his mind toward Iona again. He bid her bright eyes come to his attention, then the feel of her lips, the softness of her breasts.

Grandmother Sun, though, felt more real. He luxuriated in her. Sun warm, sea cold.

A wave whacked its way up his nose. He yelled and spat and shook his head. Ugly stuff, that ocean water, ugly stuff up the nose where air belonged.

Wide awake now, he noticed that he wasn't sailing any longer. He was bobbing up and down in one place, wagging his legs slowly, and he wasn't cloud-flying out into the everywhere-water anymore.

So this was the spot. He inspected the bottom, as well as he could see it. It looked no more distinguished than any other, and no less, for a quiet death.

His mind drifted down there.

Just then four pelicans caught his attention. They flew solemnly, gray-brown birds with jaw pouches for carrying food. Iona had pointed them out to Aku. He thought they were funny. Even now they made him smile.

And they gave him thoughts.

I promised my sister I would. My lost sister.

My mother wanted me to.

My father loves me. He wants me to live.

I don't know . . .

My mother would want me to. My mother would want me to. Look right over there.

Over there was a piece of flotsam, not big enough at all to hold a human being, but . . .

He took a couple of strokes and grabbed it. It made floating a little easier.

He held his hands in front of his face and imagined the fingernails as claws. They began to change.

Stunned, he held his feet up one at a time and pictured

them as talons. Awkwardly, with the flesh still clinging, they turned into an owl's feet.

Focusing fiercely, he made his arms into wings. He feathered his body. He altered his head, nose, and mouth.

Now he stepped onto the flotsam, and it bore his weight. He turned his head backward on its axis and looked at the land. The shore was an impossible distance to swim but an easy flight.

He jumped into the air and flapped. He teetered, swooped down, and got dunked. He climbed back onto the flotsam and launched again. The second time he achieved . . . well, it was his version of flight.

He let out a triumphant screech.

❖

"Aku!"

"Aku!"

"Hey, Aku!"

"Can you hear us?"

Nothing. Out this far Shonan and Oghi couldn't hear even the shush of the surf. The air was still, as though the earth had stopped breathing. The waves blocked their view. They couldn't have seen Aku thirty strokes away. Far off to the left four pelicans cruised low over the water, on the hunt. Nothing else on earth or in the sky moved, except for the waves, in deadly procession.

Suddenly, Shonan saw something odd. A bird fast-flapped low over the water. It had no business being there—it was an owl, and owls hunted only on land and only at night or twilight.

"A winged panther!" exclaimed Oghi.

"A what?"

Oghi repeated the words, pointing at the owl.

"We call that a great dusky owl," said Shonan.

Oghi shrugged and waggled his head oddly, like he was dancing.

The owl changed course and flew straight toward them. More amazingly, it hovered over the log they were pushing and circled, looking. It said in Aku's voice, "Hi, Shonan. Are you Oghi?" the bird said to the turtle.

"Yes!"

The owl landed. "Sure am glad to see the two of you."

Now Shonan had to watch Aku do it. Orange-faced, horn-tufted, beaked head into his son's face. Wings into arms. Feathers to skin, talons to feet. Aku grinned at his father.

Shonan said flatly, "I hate that."

Aku started to snap something back. Instead he slid into the water, so he could help push their log boat back to shore.

"You could have flown all the way back," said Oghi.

Aku bit a lip. "Sounds weird, but flying so far makes me nervous. I'd rather be with you."

They swam the log back toward the shore. It took forever.

Before long Shonan noticed that Aku seemed lackadaisical in his kicking, and unsure in his grip on the log. He put his arm around his son. Aku gave him a dazed smile.

"He's chilled," said Oghi. "When we get to shore, we'll warm him up."

Before long the three of them and the dog sat next to a driftwood fire. Aku managed a few words, and an occasional nibble on the parched corn they'd brought. Mostly, his eyes were busy soaking up the sea turtle man, who was no longer a man and was munching some grass in the shallow water.

Aku felt carefully, one by one, each of the owl feathers tied into his hair. He hadn't lost any. Wondering how he got back into human form with all his clothes and gear, he drifted into slumber.

❖

Shonan half-heard quite a few words but stayed in his hide blankets. He wanted no part of this conversation. Aku and Oghi—who were both human beings again—were locked in some deep discussion. Oghi was advising Aku on how to be a shape-shifter and a seer and a . . . magician. Shonan swallowed spittle, and it felt like burying the word. *Meli*, he thought, *Meli* . . . But he couldn't curse the dead wife he still loved.

Meli had spoken to Aku about following his nature. Shonan put no stock in that idea. He saw life as choices. A human being was clay, like a pot. Your parents gave you the raw material. You yourself made the shape of the pot you wanted. Will mattered. Making decisions mattered. Determination. The clay was just clay, and it would take any form.

Now Shonan felt a sharp twist of pain in his loins, as though they were responsible for this unnatural creature who sat by the fire talking foolishness. He stifled a cry. What had he done wrong?

"Practice once now," the sea turtle man said. "It gets easier every time."

Aku made a murmur of protest, and then said, "All right."

Shonan sat up, rubbed his eyes, and watched. Feet to talons, trunk to feathers, arms to wings, face to that crazy orange face disc of the great dusky owl. Oghi reached out and tugged at a human ear. "Next time get rid of these. The winged panther has his own."

Aku felt his ears in embarrassment. He looked down to make sure he'd replaced his peeing equipment, his *do-wa*, with an owl's.

Aku looked across at Shonan. "I'm sorry, Father." Gradually, he changed himself back into the shape his family was used to.

Shonan stood up, getting his confidence back. "I suppose it can't be helped."

"Grandmother Tsola told me it's the way I am."

Shonan sighed. "Why don't we all eat?"

As Aku reached for meat, he felt a surge of bloodlust, the spirit of the killer. He remembered that the winged panther was a deadly hunter. It was one of the few creatures that hunted animals bigger than itself. Worse, it hunted, killed, and ate its own kind, other owls.

"You're uncomfortable with it, but it is part of what you are," said Oghi. Shonan gave the sea turtle man a dirty look. Oghi went on, "Kind of fun when you get used to it, and handy."

For a moment they ate in silence. Then Shonan said, "Let's get going."

Aku jumped up. "Yes."

Shonan asked Oghi, "We've lost our chance to get ahead of the bastards on the trail, right?"

"Yes. You can still surprise them, but now only from behind."

"Whatever," said Shonan. He got the hide with the map from Tagu's load and unfurled it.

"We're here," said Oghi, pointing, "at the mouth of Any Chance River. The next river is the one you want, Big River. You go along this side of the river to right here, where it intersects the trail. It's no more than half a day's walk."

He glanced at Aku.

"I'll be fine," Oghi said, answering the question in both of their minds.

"You're not going on with us, are you?" said Shonan.

"Fighting is not my medicine, and there's no need. The way is wide and easy now. I prefer to swim home."

Aku said, "Grandfather, do you foresee success for us?"

Oghi laughed out loud.

Shonan was surprised by Aku's question and shocked by Oghi's laughter. "Grandfather" was a term of honor not customarily given to a person outside the tribe. It was an acknowledgement of kinship and respect. Regardless, it was more of the wicky-wacky stuff he despised.

Oghi got serious. "Sometimes I can answer questions about the future, but I would have to gather materials and conduct the ceremony. You have no time for that."

"We don't," Shonan snapped out.

The sea turtle man spoke directly to Aku. "You don't need my help. Ask the owls. Ask the ones that cross your path in the ordinary world. Ask the ones you dream of. Ask the owl inside yourself. All will help you."

Aku gave a wry smile. Shonan frowned at the owl feathers tied into his son's hair.

Oghi stood up and grinned. Before their eyes he performed the metamorphosis again. Claws, carapace, beak— a sea creature on all fours.

He waggled his head at them, did a little dance with his front feet, turned, and crawled into the ocean.

"Let's go," said Shonan.

Aku stood up shakily. He made sure of Tagu's lashings, stalling. He looked up at Shonan. "Father, do you want me to fly ahead and find them?"

"No," said Shonan. It came out as a growl.

That was fine with Aku. When he touched the feathers in his hair, they said, *Trouble ahead.*

9

Walking, Aku got oriented again. His father in front of him, their dog half a step behind him and just to his right—it all felt good. The Earth, at the fullest bloom of summer—all of this world felt new to him. Yesterday he had surrendered all that was above water, he had said good-bye. Twice in two days he had transformed himself into an owl, once saving his own life. Now every sight, the feel of the path under his moccasins, the sun on his skin, all of it felt like a hello. And if the father was distressed with the son right now, Shonan had helped save his life yesterday. That made Aku feel good.

Aku liked people. All the different ways they were, the odd ways they did things, the peculiar ideas they held to (sometimes held *fast* to), the way they loved each other and disliked each other and had fun together and quarreled and baited each other and somehow made a bond—every bit of that pleased Aku. He couldn't explain why.

Some things grieved him. Having his mother die. Missing her every day. Shonan being gone hunting or fighting wars. Feeling like he had no real home.

He liked going to see his great-grandmother Tsola at the Emerald Cavern. That felt like home, and Tsola was the one person who would understand the strange things that went on in his head. But no one could live with her in the Cavern, no one could interfere with the sacred duties that occupied her life. She would help him develop his powers to the highest, as she did for every seer, but that was all.

Well, I am what I am. And I am alone.

If enemies hadn't stolen his sister, and he didn't have to walk until each muscle nattered to every other muscle about hurting, life would have been halfway decent.

I am what I am.

Aku remembered well the day he'd met the tribe's Seer and Wounded Healer. He'd been ten, and his mother walked him up to the Emerald Cavern, Tsola's home. Though his great-grandmother was the most respected person in the tribe, with several titles and powers, she was also extraordinarily old. The tribe's Wounded Healers lived far past a hundred winters, and she was the oldest of them.

Beside a low fire, Tsola poured them tea. His mother had told him that Tsola had lived in the Emerald Cavern so long she couldn't see outdoors anymore—she lived entirely in these depths. "But she'll see us coming with her special power."

After they sipped, his mother said, "He shows signs of the gift."

"Yes, I see that. You sometimes look beyond the appearance of the things of this world to what they truly are."

The ten-year-old nodded. He had always seen things invisible to other people, but he'd kept his mouth shut about it.

"You also have your mother's talent. You can change into the shape of another animal."

"That scares me," Aku said. His hands shook.

"It's powerful," said the old woman, "and it's your nature. Every creature must follow its nature, or it destroys him."

She spoke casually, but the words petrified Aku. He was tongue-tied.

"If you watch the animals, you will know which one you can become, or more than one."

Aku stared at his knees.

"It's not hard, for those who have the gift. Look at your feet and picture them as talons. Look at your arms, hold them out, and see them as wings."

Aku shuddered. His great-grandmother had guessed that he pictured himself as winged.

The expression on her face changed. "When you're older, when you want to know more, come to see me. I will help you."

He'd never been back.

Now, following his father on the trail along Big River, he reminded himself: he was about to get a real home. Iona would give him one. Even if she didn't have many relatives— just Oghi—it would be a real home because she would be there. In rhythm with his steps he daydreamed about her.

Shonan's voice interrupted his reverie. "There's the trail."

They stopped at the crest of a hillock and looked carefully at all of the path they could see, which wasn't much. It sloped to the river from the hills on both sides. No one was in sight.

"They're well ahead of us," Shonan said. He was impatient today, and moving fast eased his mind.

"Let's have a look at the ford," he said. The crossing was probably at the shallowest place in the river that was handy, because women and children sometimes had to cross, too. "Full and fast," Shonan said. They'd gotten a lot of rain over the last week.

Without hesitation, Shonan stripped to his breechcloth, tucked his shirt and moccasins under Tagu's lashings, held his spear and club two-handed over his head, and waded in. If Shonan ever got hurt, at least he wouldn't suffer from fretting about it first. Aku did the same with his clothes, lifted his spear and blow gun, and followed his father. Why he bothered carrying weapons he didn't know. He couldn't do any more than scare someone with them.

A third of the way across, Aku stepped into a hole and went down. He scrabbled along the bottom like a crab, felt for something higher to stand on, pulled himself up onto a rock, and stood up. Then he had to swim several strokes to catch up with his weapons. When he got them, he turned to look at Shonan, who was grinning. Aku grinned back.

As they got to the far side, Big River curved toward them, and the current clawed hard at the bank. The stream deepened and picked up speed. Waves splashed Aku's underarms, his neck, his chin. He sloshed his way forward hard because there was nothing else to do.

Shonan got to the bank, reached his weapons onto the grass, hoisted himself up with both hands, and raised a knee onto the lip. At that moment a spear ripped through his thigh.

Shonan splashed backward into the river, bleeding. The spear floated away.

Without thinking, Aku leapt for his father and missed. He lost his footing and banged to the bottom. When he surfaced, he leapt for his father again. He barely caught the floating hair.

Two enemies howled out of the trees, jumped off the bank, and landed on top of Aku and Shonan feet first. Father and son went under. Aku flailed at enemy legs with his fists. When he managed to stand up, pain lightninged the back of his head, and the world went topsy-turvy.

When his mind stopped reeling, Aku felt himself being lifted onto the bank. Shonan was sitting up, a hand on his torn thigh and both legs splashed with blood. Tagu was raising a ruckus.

The enemies laughed at the dog and slapped at its face. Tagu barked louder and jumped harder. Two men got in good rib kicks. A commanding voice stopped the play.

The commander stood over Aku and Shonan. "Good," he said in the Galayi language. "You came after us—that showed courage." He smiled his victory. "In return you get to see your woman die."

"Where is she?" demanded Shonan. His voice sounded a little shaky.

The commander pointed north. "Headed up to—"

His words turned into flying vomit. A rock the size of two fists bounced off his skull, and he collapsed.

Aku heard a *pffsst* and a dart stuck into the neck of the warrior behind him.

A buffalo dropped out of a tree. No, it only looked like a buffalo—it was a shaggy human being with a hump. "Get the bastards!" he yelled, but his words were smothered by everyone's yelling and hitting.

The nearest enemy turned to run. Aku grabbed his ankles. The man fell and twisted his feet free by rolling.

Flat on the ground, Shonan flung himself across the enemy commander, grabbed a rock, and banged it onto the man's skull again.

A skinny soldier swung his war club at the buffalo man. The monster grabbed the handle of the club, twisted it out of the skinny enemy's hand, grabbed him, hefted him into the air, ran at the tree yelling, and rammed his victim head-first into the trunk.

One warrior skittered away like a mouse.

The one Aku had grabbed tried to run away, but Tagu fastened his jaw into the man's calf.

The last enemy swung his club and caught the buffalo

man on the point of the shoulder. The man-beast bellowed, lifted a leg high, and smashed his enemy in the face.

Shonan banged the rock down on the commander's skull one more time.

Aku found an enemy club, got next to Tagu, and whacked the dog-bitten man on the back of the head. He fell like a dropped rag.

The humped beast stomped the smashed man.

It was over.

Aku breathed.

Shonan took some lashing thongs off the dog and tied the dazed, skinny man, hands and feet. Then he rolled onto his back and looked up at his son. "That was a lucky blow. Maybe you'll let me show you how to swing a club so that it delivers next time."

For the first time in his life Aku tasted a coppery bloodlust on his tongue. Yes, maybe he did want to learn the skill of using a war club.

He said, "Let me treat that wound." Aku got out a salve of mountain allum he carried in a skin bag on his belt and poulticed his father's thigh. Finally, he cut a hand-span swath off the bottom of Shonan's breechcloth and bound the wound.

Shonan tried to stand up and couldn't manage it. "No walking for a while," said Aku.

"While they take Salya further and further away," said Shonan.

The buffalo-looking man just stood there, mute, watching. He was a giant. He had thick, matted, curly brown hair. As Aku was half a head taller than Shonan, the buffalo man was a head taller than Aku, and twice as thick and broad. The hump on his back look uncannily like a buffalo's.

The man-beast walked up to the three figures, raised his

huge foot, and smashed their necks. The sound of snapping bones told the end of their story.

Aku stifled a spasm of nausea.

As Buffalo raised his foot above the skinny one, Shonan said, "Let him be. We'll question him."

Buffalo stomped the man's neck anyway, and the bones cracked.

Shonan started to spit words out, but Aku stopped him with a hand.

"Stranger," Aku said formally in the Galayi language, "you saved our lives. Thank you."

Buffalo said, "I want to help you." His speech was a little odd, but it was in the Amaso tongue.

Aku thanked him again, this time in the Amaso tongue.

"You are welcome. My name is Yah-Su." Shonan and Aku looked at each other, amazed. It was the word for "buffalo" in both the Amaso and Galayi languages. The big warrior tapped his breastbone with his fingers, the way Amaso people did when they introduced themselves.

"Strip the bodies," Shonan said.

Aku hesitated. He'd never been to war, never had to denude an enemy of everything, so that the dead man would have nothing to help him get to the Underworld, no weapons, no clothes, no food.

First they collected the weapons. Aku threw the spears, clubs, and blow guns into the woods—they had no way to carry them. Yah-Su tested a couple of the clubs for feel and set them with his own club and spear.

"Always room for another knife on your belt," said Shonan.

Aku started keeping the knives, which had blades of stone and handles of bone or antler.

At that point Aku had to face up to the ugliness of dead

bodies. He started undoing the belts, which he kept for lashings, and throwing the shirts and breechcloths away. He avoided looking at the dead *do-was*. But on the skinny man he found something clever.

"Look, I found this hidden inside the breechcloth." He handed it to the prone Shonan. It was an obsidian blade no bigger than a thumb joint, scabbarded in rawhide. "He hung it on a thong from his belt." Aku patted his backside to show where. Nothing was sharper than obsidian.

Shonan inspected it and held it out to Aku. "It's a prize, keep it."

"I don't want to keep anything . . . down there."

Shonan smiled and shrugged. "By the spirits, I will." He tied the thong to his own belt, stuffed the holstered blade into the top of the cleft at his rear, and gave his reluctant son a fine grin. "It's a clever idea," he told Aku.

"Let's see if any of the moccasins fit," said Shonan. "Good to leave tracks that look like the enemy."

Two pairs worked for Shonan and one for Aku. Yah-Su's feet were much too big. Father and son put on two pairs and tucked one into Tagu's load.

When they were finished, they backed away. "Leave the bodies in plain sight," Shonan said. "I want to make some Brown Leaf hearts shiver."

Aku turned his attention to the humpbacked Yah-Su. "You followed them."

"Yes. They stole the pretty girl."

"Do you know the girl?"

He jiggled his big head from side to side. "Yah-Su saw her twice."

Aku and Shonan looked at each other, trying to make sense of this.

"Yah-Su . . . Yah-Su lives in a cave," the buffalo man said.

Aku nodded to Shonan. A man who didn't live in the village. A hermit, maybe ashamed of not being smart. Kind? Maybe. Violent? Maybe.

"They stole the pretty girl."

"Did you see them get her?"

"No," said Yah-Su. "Saw them carry her. Too many of them."

"How many?" Aku went on.

Yah-Su thought, then held up two hands plus one hand. Fifteen.

Aku held up the same number of hands. "This many?"

"Yes, too many. Yah-Su wants to help."

"You helped tremendously. You followed them, but there was no way to get the girl."

Yah-Su nodded, his eyes drooping with sorrow.

"When they left an ambush, you thought you might be able to save us."

"Yes. Yah-Su wants to help."

"Yah-Su," repeated Aku, "you saved our lives. Thank you."

"So what are we going to do now?" said Shonan, stroking his bandage.

"Yah-Su wants to help," said the buffalo beast.

Aku looked at Shonan's bleeding thigh, thinking, *We're desperate.* Then his great-grandmother's words popped into his mind. "If you ever need help desperately, say out loud, 'Little People, save us.'"

Aku said the words. He and Shonan disappeared.

Standing there alone, Yah-Su waggled his head back and forth, shuffled his feet, and said, "How'd they do that?"

10

Aku looked up at the sky through the leaves of thousands of ferns. The light of the sun came through them filtered, gentle, softly radiant. A stream tumbled in from the top, creating a fine mist. Millions of droplets of water wept from the tips of the leaves, creating myriad sparkles of water-diamond light.

He gasped.

"We like human beings who appreciate beauty," said a melodious voice. "Your father doesn't seem to notice it."

Aku looked up to find the speaker and saw no one.

"Here."

Behind Aku stood a smiling young man or woman with the loveliest, most perfectly formed face and frame Aku had ever seen, scalloped by cascades of curly yellow hair. He or she looked exactly like a human being, except for being only knee-high. The Little People had come to help.

"My father is hurt," said Aku. He knelt next to Shonan, who was gripping his leg with both hands, teeth clenched, breath sucked in and blown out hard.

"I think your dog bumped that leg on the journey. I apologize—we should have been more careful."

Tagu growled.

"My name is Kayna," the tiny person said. "Welcome to the land of the Little People."

Shonan said, "Have you kidnapped us?"

"You asked for help," said Kayna, "and we came."

"I *did* ask, Shonan. Grandmother gave me the words."

Shonan thought, *Her again.*

"Would you kindly calm your dog?" asked Kayna. "I'm immortal, but injuries can be messy."

Aku rubbed Tagu's ears. The dog kept his eyes fixed on Kayna but stopped growling.

"Immortal?"

"Just as you've heard."

Every Galayi knew the tales about these extraordinary creatures who, like the inhabitants of the Land Beyond the Sky Arch, lived forever. They had magical abilities and would help Galayis who got into trouble. Their special power was protecting Galayis who performed the purifying ceremony Going to Water. Sometimes these tiny folk appeared in desperate battles and saved warriors from defeat. The Little People were mischievous, though, and tricky. You had to be careful in your dealings with them. Aku was sure there was a lot he didn't know about them.

"I can treat your father's wound. Perhaps you'd like to look around."

Kayna's smile was rich with implication. Aku was getting uneasy about someone who knew more about him than he knew himself.

Still, he stood up. Tagu moved so that he was between his master and Kayna. "Do you mind if I ask?" said Aku. "Are you a man or woman?"

"Little People are neither male nor female," said Kayna. "But go see everything for yourself."

"Thank you," he said. He looked at the light-enchanted room. Something stirred in him. "It's incredible."

"Go. Take it all in."

Dazzled, Aku wandered off.

"How long before I can walk again?" muttered Shonan.

"I will heal your wound right now. Then we need to make sure you don't have a fever."

"I haven't got that much time." He sounded churlish even to himself, considering the gift Kayna was making him, but his mind was on Salya.

"We brought you here because Aku has things he needs to learn."

"My daughter, his sister—her life is in danger."

"All mortals are in danger of their lives."

Shonan was irked. "But . . ."

Kayna held up a hand. "You'll go when Aku is ready."

"I demand to go now."

"Do you?" said Kayna. The healer's eyes flickered, and a violet light emanated from them. A hand reached out and made a gentle, downward motion.

Shonan sank to the ground and slept.

❖

Aku walked with his head cocked back, studying the immense grotto. It was shaped like a cup, top and sides a little wider than the bottom. The enchantment seemed to Aku to come from two sources, the extraordinary flood of sunlight from outside and the small waterfall that curled over the edge. The lip of the cup was a profusion of ferns which diffused the light. Farther down, the waterfall splashed onto a rock shelf and burst into a delicate spray. Gradually, as the sides of the cup descended, rich green mosses took over from the ferns.

The lower grotto walls were honeycombed with small pockets which appeared to be homes. On the floor of the grotto Little People went about their daily tasks. All of them were robed in white cloth. Though Aku well knew the dark cloth woven from the inner bark of the mulberry tree, he had never seen cloth in a luminous white. The robes were trimmed in lilac, blue, orange, and red—none were the green of the grotto. He wondered if the trimming indicated ranks or skills of some kind. Though each face was different, any one would have been the most attractive human visage he'd ever seen, reduced to the size of a palm.

Aku had never imagined such a place, or such people. He had heard that the Land Beyond the Sky Arch was beautiful, but he didn't think anything could surpass this grotto, which, instead of being high above the earth, was actually beneath.

At that moment amazement blossomed inside his head. A kind of music he'd never heard before piped its way to his ears. He'd always known music—every Galayi ceremony had the beat of the drums, the rattle of tortoise shells, the throbbing melodies from human voices. But this was something entirely new. He walked toward the sound in a trance. Tagu traipsed along, looking strangely at his master.

It came from what looked like a workroom. River canes leaned against all three walls. A big flat stone served as a kind of table, and a Little Person—Aku reminded himself that they were neither men nor women—seemed to be blowing the melody from a length of cane. The musician's fingers jumped up and down on the cane, and Aku saw holes beneath the flying pads of the fingers. The tones reminded Aku faintly of the tinkle that shells made when they were strung together and moved by a breeze. The rhythm made him want to dance.

"Friendly greetings," said the piper, a twinkle in his eye— its eye?

"I'm astonished," said Aku.

"Very few human beings have heard this music." He tipped his head. "I am Rono, at your service."

"How on earth do you do that?"

"I don't know that we're properly said to be on Earth, but I'll be glad to show you. Here, let me have your blow gun."

Aku had forgotten he was toting his weapons. He handed the piper his gun, which was nearly as long as Aku was tall.

Rono plucked the dart out of one end, eyed it with a sour expression, and set it aside. "Now we'll transform something that kills to something that lifts spirits."

The musician put the cane to its lips and blew hard.

Aku jumped. The cane made a kind of blasting sound, a little like the bugling of an elk, but cruder.

The musician picked up the small, holed cane again and twittered out a little melody, very high. "I can make one like this for you, if you like." Rono reached for Aku's long cane again. "Would you like me to make this bringer of death into two bearers of music?"

Aku was stumped.

"Come, Aku, you can get another river cane anywhere."

"How do you know my name?"

"Your great-grandmother, who gave you the key to getting here, told us to watch for you. She is a mortal we respect greatly. You know, we don't bring everyone here who cries out for help. We'd be overpopulated." The musician smiled. "So, will you accept my gift or not?"

"Please," said Aku.

"Splendid. We Little People hate death. That's why we don't indulge in it ourselves."

Rono set Aku's cane on the big stone, measured it with a

string, marked a spot near the middle, and with an obsidian-bladed knife cut it into two cylinders. Rono checked one for length.

"Notice first that the tone is much higher than before." The musician blew on the shorter cylinder and got a high, sweet sound. When Rono piped on the other, it sang a lower pitch.

"First this." Rono cut a big notch near the end where you blew.

"Now I must drill some holes," said the musician. "Pretend you're my apprentice and hold this piece of cane."

With a press drill the Little Person quickly made a small hole several fingers below the notch of the short piece, and several other holes, which were almost too close together for Aku's fingers.

With a big grin Rono picked up the cane and played. It made sweet music in those hands.

"You human beings whisper sometimes that the Little People can do miracles. Here's murder turned to magic—what could be more wondrous?"

Aku picked it up and blew. The sounds he got weren't musical.

"Don't worry, I'll teach you," said the musician. "And now I'll make the other piece into an instrument that will toot nicely along with it."

❖

When Aku went back to check his father, Shonan was sitting up.

"About time you brought that dog back," said Shonan. "I'm starving." He untied Tagu's lashes.

"We apologize," said Kayna, "but we are unable to offer our guests food. You may drink water aplenty"—he pointed to where the waterfall trickled into a small pool—"but if you ate our food, you would never be able to go back to your world."

"This world is enchanting," said Aku. "I could stay."

"Sorry," said Kayna, "but no."

Aku barely noticed the words. "Look what I got," he said to his father, holding out the canes.

Shonan talked with his mouth packed full of dried meat. "What on earth!?"

Kayna took one of the canes, played a little melody, and handed the instrument back to Aku. "Rono has taught many of us to make music. Anything beautiful is welcome here."

Shonan said deliberately, "You destroyed your blow gun to get some tootling stick!?"

"Father," said Aku, "I can get another cane along any river. I still have the dart." He held it out.

Shonan eyed his son skeptically while he finished his slab of meat. Then he stood up. He walked around them in a circle. He jumped. He ran. "Just as you said," he told Kayna with a grin. "A miracle."

"Miracles are our way of life," said Kayna. "Now may I suggest you take a little nap? You need the rest."

"Actually," said Shonan, "we need to get going."

Kayna made a downward motion with one hand. Shonan lay on the ground, scooched until he was comfortable, and slept.

From behind, Rono's voice said, "Now, Aku, we have work to do."

❖

When they were back in Rono's workshop, the piper said, "Give me the flutes. I'm going to paint them."

"While Rono does that," said Kayna, "I will tell you the story, and then Rono will teach you the songs."

Aku nodded. *To hell with trying to run my own life.*

"When everything began," said Kayna, "Grandmother Sun was made first, and then her brother Grandfather Moon and the other stars, and Earth and all the plants and animals on it, including human beings. Everyone understood that all creatures would live forever. When Sun passed through the sky and looked down on the animals and plants, though, she saw that plants made more plants and animals made more animals, and one day there wouldn't be enough room. So she ruled that all living creatures on Earth must grow and die, and come back and grow and die again. And so they did.

"At that time Sun's daughter, Morning, lived among the human beings. One day as Grandmother Sun made her circuit, she looked and didn't see her daughter. When she asked, the people had to tell Sun that Morning had been bitten by a rattlesnake and died.

"Sun was angry. She scorched the Earth with burning rays. All the plants and animals, including people, suffered in the fierce heat, and many died.

"Desperate, the people asked Grandmother Sun what they could do to make things right.

"Grandmother Sun said, 'Bring my daughter back to life. I make you this promise. If you do that, human beings will live forever.'

"Live forever! What a boon!

"But the human beings were stumped. No one had ever gone to the Darkening Land and come back. They had no idea how to begin. Finally, they decided to ask for help from the only Immortals on Earth, the Little People. The wisest of the Little People put their heads together and came up with an answer. 'Make a box out of buffalo hide,' they said, 'and to go the Darkening Land. There you must find Morning's spirit. Put it in the box and bring it back. When we put her spirit back in her body, Morning will come alive again, and Grandmother Sun will shine in a good way, and you will be immortal, just as we are.'

"But the wise ones added one warning. 'Do not, under any circumstances, open the box on the way back.'

"Seven brave men volunteered for the journey to the west, to the Darkening Land," Kayna went on.

Aku wondered if that was near the place where the ocean wrapped all the way around Earth and met Turtle Island again.

"When they got to the Darkening Land, the men saw that the spirits were having a dance, just as the Little People had said, and the young woman was dancing in the outside circle, again just as we Little People said. So the men followed our instructions exactly. Each time the young woman circled past them, one of the men threw a corncob and hit her skirt. On the seventh circuit, the spirit fell down. They popped her into the box and slammed the lid quick. None of the other spirits even noticed.

"The seven men traveled fast to the east, toward their homes. Before long the girl began to cry out, 'Let me out of here. I can't stand it. It's awful being in here.'

"The men made no answer at all, but just walked on.

"Later the girl said in a pleading tone, 'Please, I'm hungry. Give me something to eat.'

"But the men said nothing and walked on.

"After a long silence the girl begged, 'I'm thirsty, really thirsty. Can't I have a drink?'

"The men felt sorry for the girl, but they remembered the warning of the Little People and trod on without a word.

"When they got close to home, the girl cried out in

a panic. 'Help! Help! I can't breathe! I'm smothering in here!'

"Now the seven men got scared—maybe the girl was about to die—so they cracked the lid open just a little. When they did, they heard a whoosh of air and saw something like a shadow dart out of the box.

"When they got home and opened the box, it was empty.

"Now Morning's body could never be brought back to life. Grandmother Sun wept copiously, and the Earth was flooded, and many plants and animals drowned. People danced to the Sun and sang songs of praise, and she quit crying. Even then, her gloomy mood cast shadows everywhere, and it was hard for either plant or animal to grow.

"Morning's spirit, set free, took herself as far from mortal life as she could get—she turned herself into Morning Star, farther from Earth than even the Sun. She is remote and beautiful, and that satisfies her.

"At last Grandmother Sun shone again. But human beings had lost their chance for immortality forever."

Aku felt dazed. He had heard splinters of this story, but to hear it all, and from the lips of the immortals . . .

"Yes, you're charmed," said Rono, "but Kayna told you this story for a reason. Your great-grandmother sent you here to get two gifts." The musician held out the flutes, the short one painted green and the other red. "You scared me when you hesitated to let me cut up your killing instrument—you would never have known what you lost.

"Yes, green and red. If you look more closely, you'll see that the holes on them are spaced differently. That's because each one is made to play a different song, and each song has a different purpose. The green one plays a song that heals spirits. It does nothing for wounds or illnesses. The red one resurrects the dead. If you're with someone who dies, before the spirit sets off for the Darkening Land, the red flute's song can bring them back to life." Rono looked at Aku's blanched face and chuckled. "I didn't mean you have to go to the Darkening Land and rescue them yourself."

The piper gave Kayna a certain look. "Why don't you check on your guest and tend to other things? Teaching a student to play a song is tedious."

In fact, for Aku the learning seemed quick and delightful. He said, "I'd like to stay here and make music forever."

Rono said, "Human beings can't. You will stay until you learn these songs, regardless of the passage of Earth time, and leave at the next sunrise."

"My sister may be killed."

"Then be glad," said Rono, "that you will gain power over death."

11

The Brown Leaf village looked like any Galayi village. Wattle-and-daub huts surrounded a village green. People began to crisscross the green on the business of life, heeled by their dogs. Mothers let children romp out of the huts, now that day was coming on strong, chasing away the cold and perhaps dangerous spirits. *Or enemies*, thought Aku.

The bay was guarded by a crooking arm of land, and farther out by two finger-shaped islands. The eastern side of the village circle opened to the ocean. On the western side rose the council lodge, an arbor with a roof circling an open space the way a fringe of hair curled around a balding man's head. From his angle on the crest of a hill, Aku couldn't see the fire at the center of the lodge, but a faint line of smoke rose from it and was blown to rags by the sea winds. The fire priest must have just renewed the sacred flame, as he probably did every morning and evening.

They may not look that different from us, Aku thought, *but they are.* He chased away a mental picture of Salya spread-eagled in front of the fire, the knife gouging her heart out.

He put a hand on Tagu's head and rubbed his ears.

Again he cast an eye around. They'd slipped past guards on the trail to get to this knob, and they were sitting in the bushes. Which didn't mean they couldn't be spotted.

"See any sign of her?" said Aku.

"No," said Shonan. "I doubt we will."

"The huts on both sides of the eastern entrance are painted," Shonan said.

Aku looked carefully and saw that his father was sharp-eyed. He could see just an edge of painting on the side of the huts toward the entrance. It probably ornamented the doors. At least that's the way his own tribe did things.

"Those have got to be the huts of the peace chief and the war chief," Shonan said.

"The colors are yellow and blue," said Aku. Among the Galayi, the peace chief's ornamentation would have been white, the Red Chief's red.

Shonan's voice had an edge. "They're different from us." He waited. "She'll be in one of those huts, probably the war chief's, whichever one that is. They'll have her tied up and probably guarded."

Father and son had a tacit agreement to speak as if they were sure she was alive. Privately, each doubted it. They had no idea how many Earth days they'd been with the Little People.

"What do you want to do?"

"Find out which hut she's in, tear her out, and go like hell."

Aku snatched his breath in.

Shonan heard it and smiled. "In war, daring is everything."

Aku voiced the calm version of his thoughts. "Incredibly dangerous."

Shonan took his time answering. "If I watched my daughter die, I could not go on breathing the air of this world."

Aku nodded. He understood. "I have an idea. I'll take my owl shape, fly down there, look and listen from the smoke holes, and find out what hut she's in."

His father humphed. After a long while, he said, "Maybe."

Aku said nothing. He intended to do it, regardless.

"Whatever, for today we just watch. Always learn every-thing you can about your enemy." Shonan thought. "Tonight we move. Unless they bring her out."

Both of them pictured her being dragged to the sacred fire for the sacrifice.

"And then?"

Shonan smiled. "Then we will taste their blood, and they will taste ours."

❖

All day they saw nothing that helped.

In the twilight they sneaked carefully uphill to a cave they'd spotted. The Galayi liked to make camp in caves—the name of their tribe meant People of the Caves. They needed to make sure of a place where they could hide with their freed captive, and tie Tagu. They would have enough problems creeping into the village without him getting the dogs stirred up.

Then they slipped down the hill toward the place the guards stationed themselves to watch the trail. Shonan wanted to kill the sentries. Why, Aku wasn't sure. To ease his anger, proba-bly.

Aku told himself, *It's my job to help, and I have to share the risk.* Nevertheless, as soon as the guards were taken care of, he would enter the village as an owl. He didn't care whether his father liked it or not. Salya was *his* twin, and owls flew at night.

Mere shadows in the twilight, sliding down from bush to bush, tree to tree, they saw an opportunity. Fifty steps above where the guards stood loomed a boulder with a split on the uphill side. Shonan nodded toward it, and Aku understood.

Using the boulder for cover, they got to its back side, crawled into the split, climbed to the top, and looked down on the guards.

The appearance of a luminous god could not have shocked them more. Even in the last of the light Aku could see her clearly. Lounging, chatting with the guards, laughing, sat Salya.

❖

For a long moment Aku felt like he'd turned, through and through, muscles, blood, and brain, into river ice.

Shonan rose to let Salya and her companions see him. Then he climbed down the boulder and stepped toward them. He held his spear and club uncertainly, neither ready nor at rest.

Aku slid down the boulder and followed his father. His legs were wobbly.

Salya jumped up, ran, and flung herself into Shonan's arms. "Ada, Ada, I'm so glad to see you. I was so scared." "Ada" was a fond equivalent of "father."

Shonan looked over his daughter's head at the two guards. "Why are you dallying with these enemies?" he asked. His speech got stilted when he was ill at ease.

"Ada, these are the furthest thing from enemies. These are my friends." She mentioned names Shonan didn't make out.

Shonan looked at the two young men with hard eyes and barely inclined his head. Aku nodded to them and said, "I am Aku."

"Oh, Ada, I've been coming out here with them each night, hoping you would show up. They said you wouldn't. They were worried that you might come later with an army—they wouldn't have grabbed me if they'd known I'm Galayi. But if you followed right away . . ." She hugged him hard again. "Oh, Ada, I was so scared."

"I think there's a lot to be explained."

"In the village. You'll be treated as special guests—they'll give a feast for you. I've told them about my father and my brother."

She let Shonan go and hugged Aku. In the last of the light he couldn't quite meet her eyes. Then she took both their hands and danced, pulling them gaily toward the village. Shonan kept glancing back toward the guards. He didn't like having them behind him.

"Ada, these are wonderful people. Whatever you've heard, it's not true at all. I've met a wonderful man. He's a shaman." She turned to Shonan, took both of his hands, and held his eyes with hers. "I'm going to give you grandchildren by him."

Shonan kept rotating his head in every direction. "But they stole you. They've stolen lots of women. And none of them were ever seen again."

"That's because they're living in the Brown Leaf village, married to good Brown Leaf men, bearing children and living happily."

Shonan knifed her with his eyes.

"Ada, your doubt hurts me. I know what I'm doing. And you'll see. It all has to do with a revelation . . ."

Warriors rushed out from every tree in the forest. From behind, the guards tackled Shonan and Aku. In an instant they were on their faces in the dirt, their hands being tied behind their backs. Feet bore down between their shoulder blades. Their weapons disappeared into the crowd.

Shonan twisted his head to the side and looked up at Salya. From the edge of his mouth, he squeezed out, "What's going on?"

"It's classic, Father. You've been betrayed by a woman."

12

M ake them face each other," said Salya, "so they can see each other's pain."

Aku fought his fear—he had to understand. He looked into the evil in Salya's face, a fire that consumed everything good. Her eyes were his, and they made him teeter on the abyss of his own darkness.

A man of authority nodded to his warriors, and they sat Aku and Shonan, firmly bound, face to face. In the dark they could hardly see the hundreds of people gathered around, a pack of hungry dogs at a slaughter.

"It is worse than terror," Salya said. "You are father and son. Each of you will feel the other's agony more than his own." She made a sound that mixed cackling and chuckling. "Until pain floods the mind to oblivion."

Even through the waves of dread Aku understood. In the council lodge guests were greeted. Here on the dance ground enemies were tortured. Salya stood next to a thick post sunk into the middle. On one side of her stood a white-haired man of great beauty and dignity. Aku did not need to see his head-dress clearly to know that he was the chief of chiefs. On her other side gangled an enormous man, hooded, and robed in a cloth rubbed black with ashes. A shaman, presumably, though

Aku had never seen a costume like that and couldn't imagine the face of a holy man beneath that cowl.

Father and son held each other's eyes. Though men were building a fire to hold the darkness away, there was little else the two could see, and nothing else in this world they wanted to see.

Salya touched the elderly man on the hand. "This man who condemns you to death is Guna. If you were not Galayi, an ignorant people who live in caves in the mountains, you would know him as a great chief, none greater in the memories of the grandfathers of the oldest men. Our people revere him." Aku didn't even glance at the chief—he was transfixed by the triumphant wickedness in Salya's eyes, evil mirrors of his own.

Now she caressed the shaman on the neck, shocking behavior at a public gathering. "This is the man I told you about, Father, Maloch, the most powerful shaman in all lands between where the sun rises and where it sets." She looked at Maloch lasciviously. "His power has entranced me." She slid in front of Maloch, embraced him with both arms, wound a leg around one of his, and rubbed her body against him indecently. Women in the crowd trilled. Men shouted or laughed.

Aku could not look away from her.

"Understand, my father, understand, my brother, Maloch is not my husband. I am his whore. I open my legs to him as the ground splits in an earthquake. His seed floods me as the ocean tides turn a river back up its own channel. He volcanoes forth his seed and fills my belly.

"Oh, oh"—her moan was a song and she writhed in a wicked ballet—"never have I felt such pleasure. Every day of my life I will degrade myself before him. Every day I beg for his humiliation."

Shonan heard only half of it. His eyes flicked over the chief, who seemed mesmerized by the fire. There lay the beginning of the pain.

"Sing for death," he said quietly to Aku. The tradition wasn't to ask for death, but to be ready for death if it came, as it did to all things.

"Yes!" said Salya, and again in exultation, "Yes! Sing for death."

A drum started, and Salya danced around them. "Our women will bring it to you now, first as a seduction, then as a rape, and last as the holocaust of fire." She waved a languid hand toward the blaze, which now burned brightly.

Shonan said quietly, "Remember that a warrior who dies fighting the enemy goes quickly to the Darkening Land and immediately is reborn on earth."

Salya cried, "Do you, the war chief, believe such an old wives' tale?" Her laugh exploded up and down in great arpeggios.

"Reborn immediately," Shonan repeated. Then he sang,

"All things pass away,
Plants must die,
Animals pass on,
Even the rocks crumble
And blow in the wind.
All things pass on.
Only spirit is eternal,
Only spirit.
Only spirit."

Salya stepped close to her father, a burning stick in her hand. "Only spirit?" she asked with a sneer. "Let me remind you of body." She jammed the flames into Shonan's belly.

Shonan howled. Salya cackled.
Shonan croaked out,

"Only spirit.
Only spirit."

Aku could only pretend to sing. He stared at the hideous burn on his father's belly. He gazed at the lewd, shadowy dance of Salya and the shaman. From the burn to the dance, back and forth. The sinuous movements of the dancers made their bodies look like one, her face grinning out from the shaman's cowl.

"You will wish your life was more frail," Salya chanted. "You will yearn for the embrace of death. You feel a splinter driven through your nipple. You get a hint of the flame as one of our women lights it. Slowly, the flame eats the wood. At last it takes the flesh in its fiery mouth."

By the flickering firelight Aku now began to see. Many times he had gotten a glimpse of what resided beyond the apparent, beyond the physical. For the first time he welcomed this sight. It stirred his heart. It was possibility.

"All things pass on.
Only spirit is eternal,
Only spirit.
Only spirit."

"Yes," sang Salya, "it will make you croon for the solace of death, but the slut has no ears. Ten times you will sing to her, but she enjoys your begging. 'More!' she demands. 'More! More!' A hundred splinters and your body lives on. Oh, what a bitch death is, how evil! But not as evil as your daughter Salya. Let me show you."

She bent over Aku, a sharp knife in her hand. She cut a thin line from his widow's peak down his forehead and his nose, to the edge of his upper lip. He moaned, and Salya cackled. Aku felt the blood run into his eyes, and he could not wipe them.

Salya's dance turned obscene now, her hands wildly suggestive. In the red light of the flames she was evil incarnate.

Something strange happened to Aku. With his vision blurred he began to see the truth.

The crowd doubled its uproar.

Shonan sang,

"Only spirit.
Only spirit."

Aku noticed that his father was twisting his hands against his bonds. Probably he wanted to use the half darkness to free them. *Foolish*, thought Aku. He turned his mind back to seeing what his eyes could not, the essence of things that lay beyond appearance.

"When our women tire of burning your flesh," Salya chanted, "when they see that the pain is too familiar to you, they will inflict an agony you never imagined. Its strength will be as the blazing sun is to starlight. They will bring stone knives, force them under your fingernails, and hammer them deeper and deeper, until the nails peel backward. And when they finish with all ten, they will eagerly remove your toenails."

Aku's mind was torn between his pain and what he was struggling to understand.

"All this time the crowd will cheer. By the time they are working on the toenails, their bloodlust will be the very air you breathe. They will glory in your pain.

"As you will exult in it. Galayi warriors like you seek nothing more hungrily than a call to show courage. A warrior rejoices in pain. As pain rampages, honor swells, courage soars. As the body suffers, the spirit triumphs."

Women raised tortoise shell rattles to spur on Salya's dance with Maloch. In the firelight the scene was phantasmagoric.

"Only spirit.
Only spirit."

"After the toenails, our women will cut you wherever they like. From your lower eyelid down your cheek. Across the arch of your foot. Between your toes. Inside your nostrils. Eventually they will cut your fingers off, joint by joint. And while you can still see, they will chop off your balls, and your cocks. While you can still feel pain, they will gouge out your eyes.

"All this time only they will touch you, our men will not. Meanwhile I will stroke Maloch. I will dance. I will sing. I will arouse him. I will suck his nipples. My depravity will inspire the women watching to depths of savagery with their own men. But none of them will be as black as the evil that inspires your Salya, your sister, your daughter."

In a booming voice Aku said, "You are not Salya!"

Silence. Salya stopped dancing, the drum stopped, the rattles stopped.

Now louder: "*You are not my sister.*"

Salya smiled nastily at Maloch. "Clever boy, isn't he, this twin of mine?" She stooped and ran her fingernail along his cut. It screamed.

"You're not my twin, not my anything. Where is Salya?"

Now the shaman spoke in a crawling, lascivious voice. "You're right, young man, quite right. This marvel is not Salya. She is whoever I want her to be. As I myself am."

Salya-who-wasn't-Salya pulled her dress over her head and tossed it away. Underneath was . . . Aku couldn't have said what. Something yellow-green that was turning itself from flesh to scales.

Subtly, Aku began his own transformation.

The shaman said cheerily, "I'll join you, my dear." He dropped his ashen robe and hood. His naked body was greenish yellow and serpentine.

Aku concentrated hard—feet to claws, and claws out of the rope. Maybe the shadows, and their self-absorption, would blind the evil ones for long enough.

Salya called out, "Drum! Rattles!" and undulated back into her dance. Her body was a dragon's, head held high, pulsating forward and back, gliding from side to side, tail undulating behind.

Wings! Aku shouted in his mind.

To the rhythm of the drum Salya and the shaman slithered toward each other, their reptilian bodies swaying to the beat, their tongues flickering. Their heads began to sprout horns.

"Yes," cried the creature that had once been a shaman, "unite with me, my love!"

Hundreds of pairs of eyes were transfixed by the serpentine twins, all except for Aku's.

Now a hideous chartreuse, the dragons slowly entwined their bodies like the tendrils of ferns. They squeezed each other and melded into one saurian monster, thick as the torso of a big man. Thick fish scales with spots of every color popped out on their skin.

"Where is your sister's body?" roared the whore's dragon head. "In the Darkening Land."

"Where is her spirit?" cooed the shaman's reptile head. "I ate it!"

Aku flapped to the top of the torture pole.

The two serpents were wholly one. They grew a single eye, and it was a diamond, one said to have the power to foretell the future. In sunlight the diamond would have blinded the hundreds of people. In the firelight it shone enough for the monster to see Aku.

Aku raised his wings to take to the air.

The monster let out a hissing roar and, faster than anyone's eye could follow, sunk its fangs into the owl.

Aku rowed the air, hesitated, faltered, fell a few feet, and with a burst of effort pulled away. His tail sent up a rip of pain. The monster had only feathers in its maw.

Aku felt the night air give lift to his wings. Over the pounding drum Aku heard his father cry out, "Meet me in the Darkening Land!"

13

High in the charcoal sky Aku circled the dance ground. It was bedlam, bodies surrounding his father, arms flailing, legs flying. Maybe in its indignation at losing one of its victims, the crowd loosed its rage on the other. *If so, maybe my father is lucky. Ada, I wish you the blessing of the warrior's death and rebirth.* Aku meant these words, but they gave him no comfort. With a start he realized he had called Shonan "Ada" for the first time, in his mind. *As I am losing you.*

He circled a second time but saw only riot. If he flew close enough to tear at his father's bindings, the dragon would kill him.

He noticed something very odd. His tail hurt, but his face didn't. He left that pain behind with his human body.

"Meet me in the Darkening Land!" Those were his father's instructions. Aku couldn't think what to do. He had never felt so confused. Pathetically, he winged toward the cave and landed just outside the entrance.

"Hello, Tagu. Good Tagu."

Silence.

"Hello, Tagu."

Nothing.

Shards of thoughts broke in Aku's mind. Tagu, run off.

Tagu, dead inside. Tagu dead inside and an enemy hiding behind him, waiting.

Aku's breath seized up.

Think, he ordered himself.

Nothing.

Think!

Nothing.

All right, human or owl? Go for surprise.

He went in, flapping his wings and flashing his talons.

The cave was empty. No enemy, no dog, no blankets, no lashings, no meat, no nothing.

Someone stole Tagu.

Which meant they knew his hiding place. They could be waiting outside right now.

He shot out the entrance high and hard. No enemy shouted, no enemy struck him.

He floated back into the cave and got the flutes out from behind the stones where he had hidden them. When he had them in one claw and stood on the other, he looked around. *This is the home of my enemies.*

❖

He launched into the air. He circled. He sought to order his thoughts. Instead wild pictures and insane sounds inflamed him. Twisting flames scorched his mind. Rampaging drums tore his thoughts to tatters. Screams howled within him like wild winds. His mind shrieked with gales that were songs and songs that were screams—in the racket he couldn't tell which was which. He thought he would go mad. He circled. What choice did he have?

He lit in a snag. He commanded himself to calm down, but his body didn't obey.

"Meet me in the Darkening Land!"

Surely that meant Shonan accepted death. Did it also mean he wanted Aku to die? Or did it mean that Aku was somehow to make his way to the Darkening Land and enter as a living being? Once before, in the most ancient times, that had been done. Seven men went there to bring back Morning, the daughter of Grandmother Sun.

Aku got out both his flutes, stroked them, and held them up in the moonlight. The red one had the power to resurrect the dead, but only in the moments just after death. Maybe he could help his sister, his twin. But her body wasn't dead—her *spirit* was. And it was not in the Darkening Land—it was in the heart of the Uktena, adding fire to the dragon's life. His green flute healed spirits, so the piper told him.

It was all bewildering. "What am I supposed to do?" He was shocked and hurt by the wail of his own voice. He sounded so young to himself, and so helpless. He hated that.

He thought. After a few minutes, he told himself, *I don't know what I'm supposed to do, but I'm going to take action. Take action,* he repeated to himself.

He threw himself off the snag and flew in a wobble down the hill. Ahead, far ahead, he could see the bay, and beside it the village. He exerted himself and mounted into the sky. He had made up his mind. He would fly over the dance ground until his father was dead. The Brown Leaves would abandon his father's body—they would not give it the honor of burial. Then he, Aku, son of Shonan, would bring his father back to life.

Yes, I'm disobeying you. And if we go to the Darkening Land, we'll do it together.

He flew along the trail to the village and . . .

The dance ground was empty.

No human figure, living or dead, hung from the stake.

The village was asleep.

They had already killed his father. *And where did you put his body?*

❖

Aku spent all night and all the next night winging from tree to tree across the plains and through the hills that surrounded the village, always carrying the flutes, the instruments of hope. Aku was no buzzard or eagle, able to soar with fixed wings, attaining great heights on warm winds, capable of covering ground ten times as fast as a man, or faster, and surveying enormous expanses of country. He was a wing-beater, flapping from spot to spot.

Part of what he learned in those two nights was that his owl sight was very keen, and he was a lethal hunter. His belly yearned for rabbit meat. As twilight slid into darkness each day, he easily spotted hares, dived on them in aerial silence, and killed them with a squeeze of obsidian-sharp talons. He relished the bloody meat.

At the earliest glimmer of light the first morning, he found still water in a creek and looked at himself. Orange face, beak like a tiny dagger, outcroppings of feathers where his ears might have been but weren't. Most important, he was huge. His wing span was wider than his human arm span. He had never seen an owl so big. Maybe he could intimidate other beasts—that would be good.

All night, each night, he flew over, through, and around the village. He learned nothing about his father. Presumably, they had stripped him naked and left him with no food and no weapons to make the journey to the Darkening Land. Presumably, they had dumped his corpse in any convenient place, vulnerable to wind and rain, to insect, rodent, and scavenger. *Where is it?*

He saw no body, no buzzards circling, no ravens hopping around on the ground.

When he checked the village at dawn and dusk, he only saw people going about the usual tasks of living. He circled farther and farther away, into the hills, well beyond where anyone would have gone to the trouble of carrying an enemy.

Frustration twisted in him, like a rag wrung tight and tighter until the last drop of hope was squeezed out.

As he settled onto his perch the second morning, the sun streaked itself across the eastern horizon far out to sea. And with the light, he got the idea. Probably the Brown Leaves had thrown his father's body into the sea. He had heard of barbarous peoples who did such things.

Though he should have avoided the visibility of daylight, he beat his way up and down the shoreline. He looked at every rock that jutted out of the ocean. With his extraordinary vision he studied the tide pools. He saw nothing. On a double-check he saw nothing. But no other explanation was possible.

He winged his way to the hills, downhearted. He would sleep all day and start tonight. He had lost his father. Now he couldn't do anything but go home, home to Iona.

14

The serpent monster roared hideously at the huge owl in flight. Several hundred people craned their eyes starward, but Aku was invisible in the darkness, and his flight silent.

Shonan didn't waste time looking for his owl son. He seized his opportunity. For some time, as he sang the death song, he had slowly tugged on the thong that concealed the scabbard in the top of his butt crack. Every movement made his belly burn scream. He ignored the pain.

When the blade reached his belt, he eased it out by its handle. Awkwardly, gradually, barely moving his fingers, he sliced the rawhide ropes that bound his hands. Now, with every pair of eyes on the sky, he threw himself into action.

One stroke, two—his feet were free!

One bound, one swing—the neck of the old chief was slit and pouring out crimson.

Shonan leapt away from the fire and into the crowd. Action blotted out his own hurt.

Eyes saw the chief fall, the neck gouting blood. Voices raised piteous cries.

Of the hundreds of spectators, several score glimpsed or felt Shonan. He sprinted between squatting figures, kneeing them, shouldering those who stood up, outshouting those who yelled with a terrible war cry—"Woh-WHO-O-O-ey! Woh-WHO-O-O-ey! AI-AI-AI-AI!" This Galayi war cry had frozen the hearts of soldiers, and Shonan gloried in seeing what it did to the faces of the Brown Leaf villagers.

He stepped on chests, bounced off shoulders and even heads like stepping stones, stomped men, women, and children, and slashed a path of horror with his small knife. Instead of confronting him, they pell-melled away, screaming.

The rest of the circle of villagers crushed their way toward the center, the stake, where their chief lay fallen. They moaned and wailed.

One man depended on boldness and blade. As he went, he lashed those in his way with his fury—"Woh-WHO-O-O-ey! Woh-WHO-O-O-ey! AI-AI-AI-AI!"

❖

Shonan rolled into a ball, clutched himself, and shook. From pain? From the chill night? From fear? Relief? His disbelief that he'd gotten away with it?

No, he was shaking with laughter.

For years he'd told his young warriors that surprise and daring were everything. Now his whisper felt like a shout of triumph—"Oh, did I prove it, did I ever prove it!"

He sat up, refused to let the burn make him scream, and sobered himself. He listened carefully. A few warriors had run after him. In the darkness he'd been able to slip off. Very gradually, staying in moon shadows, he'd worked his way to a muddy ravine. Now he was hiding among the exposed roots of an oak that leaned out over the ditch. One spring before long, when snowmelt came cascading down from the mountains and ripped through this gully, it would undercut the oak far enough and the great tree would crash into the raging waters.

Shonan would crouch here for a few hours, until he believed the search had stopped for the night. The scrunched-up position eased the agony on his belly. Later he would make his way uphill to the cave where he and his son had hidden, and where they'd tied Tagu. His owl boy. That was still hard for him, a tang of bitterness swirled with love and fear—*my great dusky owl son.*

Shonan knew the Earth in darkness. He had spent many nights hunting and many nights approaching enemy camps. He knew the sounds of the winds in the grasses and the leaves, the noises of the creatures of the night. Best of all, he knew the padding of two-footed predators. And from time to time now, he heard them. They were footfalls slipping by on the grass over his head, circling around the tree he hid under. They were scuffles and mud-sucks as they trod up and down the ditch. He was a shadow in a cave shielded by a waterfall of roots, invisible. He kept perfect silence. Sometimes he thought he could sit silent for days, and maybe not breathe for hours.

Then he noticed that the world had gone silent. Where were the sounds of the hoot owls? The other night birds? The katydids? Thousands of rustlings usually echoed through the night, maybe as many as in the day. Except when the animals were stilled for a cause.

An enemy creeping up on me?

Shonan closed his eyes. He ignored his taste, his touch, even his smell. He made his ears as sensitive as taut drum heads, ready to magnify any sound. He heard an impossibility—nothing.

Perhaps some animals could deceive his ears, like a breeze too slight to feel. Shonan had watched a playful fox approach a sunning blacksnake from behind, ease down paw after paw until he neared the serpent's head, and stretch forward a paw into the air beside the serpent's ear. Delicately, the fox touched the ground with that paw but put no weight on it. He raised it high, changed his mind, laid it gingerly on the earth again, waited, eased his full weight onto it, regarded the unmoving snake for a long moment, and backed away with a sly smile.

No human being could elude Shonan's hearing the way the fox fooled the snake. And the forest might not go dead silent in fear of a human being, a creature with such poor night vision that he was more likely to hurt himself than his prey. Only for something very dangerous.

Shonan raised his bottom, balanced on his feet and hands, and holding his belly as still as possible, crabbed backward to the very rear of the root cave until his hair touched the wall. Then, bit by bit, he fitted himself to the dirt like moss.

The killer didn't come. Stopped above, waiting?

A panther, maybe? Panthers hid from the ears of the night creatures, but not their eyes and not their noses. They smelled him first, then watched him glide along, black undulating on black. Leaf bugs ignored the cat. So did tree frogs, caterpillars, and moths. He wanted nothing from them. Buzzards and other roosting birds were out of reach and out of his mind.

The panther wasn't looking for these creatures, or *looking* for anything. He hunted with his nose, and he sniffed especially for those who denned up at night with their young, like coyotes and wolves. He wanted to find them in their cuddly sleep. His paws would slay the mother with two thunder strikes, perhaps three. Essential to kill her immediately—not because she could actually whip him in a fight, no prey of the panther could do that. But a wolf or coyote mother would battle fiercely for her pups. The panther didn't want to pay for his supper with a thousand bites and scratches.

This killer hunts dens with his nose, and I am crouched in a den. Shonan got his weapon ready. *A knife the size of a fingernail.*

The biggest warrior Shonan had ever seen crashed through the roots.

Shonan slashed with his baby blade. His heart pounded its drum head. He thought, *I might as well fight a war club with a feather.* He loved it. He lunged toward the killer and sliced the air.

A paw strong as a bear's grabbed his wrist.

"Shhh!"

Shonan froze at the odd sound of the voice.

"It's Yah-Su!"

Shonan's pulsed drummed, *Strike!*

Yah-Su clapped a monstrous hand over his mouth. "Shhh!"

Shonan's belly yelled.

Yah-Su pushed, slowly but irresistibly, until Shonan crunched against the wall. Then the buffalo man-beast slipped back outside the cover of the roots and immediately reappeared. Tagu was with him, on a lead. The dog curled against Shonan's leg. "I got him from your cave," Yah-Su said, and signed the words.

Shonan's rubbed the dog's ears. He didn't dare ask, "Did you see my son, too? In human form or in owl form?" He wondered where his bird son was. Probably winging his way toward the woman he loved—that's what young men did.

Yah-Su crouched next to Shonan. The beast was taller, and the dirt ceiling crooked his head down awkwardly. He put a finger the size of a baby's forearm to his lips, slid to the floor, and was asleep.

Shonan petted Tagu until his own blood stilled.

Both men woke when they felt water lapping at their skin. Tagu was already sitting up, on guard against the rising rivulet.

They crawled *plish-plash* through the curtain of roots. High in the sky, the constellation of the Six Pigs said it was far past the middle of the night.

Shonan put a finger to his tongue—the water was salt. He rubbed some on his belly, and the coolness felt good.

This ravine was a steep-sided cut made by the pounding waves of the sea. When the tide came in, the gully was wet, maybe even full. When the tide went out, it was empty. The sea was new to Shonan, and mysterious, but he intended to learn all its ways.

Yah-Su parted the roots, motioned to Shonan to come along, and waded upstream. The Red Chief wasn't used to following, but Yah-Su was quick-minded about the ways of war.

They hurried along in silence. Yah-Su didn't hesitate to walk on the sand, trusting the rising tide to cover whatever tracks they left. Shonan put his life in the buffalo man's hands.

Before first light, the creek made a sharp left turn toward the sea. There Yah-Su lifted Tagu onto a head-high stone slab and gave Shonan a hand up. The quick lift was a lightning bolt of agony.

They padded across rock and into an overhang. In the darkness Shonan couldn't tell how much of a cave it was, but they walked back twenty or thirty paces. Yah-Su pulled on Shonan's hand to get him to sit down.

Deep in the darkest shadow Shonan found some surprises. Yah-Su had a couple of untanned deer hides here for mattresses, and soft, tanned elk hides for blankets. After some shuffling around, Yah-Su dropped a slab of dried deer meat into Shonan's hand. Evidently he intended to save the meat lashed to Tagu's back.

Altogether, Yah-Su had a camp, an outcast's camp.

One skill Yah-Su had was sleeping. He was already rolled up in one of the bed rolls and snoring like a bull.

Shonan hurt too much to sleep. He sat and thought things through. When father and son disappeared, whisked away to the land of the Little People, Yah-Su must have gone on ahead to the Brown Leaf village and waited for them. No question he was their friend. After a few days in the world of the Little People and nearly a week's travel, Shonan and Aku turned up. Yah-Su probably saw them—he seemed super-observant—and he certainly knew about the sentries. He didn't show himself, just as he didn't reveal himself at the river crossing, but let the Brown Leaves spring their ambush and then helped out when he could do some good.

But why did Yah-Su have a camp near the Brown Leaf village? Shonan thought again, *outcast*. Among the Galayi, villagers punished by banishment were utterly cut off from their people—not even relatives would spare them the slightest help. Usually such people went crazy and disappeared forever. Occasionally, the strong ones became bitter enemies of their own people. In that case Yah-Su might have a series of invisible animal dens. Shonan wondered if he would soon find out.

The notion of an outcast bothered him. The Galayi people banished members for only one reason, killing a fellow tribesman. He looked at the beast sleeping next to him. A killer? Definitely. A killer of one of his own? Possibly.

But a friend to me and Aku.

Shonan would have chewed on the problem longer, except that his breaths fell into rhythm with Tagu's, and the Red Chief drifted off.

❖

The morning showed why this was a camp. A seep oozed from under the rock at the uphill end. Yah-Su picked up two of several gourds of water beside it, handed Shonan one, and drained the other. No water had ever tasted better. Shonan had gone all night dry.

The angle in the sharp turn of the ravine formed a huge triangular room with a flat roof. The stone of the earth shaped the sea here as much as the sea shaped the earth. The water from the seep never even reached the bottom of the gully. Apparently the tide was going back out—the ravine was mud-bottomed now.

Yah-Su gave Shonan a dab of fat to rub on his belly. The war chief did it very gingerly.

The buffalo man handed Shonan another slab of dried buffalo meat and took one for himself. When he finished eating, Shonan whispered, "When you got the pack dog . . ."

Yah-Su clamped Shonan's mouth and nose so hard he felt like he couldn't breathe. After a long moment he let go of Shonan, who felt full of fire—no one treated the Red Chief that way.

Then he realized Yah-Su didn't know anything about Galayi positions of honor, and just wished the beast knew his own strength.

Yah-Su pulled out his knife, drew the point along his own throat, and then made the same motion toward Shonan's throat. Then he clamped a hand over his own mouth.

All right, thought Shonan, *we shut up and stay put.*

And hope that Aku got back to the Amaso village of the Galayi tribe safely.

15

It took four nights of flying. Days were no good. Aku could see the raptors cruising the skies—hawk, eagle, osprey, and the buzzard to clean up afterwards. He didn't have to remember how his mother died. The pictures of her and the attacking hawk played bright and deadly in his mind. He was left with nothing of her but the three feathers he wore in his hair when he took human form. Her legacy was this lesson—owl shape and night flight.

❖

In the first moments of the day's light, from above, Aku watched Iona walk toward the river carrying two water gourds. His heart was already beating fast from wing-flapping—now it zoomed. He wanted to grab her, roll on the ground with her, laugh with her, kiss, make love. Except that she wouldn't make love to an owl.

At an eddy where the river was still, Iona bent and dipped the gourds into the sweet water.

He lit in a snag. As fast as he could, he put himself through the transformation. When he was finished, Aku felt behind his ears, under his arms, and in his groin, places where, if he wasn't thorough, he sometimes left feathers.

He ran. Iona was walking briskly, barefooted. The earth

was cold in the dawn. He ran faster, thinking how he'd grab her waist and swing her around and she'd see his face and they'd both shriek with excitement. But she turned left, away from the circle of huts of the Amaso village. She headed for the brush hut where the moon women stayed.

He felt a pang. If she was on her moon, he would not be able to touch her until it was past. He could talk to her from a couple of steps away, but the medicine of moon blood was strong. Even touching a moon woman might ruin whatever medicine a man had.

Aku stopped. He had the power to metamorphose into an owl. He had some ability to see beyond appearance into the spiritual nature of things. His grandmother had told him what great gifts these faculties were, and his own experience told him some of the truth of her words. No question—he couldn't go near the moon women's lodge.

He felt a jolt. What on earth was he thinking? She was full of his child. She couldn't be . . .

"Aku!"

She set the gourds down, ran, and slammed into his arms.

He swung her. He felt a drum-flutter of joy rise in his chest, and quelled it. He set her down. "Your nose!" she cried. She barely touched the scab running down it. He started to explain, but his face collapsed. "My father is dead," he said.

Holding hands, sometimes stopping to kiss, they made their way down to where the river ran into the sea. At a glance Aku saw that the tide was flowing out, sucking the river into its immensity. They sat, and over the shush of waters, he told her the story. He wept. She wept. They lay down, held each other, and grieved.

And after a while another feeling, wild, strong, uncontrollable, rose in Aku, and they made a declaration with their bodies—*I am alive.*

Aku slept on the sand for most of the day, Iona lounging comfortably nearby. Sometimes she drew a breath in so far it hurt, and eased it out. She'd been scared. She hadn't let herself know how scared.

Once she slipped away to get some water and balls of cornmeal rolled in honey. She thought Aku must yearn for something other than dried meat.

When he woke up, only a glimmer of sun stole through the treetops on the western hills. He wolfed down the cakes. They held each other and kissed and cooed for a few minutes more.

"Harvest Dance," said Aku, a solemn promise.

"Harvest Dance," said Iona.

At that ceremony their families would sing the songs that would tell everyone that their son and daughter were become one flesh. At the council there the new, combined village would elect chiefs. But what stirred their blood was the thought of making a life together. What people would remember would be the first marriage between the Galayi and Amaso groups of the Amaso village.

What great luck. He loved Iona, and she loved him. At the Harvest Dance his great-grandmother Tsola would give them a special blessing, and they would move into Oghi's house, and sleep together in hide blankets. Iona would be his new home.

"I have to show you something," said Aku.

"I've already seen it," said Iona. She grabbed. "When it was better."

"This is something not every man has," he said. He was tickled at himself. With great ceremony he unrolled the flutes from their hide wraps. Her expression was mystified. When he played a few tones on the green flute, silvery beauty agile as sunlight on rippling waves, her eyes seemed enchanted.

She was also enchanted by the story of his visit with the Little People. "Knee high?" she exclaimed.

"Knee high," he repeated.

He explained the power of the green flute's song.

"It heals any wound?" Iona asked. "Any illness?"

"Wounds are of the body. I can't do anything for those. Sickness is of the spirit, and this song restores the spirit. That's what the Little People said." She ran her fingers up and down the flute, and her eyes glowed.

"Now I want to play the red one for you," he said in a different tone. He played part of the song. Rono had warned him never to play all of either song, not for anyone, unless it was being used for its sacred purpose.

Iona looked at him uncertainly. The section he played was slow, grave, with only hints of something celestial. "What's it for?" she murmured.

"Raising the dead," said Aku. "If someone dies and I get to them before the spirit has left for the Darkening Land, the song will bring them back to this world."

Iona looked at the father of her child, who came to her bearing greatness.

"Or so the Little People said," Aku said softly.

Grave-eyed, they squeezed both hands, looking, seeing, and feeling. Aku had lived for a couple of weeks with the understandings that were opening in Iona's mind.

Could he tell her about his ability to become an owl? Not yet, he thought—one crash of realization at a time.

He decided to tell her about getting captured by the Brown Leaves, threatened with torture, and cut on the nose. He didn't mention how the witch and the shaman united into Maloch, a new incarnation of the Uktena, and he just plain fabricated a story about how he slipped his bonds, treading carefully around the revelation of shape-shifting.

When he finished, she cocked her head skeptically. "That's not what you wanted to tell me."

Aku flushed. Caught. He juggled thoughts, possibilities. "No," he said, "I . . . I have to go see my great-grandmother." He rearranged thoughts in his mind. "I don't know where Salya is. The witch and shaman, if they were telling the truth . . . If my sister is a body without a spirit, where is she?"

She eyed him warily. "When will you leave?"

"Tonight."

"Tonight? You haven't even seen Oghi."

"I have to."

"At *night?*"

"It's safer that way," he fudged.

Iona put his hands on her hips and stared at him.

All right, evasion wasn't going to work. "The truth is, there's things I can't tell you yet."

"You . . ."

He raised a hand. "Not yet," he repeated.

With a canny edge in her voice, she said, "Let's go see Oghi."

"No!" he said too loud and too fast. Oghi would give away his owl secret immediately. "I need to leave."

"You want to make me really mad?"

"Iona, there are other things going on here. I can't talk about them. I've got to go see my great-grandmother."

Iona studied his face. At last, with the wisdom of generations of women who watched their men act bone-headed, she nodded. "I'll pack you some food, so you can go out and slay the world's demons."

16

All day Shonan and Yah-Su crouched in the shadows of the cave and listened to Brown Leaf warriors walking up and down the hillsides, searching for the Red Chief who cut a swath through their people.

Shonan supposed he was safe. The enemies were damned unlikely to find this camp. It crouched far back in a corner of the ravine, and on both sides the rock walls were overhanging. Anyone peering down would see that the muddy bottom showed no tracks. Clearly Yah-Su had camped here for years. If the Brown Leaves hadn't found his camp in all that time, they wouldn't find it today.

Shonan hated hiding. He wanted to *do* something. He wanted to find Aku. He wanted to fight. He put more fat on his raging belly burn.

At full dark Yah-Su motioned that they should go. They moved out by stealth.

It was impressive, in the Red Chief's mind, that a man the size and shape of a buffalo could weave through the forest with less noise than Tagu made. The fellow had survived for a reason. By the time the moon came up, they were tucked deep in another cave, this time with few supplies and no water. The next night they traveled until dawn and came to a cave behind a waterfall.

Yah-Su grinned broadly, jumped behind the curtain of water, jumped back out, grinned bigger, and with a hand invited Shonan in. With a couple of deft steps, you could get in without getting wet.

This looked like Yah-Su's main camp, if he had such a thing. A lovely, liquid light gleamed through the falling water and showed a room that got wider as it deepened. Yah-Su had stacks of rolled hides, all protecting dried meat. The man clearly was a good hunter, and he must have learned to tan hides himself. Against the walls leaned weapons—clubs, spears, spear throwers, all with well-flaked heads nicely lashed to the bodies. He had a pile of knives of flint and obsidian, with handles of everything from wood to a bear jawbone.

Shonan looked around curiously. Because of the water-reflected light, this was a remarkable home.

He realized they could talk—the water would cover the sound. "It's beautiful," he said.

Yah-Su smiled sweetly and said something in the Amaso tongue. Shonan resorted to signs—he hated it when people didn't speak Galayi, as right-thinking people did. "Good place."

"Thanks." Tagu came to Shonan, who rubbed his ears.

Awkwardly, he told Yah-Su with signs and gestures what was what. "I want to go back to the Brown Leaf village and kill the shaman." He spoke aloud the shaman's name, Maloch.

"No," signed Yah-Su.

"I'll do it alone," signed Shonan. Signing cut speech to the basics.

Now Yah-Su was stumped. After a few minutes he fingered, "*Big* want to?"

"Yes."

"Maloch is also the Uktena." He spoke the name of the

dragon. Evidently the two tribes called the monster by the same name.

"Yes."

"We die."

Shonan sighed. He would be glad to have the man beast as a war comrade. He fixed Yah-Su with his eyes. "A warrior dies maybe any day. A warrior, okay to die."

Galayi tradition said that two kinds of the dead were quickly reborn onto the Earth, warriors who were killed in battle and women and children who died in childbirth.

Yah-Su looked at Shonan with huge brown buffalo eyes. "They stop looking for us. Then we go."

That simple.

❖

They talked. It was damned awkward, in Shonan's mind, to talk with your fingers. But they were stuck inside, they were safe, they had nothing to do, so they talked.

Shonan told about his war exploits. If he read Yah-Su right, the young beast was fascinated. He was another man of action, he understood. You come to situations that have to be faced. You clear your mind for moments of pure action, without thought, in a way moments of pure beauty. If you kept things simple and true, if your actions were bold and quick, you probably lived. And you felt real. The rest of life wasn't like that.

Those meanings underlaid Shonan's tales. He had the impression that Yah-Su understood.

But Shonan didn't understand Yah-Su, so he asked him, "Why do you live alone?"

"I don't like to be alone," said the buffalo man. "I plan to get a dog like Tagu." He turned the dog over and rubbed his belly.

The beast was evading. When Shonan pressed him, he wouldn't answer, not really. He fingered a lot of things. He threw out quite a few words to go with them, but the words were in the Amaso language, and Shonan didn't understand them. Shonan did learn for sure that Yah-Su was from the Amaso village.

Shonan got the picture that Yah-Su had been mocked by other boys when he was an adolescent because he was humpbacked. Yah-Su felt humiliated, probably thought marriage would be impossible for him, and for that reason he could never truly be part of the village, one of the people. So he ran off and started living by himself.

"That was before you got so big?" sighed Shonan.

"Yes." Yah-Su always seemed polite and considerate in the way he conducted himself. The people who thought he was a beast had the wrong fellow.

"You learned to hunt, make lamps, everything else by yourself?"

"I saw it around the village. And my mother's brother, sometimes I would go see him at night. He helped me get good at making weapons."

"You still go there?"

"One of my relatives trades things to me. For meat. But she . . . she doesn't want anyone to know."

There were more details, but that was the story.

Yah-Su wanted to know the particulars of what happened when Shonan and Aku were captured, more than he'd been able to see from the distant shadows. Shonan told him how a creature tricked up to look like his daughter lured them into a trap, how the "daughter" taunted them with whorish talk of what she did with Maloch. She was no daughter, but a false creation of Maloch shaped like Salya. Then the two of them did an obscene dance and melded themselves into one creature, Maloch.

Then he told how Aku shape-shifted into an owl and escaped.

Shonan asked, "You don't think we can kill Maloch?"

Yah-Su shrugged the most massive shoulders Shonan had ever seen and shook his shaggy head.

"Then why are you going with me?"

"Maybe you'll be my friend."

❖

On the second afternoon Shonan asked Yah-Su if he wanted to leave that night. The buffalo man shook his head no. Shonan thought the man's reluctance was odd. He knew Yah-Su was not afraid of a fight. Bluntly, he signed, "What is it? What are you afraid of?" He didn't believe such a warrior had a great fear of being killed.

Yah-Su shrugged.

"Do you like Maloch the Uktena?"

"I hate him." The buffalo man's eyes flickered with fire. Then he lowered his head. "He took over the village. He kills the pretty girls."

Shonan nodded. Yah-Su had watched what happened. He saw the warriors go to neighboring villages and steal girls. He watched as Maloch the Uktena ate their life-fires.

"Then what's wrong?"

"No one can kill the Uktena."

"He has armor," Shonan agreed.

"No one can kill the Uktena."

"He has teeth like knives." Shonan didn't think the dragon's short arms and small claws were a big factor.

"No one can kill the Uktena."

"He has that diamond eye. If you let it blind you, you're dead."

Yah-Su said nothing.

Shonan regarded Yah-Su. In this world everything could be killed—everything died. Death made Earth different from the world above and the Underworld. He liked it that way. Battle, the risk of life, death right in your nostrils—it was exhilarating.

"Let's wait one more day," he said.

❖

"I want to practice with your spear throwers."

Yah-Su nodded.

Yah-Su had a place for his own practice. You could hurl a dart into a mound of dirt twenty paces away or arc a dart to the far end of the meadow a hundred paces away.

The weapon was a kind of spear given the speed of a shooting star. You used a lever with a cup on the end to hold the dart, a slimmer, lighter spear the length of a man. With this thrower, which increased the length of your arm hugely, the dart became the deadliest of weapons.

Shonan knew damn well that a spear-thrower dart would kill any living creature.

Yah-Su had three spear throwers—he was a real warrior— but Shonan didn't know them. He needed to throw with each one, feel its heft, test its balance, learn which one suited his arm and style. He practiced at twenty paces, not a hundred. He intended to drive the dart head clear through the dragon.

He knew by noon, and chose one. The dart was heavy for his arm, but it was the lightest of the three.

Yah-Su signaled that he would carry the others.

Shonan smiled, clapped the buffalo man on the shoulder, and they walked back to the cave behind the waterfall.

They had three shots. He would need only one.

❖

Shonan was amazed by Yah-Su's strength and agility. Not only did he have trouble keeping up with his comrade on the way back to the Brown Leaf village, they wore Tagu out. In the dark Shonan couldn't figure out the route Yah-Su was taking. Like any good fighting man, as he and Aku walked the trail, Shonan had made a clear picture in his mind of the creeks and ridges. But he couldn't puzzle out where Yah-Su was headed. He shrugged and followed. This was Yah-Su's territory, and he was its master.

The second night they camped in sand. Since the moon was dropping behind the mountains to the west, Shonan couldn't see the ocean, but he could hear it and smell it. When he crawled into his blankets, he was comfortable. He liked the soft shush of the sea on the sand.

At dawn Shonan saw nothing but the rocky point above him and an infinite ocean. Yah-Su led the way up the point, and from the top Shonan got a look across the bay at the Brown Leaf village. Their hiding place was tucked behind rocks opposite and jutting into the sea. Did Yah-Su mean for them to make their move from the ocean side? Did he have a plan?

Yah-Su signed, "Let's watch."

Watch was what they did all day. They saw nothing out of the ordinary—men, women, kids, dogs, people doing the ordinary tasks of life, others crossing the village common to visit friends or relatives, adolescent boys playing the ball game. Assuming they had quit searching for Shonan, the men were mostly out hunting deer. Dried meat, parched corn, chestnuts, acorns, and seeds would get them through the winter. A few old people wouldn't be able to chew the meat well enough to get enough nourishment, and some of them would dwindle away. That was the way of the world.

Shonan intended never to reach such a point. He wanted to die *living*, to go out in a glorious fight, all juices pumping, and then receive a warrior's honor, quick rebirth.

Maloch came out of his house three times, wandered around, and talked to a few people. Mostly, though, he stayed inside. The smoke flagging out of the hole showed that he had a good fire and probably a cozy home. Shonan got a kick out of that idea—a dragon comfortable by the fire. Since the old stories said he was male and female at once, maybe he was having sex with himself.

Yah-Su pointed out the tide several times during the day. When it came in, some of the sandy tidal flats were covered, and the bay was deeper. Though there was an outlet, it was like a saltwater pond fed by the river at low tide and the sea at high tide. Now, at high tide, the ocean came into the bay and up the river. The stream might be hard to cross. When the tide receded, the river turned into several braids of shallow water. One of the braids fed the bay, and bay water flowed out to sea.

Shonan wondered why Yah-Su was so keen about knowing the tides. Maybe he was afraid the river would cut off their retreat.

Right after the sun came down, when the tide was all the way out, Yah-Su got very excited. He started pointing and kept signing, "Watch." Maloch came out of his house, strode to the bay, took off his clothes, and bathed in the bay. Not only bathed but lolled, splashed, and played. Unarmed.

Shonan signed, "Every day at sunset?"

Yah–Su nodded yes.

"How long does it take him to change from a man to a dragon?"

Yah–Su signed, "Underneath he is a dragon."

"Beneath his human skin?"

A nod yes.

Shonan considered. He considered longer. Then he said, "We've got the bastard."

❖

They watched another entire day. Shonan wanted to see everything again, soak it all up, make sure of his plan. He liked it. It was bold and decisive. Best of all, it wasn't to be executed by the mixed bag of a war party but just two good fighters.

That night, before the moon came up, they walked upstream, found a place to tie Tagu by the river, and left him enough meat. Then they roamed the coastline in the dark looking for flotsam. Shonan wanted a hunter's blind. Finally they found a thick log as long as two men. One on each end, since the tide was against them, they slogged their way toward the bay on foot. Before long Yah–Su snatched the log, slung it onto his shoulder, and stalked forward bearing the entire weight. They slid it into the bay well away from the outlet and crept back to their hiding place. The next tide would wipe out all tracks.

From first light on they watched the village as fish–hunting birds watch the sea. All the normal things happened, including a catch-as-catch-can ball game without the full number of players. Shonan thought it was odd that the Brown Leaves played the same game as his people, a ball thrown with long-handled rackets, very rough, a way of preparing boys for the violence of war. Though he observed scrupulously, nothing happened to change Shonan's plan.

At midafternoon, they walked upstream behind their ridge of land. Shonan carried the one spear thrower he was familiar with, Yah-Su carried two. Shonan was confident that his single dart would do the job.

At the spot he'd picked out, they eased up to the top of the ridge and watched. Normal village activity. When the two were sure they wouldn't be seen, they slipped down the hillside and into the river.

Yah-Su signed, "Success or failure, we stick together afterwards."

Shonan answered, "And go to the Amaso village."

Yah-Su pursed his mouth and gave a reluctant yes.

They floated downstream. This was the dicey part. Mostly the riverbank hid them from the village, but not always. They stayed in the water up to their eyes and floated their weapons like sticks. Where the bank got low, they turned onto their backs and floated downstream with only their noses above water. They slipped into some river cane and squatted in the dense foliage, heads above water, to get a break from floating. Shonan fingered the cane, remembering that he needed to make weapons when he got home—knives, a couple of war clubs, a couple of spears, a couple of spear throwers, even a blow gun. The damn Brown Leaves had taken all his weapons except the little blade that saved his life, the knife in the cleft of his bottom.

They floated.

The river braided, and they eased into the left-hand fork, toward the bay. This braid was closest to the village, but it was also the deepest and brought them to their prey.

Shonan motioned toward the left bank. When they beached, he signed that he was going to take a look at the town. He crawled up a short gully in the bank, raised his head behind some weeds, and peered toward the village. Everything as usual, even another ball game. Some villagers were watching the boys play, which was good—it held their attention.

He crawled back down the gully and nodded at Yah-Su. They slipped into the water and floated on. Shonan thought, *I've never gotten a ride to a killing before.*

Around the bend a young man stood waist-deep in the water cutting cane.

Damn!

Shonan kicked his legs silently and eased to the far side of the narrow stream. Maybe the young fellow wouldn't look up. If he did, maybe he wouldn't see them.

Shonan saw that Yah-Su was swimming quietly closer to the Brown Leaf. The Red Chief yearned to scream, but noise was exactly what they didn't need.

The young cutter got a piece he wanted and raised up. He put one end on the river bottom to measure it. Just right, his own height. He put it to his mouth to blow through it. Then, terribly, he swung the cane upriver, as though to shoot at something there.

Two steps away the cutter saw the face of a beast in the water. He screamed.

The beast rose up hugely—now the young man's lungs froze—and plunged a knife deep into his chest.

Shonan swam like the devil for the village side of the river. He scrambled up and looked.

No one was disturbed or excited. The ball game was in full swing, and some spectators were cheering. As Shonan watched, one team scored a goal. The players tucked their rackets under their arms and talked idly with each other.

We got away with it.

Shonan looked back toward Yah-Su. The buffalo man had heaved the cutter's body onto the bank. Unless someone found it this afternoon—unlikely—the high tide would probably take it to sea tonight.

Yah-Su himself was already back in position, floating downstream. Shonan followed suit.

When they came into the bay, at first they couldn't find the log. Then they saw it, beached on the sand, probably by tidal action. They swam to it—nothing to do except take the risk—and pulled it into the bay.

Communicating by nods, they decided to swim the log very slowly, so that an observer wouldn't realize it was moving, to some reeds on the village side of the bay. This was close to where Maloch customarily undressed and came into the water. The tide was sucking water out to sea, so the movement of the log from the reeds toward the middle would look natural. This was the way Shonan planned it. Silently, he thanked his comrade for showing him how the tides worked.

Nothing to do but wait.

Some fighters hated this part. Shonan loved it. He taught his young men—would have taught Aku if the boy had let him—how to be patient. Patience was one of the warrior's critical skills. To be still, to be quiet, to observe. To watch all day if necessary, in a relaxed but alert way. If you were still enough in mind and body, the creatures of the forest ceased to notice you. The birds started singing again, the rabbits foraged, the deer browsed, everything went back to normal.

Then, when your enemy came, he would have no warning, no signs.

The quality yoked to patience was readiness. Shonan crouched in the reeds, head behind the log, ready.

The bay fell into shadow, and deeper shadow. The light faded to almost nothing. Just as Shonan was deciding the bastard had decided to skip his daily bath, Maloch came over the dune. He took off his clothes—*That disguise of human skin is stupid!*—and clomped into the water. Shonan noticed what he had forgotten, how huge the dragon's hind legs were—how huge the man-monster was.

Fear trilled up and down him. He looked sideways at Yah-Su. He was sure the buffalo man knew as well as he did that when you're scared, use that feeling to propel yourself.

A quick glance and the two killers began to push the log toward the monster, at the speed a nearby leaf was floating toward the sea.

Wait for twenty paces. All I have to do is get the spear thrower ready, stand up, and I will kill you.

Maloch first dipped himself several times. In this shallow water, at ebb tide, he had to lie down to get all of his body into the water at the same time. Once he lay underwater for several seconds, then raised up and shook himself like a dog. He was like a dog playing in the water. A monster dog.

Down to forty paces.

Maloch began to cavort. He splashed water on himself with his hands. He kicked the water in every direction, yelling on every kick.

Down to thirty paces. Poor light. Breath hard to get.

Suddenly Maloch did a stroke like a dolphin, or maybe a serpent monster, straight toward them.

Twenty paces.

Both men got their weapons ready.

Ten paces. Is he charging us?

No, the angle was off to the side.

Still ten, still about ten.

Suddenly, Maloch turned and his chest faced straight toward Shonan. *Better than anything I hoped for.*

Shonan hurled his dart with all his strength, straight into the chest.

It hung there for an instant and dropped into the water. The human skin ripped, and green scale showed underneath.

Maloch roared, and his face began to change. Immediately, a diamond shone on his forehead, but in the twilight it didn't reflect enough light to blind anyone.

Yah-Su threw his dart like storm winds fling a heavy branch of a tree. It rammed its way between the monster's teeth and into the roof of its mouth—a sure death shot.

Maloch bit the dart and broke it like a toothpick. He launched himself through the air at Yah-Su.

Yah-Su dived to the side.

Shonan jumped onto the serpent monster's neck, drew his knife, and stabbed furiously, over and over, at the beast's heart.

Maloch roared at every blow. He tried to reach for Shonan, but his little arms wouldn't reach far enough backward.

Maloch writhed and shook violently. Shonan flew back a dozen paces and splashed into the water on his butt.

Yah-Su gripped his second dart and hurled it as far down Maloch's gullet as he could. Then he yelled, "Run!"

They waded, splashed, and ran. At the far end of the bay, where the river entered, Shonan looked back. The serpent monster was walking back toward the village, pulling at the dart with his puny arms, unable to jerk it out of his throat.

They hadn't killed it. Shonan wasn't even sure they'd hurt it.

17

The owl man Aku flew for four straight nights—across tidal plains, through the hilly piedmont, and toward the distant Galayi Range. No human being could have kept up. He followed the big river upstream, and up, and up, all the way to the base of the Galayi Mountains, which his people believed to be the center of Turtle Island.

He flew over Equani and over his home village, Tusca. Three generations ago his hero-ancestor Zeya, the Hungry One, had defeated a Tusca army of overwhelming numbers here, using his marvelous power as a shape-shifter. Then he restored the village of his enemies, a humanitarian act that made his memory live forever.

And there Aku was born and raised. His lifelong friends and members of his family still lived in the huts below. Part of him wanted to drift onto a branch, change into the form everyone knew him by, and walk into the town. He would eat a good breakfast, catch up on the news, hug his women relatives, and slap the shoulders of his uncles, cousins, and the comrades of his youth.

Another part of Aku the owl man, though, wanted to avoid all the people who once knew him. He could feel inside that he was different. They might recognize his face but would not know his spirit. He did not fully know himself.

He cruised over the shadowy buildings, soaking up the sights with his owl eyes, filling the dark spaces with warm memories.

Then Aku left the river and followed an ancient trail up the steep mountainside. At night there were no thermals to ride, so he labored up into the range, and then across several canyons and more ridges to the Cheowa River and upstream. Here in a broad valley spread the tribe's principal village, Cheowa, four separate circles of wattle-and-daub huts, smoke drifting out of holes at the tops, the fires glowing to keep away the night freezes of autumn. Aku the owl hoo-hooted in honor of this sacred town, the breeding ground of the tribe's chief shamans, the Wounded Healers.

Behind the village on the western side loomed Emerald Mountain, and halfway up its forested side, the entrance to the Emerald Cavern. Deep in this cavern lived Tsola, the woman he called Grandmother, though she was actually his mother's grandmother. Here, since before the memories of the grandfathers of the oldest men, had lived every Seer and Wounded Healer of the Galayi people.

Tsola would know this human owl man. He wingflapped straight up the mountain.

Aku was queasy. First, he was coming to confess he had a gigantic favor to ask, and he hated to be a beggar, especially before this powerful woman. Second, he had to humble himself and admit to his mother's grandmother that he had never known himself as well as she had.

Now he approached the Healing Pond, the pool of waters just outside the cavern. Here seekers came to ask the help of the caretakers who lived in the little hut. For a day or two they dipped themselves in the cold, fizzy water and then went home with their aches and pains eased. Aku lit in a great chestnut tree to look not at the pond or hut, but be-

yond them at the entrance to the cavern. His feathers ruf-
fled, and he felt a chill that did not come from the breeze.

Like many holy places, the Emerald Cavern was mostly
unknown. As a center of power and magic it was as much
feared as loved. The reports of its mysteries passed from
mouth to ear in whispers. It was a vast spiderweb of earth and
stone hallways, flowing black waters, and weird shapes from
the darkest of night-haunted dreams.

Like the cavern, the shamans who lived in its depths were
strange, eerie, tinged with danger. These men and women
had explored the odd fingerways, the passages that seemed to
be not only the inner mountain but somehow human consciousness itself—they had come to know this vastness over
many generations by wandering through the passages, crawling and squeezing through some of them, and swimming
through many.

Nothing made people shiver like the rumors that the cavern arteries were subterranean rivers. Who knew the source
of such rivers? Perhaps the Underworld itself, the Darkening
Land. Yet the stream that issued from the main entrance to
the cavern brought healing to human beings.

The cavern was honored and feared—its masters and mis-
tresses were honored and feared.

Aku looked at the entrance and wondered. Or was it the
owl man who looked and wondered? He and Aku didn't
seem identical at that moment. Aku's knowledge was the
merest shadow, his ignorance vaster than caverns.

Something near the entrance shifted. A strange feeling
came into Aku's chest, like a cloud of ice crystals.

❖

Across the pond came a deep voice. "Good morning, Aku."

Aku was speechless.

"You could try being friendly," said a similar voice.

Still speechless.

"Get your tail over here."

"Wing feathers, too," echoed the other voice, teasing.

"You know us, Aku," said the first voice. "I'm Bola, my son is Bota."

Aku remembered. He could also make out their shapes faintly, ink against the black of night, the panther son and grandson of the Seer, her guardians. He remembered that the Powers gave the ability to see at night only to Panther and Owl, because of all animals only they passed the test.

"You could shed those feathers, Aku," said Bola.

Here came the Feeling again. One previous visit and the panther remembered his name?

"Hoo hoodoo hoo hoo," called Bola. "Get over here."

Human owl man fluttered over to them and lit on a waist-high boulder, carefully out of reach.

"So," said Bola, "are you a human being or an owl?"

Neither Aku nor owl man knew what to say, and he couldn't tell the panthers apart.

"If you're the Seer's great-grandson, you have a claim to see her. If you're just any old owl, you're . . ."

Bola leapt as fast as sunlight glances off water and into an eye. In that flicker owl man was in the panther's mouth, pricked by cat teeth, pain shooting from talons to skull.

The other panther, Bota, said, "My father was going to say, 'You're a snack.' Maybe it's time to tell us that you're a human being."

"Human being," squeezed out Aku.

Bola dropped him like a hunk of meat. "Show us," he said.

Orange feathers to face of flesh, beak to nose and mouth, wings to arms . . . Aku had never changed so fast.

"We know your gifts," said Bola, with deliberate indif-

ference. "Don't try to fool us." Then, sharply, "What are
those things in your hand?"

"Gifts from the Little People."

"The red and green flutes," said Bola.

"That's a lot of respect from the Little People," said Bota.
Bola cut off the talk. "No need to wait for light, let's go."
The Feeling raged now.

Bola motioned with his feline head, and they were off.
The first cave room was twice the size of any house Aku
had ever been in. The panther leapt across the stream that
formed the pool below. Aku jumped, dunked one foot,
slipped on an algaed stone, and soaked his moccasins, breechcloth, and leggings. Though he couldn't see the panther's
face, Aku heard his chuckle-growl.

He felt the flutes to make sure they were all right. Their
wood was thick, unlikely to break.

They turned right, out of the big chamber, into a tunnel.
Within a hundred steps the light disappeared. He couldn't see
how big the passage was, or how small. He bumped his head
on something stony overhead.

"You can't see now, can you?" said Bola. "That's why we
don't invite your owl eyes in. Even Tsola doesn't see as well
as an owl."

Aku bumped his head again.

"Better get down on your hands and knees here."

The trip Aku made into the cavern as a child hadn't been
this scary. His mother had carried a torch. Now he was blind
and lost. He'd crossed into a different reality-darkness, an
absolute, soul-numbing darkness. Here the Feeling was
breath itself.

"Now grab hold of this rope and use it for a handhold,"
Bola said. He thrust it against Aku's hand. "You'll need it,
I won't."

Aku heard scratchings on rock from below. Not only could the cat see in the dark, he was ten times as surefooted as Aku. He wound the rope around both hands. It felt like thongs of rawhide twisted together. He hesitated.

"Just trust it. Step off and work your way down."

Into pitch blackness, his feet groping for holds, his hands and arms his lifeline. The slope felt almost vertical.

Suddenly his feet pawed at nothing but air.

"It's all right," said Bola. "Just slide down the rope itself for a way."

Aku squeezed the rope for dear life, rubbed his forearms and thighs raw as he slid, and was surprised to land on sand in a stream.

"This way," said Bola, and Aku followed his voice. He'd never been turned so topsy-turvy.

They wandered. That was the only sense of it Aku had— they wandered. He lost all sense of place. Though the sky was trackless, a flier could see exactly where he was in a vast panorama. The cavern was genuinely trackless. Here the traveler didn't know what was a hand span from his face. This was a new meaning of *lost*. You could walk a day and touch nothing but the stone and clay under your moccasins, not knowing whether the walls were a breath or a hundred steps away. You could move an inch and fall off a precipice.

Lost. Occasionally, a word from Bola reminded Aku that he was not alone in the world. Otherwise he was utterly disoriented. The feeling of ice crystals in his chest was more real than the cavern.

"We clamber up some rocks here," said Bola. Climbing by grope—another new experience for Aku. Climb on and on—he pulled himself up forever.

And at the top a shock. He could see dark shapes. Gradually, his eyes put together recognition. A large room opened to shadowy sight. Slender columns of stone ran from floor to ceiling, or ceiling to floor, as though holding them apart. He remembered this room, and knew where to look. Far to the left he saw a faint glow, and a dark figure beside it. Grandmother's fire. Beyond it, he recalled, a flowing stream formed a pool of water the shape of a maple leaf.

"Welcome, Grandson." Her voice was soft and gentle, like the flutter of wings.

"It's good to see you, Grandmother." He and Bola padded toward her.

"I imagine being able to see anything is a relief." He could hear the smile in her voice.

When he got close enough to make out her face, she embraced him. She was elfin, slender, silver-haired, and had a graceful carriage. Her face was like the tobacco she was named for, a leaf that had been wadded up and pressed flat again. He felt a welling of love for her—or was it for any human creature? He hugged her back.

She sat back down near the fire and patted the ground. Bola curled up beside her. She looked up at Aku. "Sit," she said, "and we will eat and drink."

He folded his legs in front of the fire. He knew that she didn't keep it for light or warmth—the dark, cool cavern was home to her, had been for more than a hundred winters. No, this fire was sacred. It had been carried as coals from the council lodge at the Cheowa village, and that fire was said to be descended directly from the fire given to Earth creatures by Thunder, and never allowed to go out.

She brought him tea and a bowl of acorn and berry mush. All the Galayi people brought her food, in return for her guidance and in thanks for the benefit of the Healing Pool.

When they had eaten and traded pleasantries, Tsola said, "All right, Grandson, you haven't come all this way to gossip with your ancient relative. You want something. Before we can begin, I must ask you a very important question. Are you afraid?"

Aku hesitated. He had to show some gumption. He bumbled out, "No."

Her words were like stones being cracked together. "Of course you're afraid. Human beings are naturally afraid anywhere they can't see. I took your owl eyesight away from you and then told Bola to make the trip as frightening as possible." She patted the big, black cat. "That trick of grabbing him with your teeth was a devil of an idea."

"Thought you'd like that," said Bola.

"I asked Bola to bring you here a roundabout way, to put the fear of the cavern into you.

"Everyone of good sense who travels in the cave is half-terrified. They sense that they have entered an alien world, a place that is exotic, fantastic, and mysterious. Which is true. Physically, the cavern is incredible. In its curling passages you could walk all day every day for six moons and never take the same step twice. There are wonders here more amazing than sunsets, more beautiful than rainbows.

"The cavern is dangerous, too. Cliffs, rivers, every trick of direction you can imagine.

"Also, after the death of Zeya, an earthquake changed its shape completely. The sacred chamber, the Emerald Dome, was shut off. The course of the main river changed. Almost every passage was altered. Where the ground had been level, suddenly there were drops taller than an oak tree. Except under the sea, the cavern is the most dangerous place in the world to travel. And the earthquake destroyed all our knowledge of it. Bola, Bota, and I have had to re-learn it."

Wounded Healers sacrificed their eyesight in the outside world to be able to see in the cavern.

"I wanted you to sense the danger as vividly as you feel a knife wound. I wanted you to be scared." She smiled. "Well, what do you think of your great-grandmother now?"

"I've had an awful sense of dread since I arrived." The Feeling.

"Excellent, because it's the truth. Now why don't you tell me what you've come all this way for?"

Aku suspected that his grandmother already knew, but he told her the story of how Salya was kidnapped, how he and Shonan went to the village of her abductors and were captured. "I . . ." He didn't know how to say it. "I changed myself into an owl and flew away."

They looked at each other.

"They tortured and killed my father."

"So you used one of your abilities. You're not avoiding them anymore."

"I didn't have any choice. I was way out on the ocean, carried by a riptide. I couldn't swim back. My only chance was to fly. So I took it."

"Very good. I was worried that your father would force you to follow his path. Which isn't yours." She looked at him. He saw the fire reflected in her eyes and thought, *She's much more than my great-grandmother. She has a power I don't understand.* It gave him the Feeling.

"And what do you want to do now?"

"I don't know who to speak of first, Salya or my father."

"Tell me about your twin."

"Maloch said he'd eaten Salya's spirit but not her body. I don't know where her body is. I want to . . . I have to try to save her."

"He ate her spirit." Tsola's voice was contemptuous. "He consumes other people's life-fire and adds them to his own." She thought. "Do you know what that means?"

"No."

"Every living creature has a *yuwi*, a unique spiritual energy. Yours makes you what you are, mine makes me what I am. The same goes for crawfish, a sparrow, or a dandelion. It is your *life*. It never dies—but this is not the time to talk about that. If Maloch the Uktena steals your *life* . . ."

She held up a hand for a long time, thinking. When she spoke, she changed the subject. "Now speak of your father."

"His last words to me were a cry, 'Meet me in the Darkening Land.' I don't know what he meant. Die along with me? I don't think so. I think he meant, 'Meet me there and we'll get Salya's body out.' It's scary."

"Worse than scary. Your father will reappear in this world soon. But living people don't go into the Darkening Land and come out."

"She's down there. My father's down there. I have to go."

Tsola thought for a while. "Two reasons. You have to save your sister. And you have to be loyal to your father."

"Yes."

"And you're scared to go, so scared your pee comes out cold."

"Yes."

"If she's a body without a spirit, how will you save her?"

He showed her the flutes, the one that healed wounds of the spirit and the one that resurrected the dead.

"I don't know whether the powers of the Little People can accomplish something so enormous against the greatest of enemies, death itself." She pondered. "Are you sure you want to risk your life for this?"

"She's my sister. My twin."

Tsola gave an odd smile. Maybe she thought she was looking at a simpleton or at sublime simplicity. "You alone. I don't believe I will see you again."

"I know."

Unreadable changes ran across the old woman's face. Or perhaps that was a trick of the firelight. She took a huge breath in and let it out. "You have earned the chance to try." She looked at him for too long a moment. "You may become someone great. Or you'll become nothing at all."

He felt too small to speak.

She held his gaze, taking his measure. "This is what you're going against. The physical danger is trivial. To die physically is a small thing, compared to dying spiritually. It is an ember trying to glow next to the sun.

"Children imagine monsters in the dark." She shook her head. "The monster here is fear. I gave you the feeling of a cold cloud in your heart because I wanted to intensify your dread of being lost and blind in the cavern. Imagine a fear like being lost and blind among the stars. If you let yourself feel that fear, your spirit shrivels."

He didn't dare ask a question.

"Only those who become seers are able to look beyond the monstrosity to the truth." She got a faraway look and then returned her eyes to Aku. "Did Shonan ever tell you that on the battlefield the true killer is fear?"

"He said it over and over."

"In the spiritual world the true killer is also fear. If you quail, you die."

"I'm ready."

"No, you're not. You're a beginner as a shape-shifter, you haven't apprenticed yourself to a seer, you haven't learned a thousand lessons you needed before you came to me. You have no idea how ignorant you are, or how hard it will be. But for whatever reason life has put this task in your hands. For the coming days you are not a relative, and I am not your great-grandmother. I am Tsola, the Seer and Wounded

Healer. You seek to discover your powers. I am your daunting taskmaster."

She mused. "Do you know how to begin?"

"No."

"Good. You tell the truth. Which you didn't do with the mother of your child, which you didn't do with me. Because you were afraid of her reaction, you didn't tell her you are a shape-shifter. Because you were afraid of losing my respect, you denied your fear of the adventure in front of you.

"So now we must make a bargain. At every moment, in every word, with every gesture, you will tell the truth. Not only to me, but to yourself. That is your pledge. That is the cost of crossing the threshold of the world you want to go to. You will tell the truth to me, and you will tell it to yourself."

She raised her hand for the traditional gesture of sealing a pact, and he followed her lead. At the same moment they slapped the ground.

"And right now, Aku, son of Meli," the old woman said, "what is your truth? The spirit inside you, how does it feel?"

He nodded once before he spoke. "Scared and excited."

"That's a good beginning," she said. "Now get some sleep. We have hard work to do."

18

Tsola waited for Aku to wake up, sit up, and focus his eyes across the fire and on her. "Truth," she said.

Aku shook his head, held it still, and shook it again hard. His mind was still cobwebbed from sleep. He was trying to grow, half consciously, into his powers. While he was awake, he grew by thinking about being as much owl as man. While he was asleep, he grew by dreaming himself as an owl. He was exhausted from working in both states.

She handed him a tea she'd brewed to snap his mind awake. The young man—she refused to think of him as the boy he was—took a long swallow. She looked over at her son Bola, curled up in sable elegance. They both felt for Aku. Bola had guided many seekers through the cavern to her, and she'd initiated most of them—nothing she did was more important than creating shamans to guide the people. Generally, the seekers brought nothing but the awareness that they were different, that they bore the talent and responsibility of some kind of special powers. They came, learned something, and came back year after year before coming to the trial. Even after the most patient training, some failed the trial.

So why the dilemma of this young man, her own great-grandson? He had a genuine gift, and in time he might become a true shaman. Why, then, why, did he have to risk the trial now, when he was a spiritual infant? She was probably guiding him to his death. She shrugged inside herself. Her skills let her see and hear the Powers, not question them.

"Truth?" she repeated.

"All right," he said.

"You came a long way to see me. What do you want?"

"You are a seer. Tell me where my sister is."

"If Maloch ate her spirit," she said, "she's in the Under-world. But that's not what you came for."

"It isn't?"

Bola growled.

"You can do better," Tsola told him.

"My father is waiting." He felt a searing hurt. He owned a flute that would save the dying, but he had not been able to help his own father. "Is it possible to bring him back? Or her?"

Bola screwed himself into a different curl-up and gave Aku an impatient look.

"Yes." Tsola deliberately didn't tell him the rest. "That's still not what you want."

"I'm tired of this playing around."

Bola growled loudly, but Tsola liked the young man's spunk.

"I'll get you started. Look inside yourself. Did you come to get me to save your sister? Your father? Or to help you find the power you need within, so you can do it yourself?"

"That's a big bite," said Aku.

"Find the courage to tell the truth," said Tsola. She cocked her head and waited.

He waited several heartbeats. "Tsola, Seer, Wounded Healer, Grandmother, I want to find my sister and father and save them. Show me the way."

"Better, but not enough."

"Give me the strength to do it."

"No one can give you that strength. But you can discover it in yourself, if it's there."

"Help me."

"I can help you begin. You need more than you realize. You need courage. You need wisdom. You need to understand your powers. What it means to take the form of a human being, to take the form of an owl."

"Or a panther," said Bola.

"Yes," said Tsola, "some shape-shifters can become several animals. Bola and Bota are human beings, panthers, and ravens. They spend most of their time as panthers because that's the best way to protect me."

"And because I like it that way," said Bola.

"I can't wait to learn all this."

"Then learn fast. You also have to get some idea of what it means to be a seer."

"My father is in the Underworld. My sister is in the Underworld. Her spirit, her life-fire, is inside another being, a monster."

"I will show you how to begin if you will show me the respect of learning what you can. If not, I will only be giving you to Maloch the Uktena."

"I have to find my father and sister."

"First you have to find yourself."

19

As the three of them walked, Aku holding a torch high, Tsola issued her warnings.

"I've never sent anyone across who was so unprepared."

"I want to go." It was a flat, firm statement.

Bola led the way into a passage where the human beings had to crawl. Aku was tempted to flutter through as an owl, but crawled with his great-grandmother.

"The entrance to the Underworld is guarded by the Great Dusky Owl. You have to ask his permission."

"He'll see you're not ready," said Bola.

"What do I do?"

They stood up and walked through a graceful passage. She thought about her answer and couldn't find one. They squirmed through worm holes and waded down streams. They skirted a pond that appeared to have lily pads, except that the pads were pale stone. They strode into a room so bright with light from above—the outside world!—that Tsola had to shield her eyes. They scared a thousand bats into wild flight.

For Aku the cave was drenched in dread. He wanted to be somewhere else, anywhere else.

Bola and then Tsola stopped in a round room that was a dead end and lit two lamps of animal fat from the dying sparks of the torch. She handed Aku one lamp and kept the other. Aku saw a small stack of torches, hides, and gourds with food and water, all the signs of a long-term camp. Since he'd never seen a stone lamp, he inspected it. It had a handle and then a surface the size of a hand, with a place scooped out to hold rendered animal fat, all carved elegantly. A wick of cloth burned slowly.

"Hold it up and look at the bottom." Tsola held her lamp beneath his so he could see. Inscribed into the underside was a large eye, not a human eye, but a round one, like a bird's.

"An owl's eyes," she said, "because the owl is the master of the knowledge of life and death."

"It's beautiful," he said. And very different from the workaday lamps the people used, made of buffalo horn.

"Aku, lift your gaze."

The walls were covered with drawings of animals. Some were pecked into the rock, some stroked onto them in black and shaded with grays and blues, some painted in bright reds, oranges, yellows, greens, and purples.

Among the Galayi, drawings were common enough. If a man had a vision, or acquired an animal helper, or if he brought down a buffalo or slew an enemy, he might draw the event on a hide. But those drawings were childish compared to these.

These were . . . they had power. The power of beauty and the power of magic at once. They hummed with it.

"Unbelievable."

He studied a big painting of two buffalo that were, comically, facing each other not head to head but bottom to bottom. They were big, magnificent creatures, their heads turned toward the viewer with expressions that seemed to say, "I am Buffalo." The bull was solid black, the cow black with a large area on the flank colored red-brown, the color of a new calf. Aku wondered if the color was meant to suggest the next generation within the buffalo belly.

He stepped sideways and looked long at one that felt different. The artist had started with a bulge in the rock for a basic shape. By incising he had made the bulge into a large great dusky owl looking straight at the viewer. The rock was cut away to let the head, tufted horns, beak, and body stand out in relief. For the moment Aku had to avoid looking at the eyes, which drew him powerfully. He forced his eyes along the head and body of the bird, which were spotted black on the gray rock, and the legs striped with black. There were no talons.

From the spot where the claws might have grown issued a different feature of the rock itself—it seemed to be weeping huge tears, thicker than thumbs and long as arms. The tears ran down the rock until they were longer than the owl, and where the wall cut back, they dripped off it into mid air. King-sized stone tears, frozen in their grief.

Aku loved the way the artist had used the natural shapes of the rock, both the bulge and the drippings, and made them into what he saw in his head and felt in his heart. He stood transfixed.

After a while he let his eyes sail up to the eyes. They were huge orbs, out of proportion to the body, and painted a yellow that radiated energy, like mini-suns challenging observers with light and heat.

Grandmother interrupted his study. "Don't look into his eyes," she said, "not yet."

Aku felt her voice jerk him back into the ordinary world.

"Keep in mind that Owl is your spiritual ancestor."

He wandered a few steps and looked back up at the magical animals.

Aside from the power, what surprised him was that some of the animals were unrecognizable. Yes, there were deer, elk, buffalo, and rabbits. But the other animals didn't exist, as far as Aku knew.

"They do exist," said Tsola, "or have walked the Earth at some time, or they are Immortals."

Aku snapped his head around at her. Again it gave him the willies for someone to look into his mind.

"This is called a horse," Tsola said.

It was a beautiful, red-orange creature with four feet, a flowing mane, and a long black tail.

"This is a woolly mammoth."

It had a nose as long as a man's leg and horns too big to chase any animal that Aku knew about.

"This is a rhinoceros. That's an ibex. All of these creatures, well, the originals of them, live beyond the Sky Arch. You'll see some of them there."

Aku shook his head hard. He wondered if he was really awake.

"This is one you need to study," said Tsola.

Aku turned his attention to a vivid painting of the sun, flame-colored rays shooting out from a coal-hot center. Feelings welled in him that he could not speak aloud. He stepped back and took time to survey the room.

"These are the dwellers of the world above."

"Yes, among many others. The beings of that world are immortal. We mortal creatures are shadows of them."

"The drawings are ancient."

"Old beyond imagination, but the artist is me, with Bola's help. I saw them with the eye of the spirit, not the eyes of the body."

"Then why do you call them old?"

"Because they exist outside of Time."

Aku pondered that and asked, "Why hidden away in this cave?"

"Hidden away." She hesitated, smiling. "I don't think of them that way. These paintings are doorways to the world of the Immortals."

"You mean . . ."

"Years ago, when I made a journey to the Land Beyond the Sky Arch, I would come back and paint an Immortal I had met there and learned something from. I made the paintings an act of homage and looked at them as a way of honoring the Immortal creatures. Then I began to use the paintings themselves as gates to the Immortal world. If I wanted to visit Buffalo, I would look at his image and pass through to the world where he lives."

She looked for a moment at the buffalo bull and cow.

"Finally, I started using them as gates for the shamans in training who wanted to visit the Land Beyond the Sky Arch. Now they use the paintings as wings."

Aku looked at the paintings, stupefied. This was the Seer's real work. In a way it was much more real than the ordinary tasks of fetching water, growing corn, cooking, and other daily jobs of women in the village.

"It's hard to find a place for you to begin. Maybe as good a way as any is to tell you some of the big stories. Why not start with Grandmother Sun?"

❖

Tsola built a little fire, took shredded tobacco from a pouch, dropped it onto the flames, and said quietly, "This smoke, my breath, breath of the Earth, carry my prayers to the spirits above. May I see truly and speak truly."

She sat cross-legged and motioned for Aku to sit across

the fire from her. Bola padded to a wall and scratched his ribs on it.

"In the beginning, the Land Beyond the Sky Arch got too crowded, so everyone began to look down at Earth and think, 'Maybe we could live there.' But Earth was nothing but water, water everywhere. Well, you know the story of how Water Spider dived down and got dirt and made Turtle Island, the land we live on now, even though there's still a lot of water.

"So down the animals and plants came, and when they got here, they found out everything was different. They were missing something—they were like shadows, ghosts, not living beings, not running, jumping, laughing, loving, blood-pumping beings like we are now.

"Eagle, the highest flying of all birds, is the messenger between the world above and the world below, so he soared upward, beyond the sun, and asked what was wrong. 'You need fire,' he was told. 'Fire is energy, fire is vitality, fire is life.'

"Eagle lifted his voice to Thunder, 'Give us fire. We will die without fire.'

"Thunder gathered his strength and shot a bolt from the heavens. It split the sky and blasted into a hollow sycamore tree. Everyone watched, worried. When smoke wafted out of the top of the tree, they all rejoiced. Thunder had made the Earth the gift of fire.

"Even today Eagle is known as the bringer of thunder and lightning.

"Fire is a good example of how we don't see deep into things, beyond appearances to reality. Let's talk a little about the essence of fire. Our first idea about fire is that it keeps us warm, and it cooks our food. These are trivia. Fire is the spark that burns in all living beings. It is energy. It is life itself. Sometimes it seems to destroy. But watch fire burn a stick of wood. It doesn't destroy the stick—it transforms it into energy. You can feel the heat with your hand. You can see the light from the flame. You can even see the waves of heat rising up. And when fire burns a field of grass, or a patch of forest, it renews the earth to grow younger and greener grasses and trees. Fire is not just one flame. It is a life-giving energy, a gift of the spirits to the Earth.

"There, now you see part of what I mean by seeing be-yond the appearances of things to their spiritual reality.

"So, back on Earth they still needed fire. This burning sycamore was on an island, and the animals wondered how to get the fire. As they thought, they suddenly noticed that they were feeling better. Animals' bodies began to take on substance, muscles thickened, bones formed in their shadows. Soon everyone began to move around and talk and smile. Plants picked themselves up off the ground, rose into the air, and faced the sun. As everyone breathed in and out, they felt more vigorous. Dusky Owl, who is wise, guessed the truth. 'Smoke is fire's breath, and as we draw smoke in, we come alive.'

"They were concerned, though, that the sycamore would soon burn up and the fire would go out. They needed to get hold of that fire and make it grow. So all the plants and animals, including human beings, held a council. Every one that could swim or fly wanted to be the hero to get the fire.

"Because he's big and strong, Raven went first. While he was standing on top of the tree, the heat scorched all his feath-ers black, and he flapped back fast, without any fire. Screech Owl went next, but when he looked down into the tree, a blast of hot air burned his eyes. He zigzagged his way back, but for a long time he was nearly blind, and even today his eyes are red. Hoot Owl and Horned Owl tried next, but the smoke blinded them, and the ashes made white rings around their eyes. As anyone can see, they have never managed to get rid of those white rings.

"When the birds had failed, Blacksnake said he was sure he could do it. He swam across the water, wound his way up the tree, and peered down. The smoke immediately choked him. He fell into the tree, got burned, climbed back up the inside, and got back to shore as blackened as he still is.

"Now all the animals were afraid to go. Everyone tried to talk someone else into going. Eventually, one of the smallest animals of all volunteered, Water Spider, the one with black hair and red stripes. 'You can swim over there,' everyone else said, 'but how will you bring the fire back?'

" 'Just watch me,' said Water Spider.

"Out of her body she spun a thread in the shape of a small bowl. She swam across the water with the bowl on her back, plunked a coal into it, and swam back. Ever since, we've had fire.

"All living creatures came together then for a giant council. Remember, this was when all the animals were still friendly and still talked to each other, before death came into this world, and creatures started eating one another. They put Water Spider's fire at the center of the lodge and built it high, so they would have plenty of fire. And then two peoples made great gifts to the human beings.

"Tobacco spoke first. He said, 'If you will pluck my leaves, cut them up, burn them, and breathe in the smoke, I will give you health of body, clarity of mind, and spiritual insight.'

"First Man, Kanati, asked, 'What do you want in return?'

" 'We want you to plant us everywhere we can grow, so that our tribe will grow larger and larger.'

"First Man and First Woman agreed, though their descendants later forgot.

"Then the Stone People made First Man and First Woman a generous offer. They said, 'Build a low, tight hut that holds steam. Make a fire, heat us very hot, and put us in the hut. Then pour water on us and breathe in the steam that springs up. Draw in the breath of fire this way, and soak your bodies in it. We will be a furnace of life for you, body, mind, and spirit.'

"First Man and First Woman were so grateful and humbled by this generosity that they could not speak. You know that we still perform the ceremony of the sweat lodge today. Unfortunately, the people have forgotten that the ceremony is to renew the mind and spirit, and not for the body only.

"First Man and First Woman realized now that fire was a supreme gift and that it must never be allowed to go out. They kept it going in the council lodge, and they put it at the center of their home for warmth at night and in the winter. One of them always stayed home to keep the council fire going. And when First Man traveled, he learned to carry fire along in a pouch of thick buffalo hide, so if he camped in a cave, he would always have fire. Later the people learned to create fire by rubbing the fleabane stalk against the hard fungus that grows on the underside of locust branches. You know that every year at the Planting Moon Ceremony we still put out the blaze in every house and take to each house new fire from the sacred fire in the council lodge.

"But that original fire, the one Water Spider brought back, it is the grandfather of the fire that burns in the council lodge in our own village now. The priest tends it so that it never goes out.

"So, Grandson, that is how this world got fire, and how human beings use its gifts. Fire is life itself in this world. The sun is fire. A star is distant fire. A lightning bug is fire. The life of every living creature is fire. Your spirit is fire. In the Galayi language we have a single word that means your spirit, your soul, and your heart—your *yuwi*. That is your fire.

"Listen to this lesson carefully, keep it close within your heart, because it is an elusive one. Fire—spirit, soul, and heart—is not physical. It is the essence of life, and it cannot perish. Here on Earth, as long as there is fire, there is life, and as long as there is life, there is fire.

"That's why, every winter solstice, when the sun is weakest, I come to this room and paint the sun the color of fire."

They sat together for long moments, Aku's mind sifting through what he had heard. Finally, he said, "When I change myself into an owl, I make no change at all. My fire is the same—I am the same."

She came around the fire and squeezed his hand. "That is a great secret. When you know it as experience, not just thought, you will be more powerful."

Aku went on, as though watching something at a great distance. "Your son and grandson are the same. They are the fire born into them, whether in human shape or panther shape."

"Yes."

"This is part of what you mean when you ask me to see beyond appearances to reality."

"It's one part, beginning to see the bones in the shadows."

Aku swiveled his shoulders and stretched his back like he was uncomfortable.

"Who else are you thinking of?" asked Tsola.

"Salya."

"And what do you see?"

Aku clasped his hands on top of his hair and shook his

head fast. "Maloch has stolen my sister's spirit." For a moment he lost his tongue. "That is beyond horror, and I must set it right. Now."

"Drink this," said Tsola. "It will help you get ready for the next step."

Tsola and Bola watched each other for long, silent moments. When they knew their young kinsman was asleep, Bola said, "Maloch the Uktena won't just kill him. He'll eat his spirit. And you're sending him there."

"Not I. It's what he's born to."

Bola heard a scraping in his mother's voice. A rare thought zinged through him. *She's getting too old.*

❖

"Every one of them has something to teach the seeker," Tsola said. She held her torch as high as his own so Aku could really study the painted images.

He checked out Rabbit, with its split nose. "What does Rabbit have to say to me?"

"He's the trickster. But every seeker has to learn the teaching from every animal. It's like giving birth, or having sex. No point in knowing *about* it—you have to experience it."

"I don't understand." Well, he did, about sex.

She didn't respond.

Aku held his light close to Little Deer, who was only knee-high and entirely white.

"Do you know the story of the King of the Deer?"

"No."

Tsola grimaced. Meli, had she lived, would have made sure her children knew the old stories. Shonan thought they were the ghosts of the past. "The seekers of wisdom who come to me, each one gets to know some of these figures and the spirits they represent. Seekers make different discoveries in different paintings—sometimes, in fact, within the same painting. Each seeker takes home his own wisdom, and usually they come back several times to learn more."

Aku considered Rabbit for another long moment and passed on to Wolf. "That seems strange to me," he said.

"What?"

"His fangs are showing, but his eyes, his eyes, they're . . ." Aku rummaged through his mind. "Compassionate."

"Very observant," she said. "Wolf was the companion of First Man, the lucky hunter." This was mere information—she could talk about that.

"That's why no Galayi will kill a wolf," said Aku, "except for the one man in each village who is given that power."

At least her grandson knew some of the old lore.

Aku stopped in front of the drawing of Panther. Behind them Bola thumped his tail. "Look at the eyes," Aku said. "They see in darkness but . . ." He considered the strange luminescence in the orbs. "Bola," he said, "do you also see into the darkness of the spirit?"

"If you want the knowledge," Bola said, "you have to take the journey."

Aku turned and looked Bola straight in the face. "Can you see into the Darkening Land?"

Bola snapped out a roar.

Aku's knees shook as he turned away. He pretended to study the next figure, Bear, for a long time, but fear lashed every thought out of his mind. Finally, he said, "Grandmother, why is Bear white?"

"If you walk with him, you will know."

Aku cocked his head at Bear. "I think he looks like an uncle." Among the Galayi, a boy's maternal uncles were his particular guides and teachers.

He walked onward to look at Great Dusky Owl.

"Don't gaze at him now," said Tsola. "That's for later."

"Will these paintings last forever? Down here away from the weather?"

"I don't think so, not on this limestone. I've already re-painted some of them. Besides, I'd hate to think that in a hundred generations, when no Wounded Healer might be here, people would come and use the power of the paintings without guidance."

Aku sidestepped to look up at War Eagle, the highest of all the paintings, curving with the wall so that its head and its amber eye glared down from the ceiling.

This was not the white-headed, white-tailed eagle, but the dark red-brown bird with the red-gold throat. He was sacred to the Galayi for two reasons. He carried messages between the people and the Powers who lived in the Land Beyond the Sky Arch, and they thought him the perfect warrior, the essence of courage. When a Galayi warrior acted bravely, the Red Chief gave him the feather of a war eagle to tie into his hair.

Tsola watched Aku keenly. He tilted his head far back and stared into the great eye. Quietly, she reached for a cup of special tea she had brewed.

"I could fly into his eye," said Aku, drone-like.

She handed him the tea. "Drink this."

Beyond thought, he drained it.

Tsola reached for her drum and began a gentle tap, *tum*-tum, *tum*-tum, like a heartbeat.

Aku felt a wobble inside, and in the next moment he was flying.

20

The wind was cool and bracing, its damp edge intoxicating. He swiveled his head in every direction. A jolt of fear thrilled him. His first measure of height was the distance the tops of the mountains rose above the plains. His second, equally helpful, was a thin gauze of clouds that shadowed the mountains. Aku glided to that height again, three mountain measures above the earth. His wings were spread, and he was floating, effortless.

What's it like, wing-flapper?

Tsola's words, without a voice.

Where are you?

His own words, without a voice.

In your mind.

Inside my mind?

I can see out your eyes.

The drumbeat insisted a little, and for the first time Aku noticed it.

This is our connection, the beat. It binds you to the world of Earth and lifts me to your world.

Some tricks you play.

What if this is reality? What if your ordinary world is the trick?

Jabber-talk.

She laughed. *What do you want to do?*

Fly!

Pay attention!

In fact, he could feel it now, he was not only flying, he was rising without any effort on his part. Somehow the invisible hand of the air itself was lifting him.

So, wing-beater, how does it feel to be a soarer? A high-flier? A cloud-dweller? Scary?

It feels supreme. He didn't add that a portal in his mind had been kicked in and a new world of infinite vistas spread before him. Aku was a man was an owl was an eagle was a life-fire.

Good, said Tsola.

He felt a pang. *Grand,* he thought out loud, *but lonely.*

Power is always lonely. But that doesn't mean you can't have a little company.

Wing tip to wing tip he flew alongside another war eagle. They met eye slit to eye slit and knew each other. Mates, life partners, male and female.

Aku's spouse arced her beak downward, folded her wings, and dived. Aku zoomed beak to tail behind her. Down, fast as any living creature could go, plummeting like drops off a high waterfall.

After shrieking down forever, his mate suddenly stuck out her wings and glided.

You're a little confused, warned Tsola. There was a tease in her voice.

Aku followed his mate into the glide, and they coasted toward the top of a mountain with sharp, jagged promontories, peaks pointed like the tips of awls, or the splinters of broken bones.

Where do you think you are? said Tsola. *Earth?*

Aku was busy noticing something else. He was the bigger eagle, length greater, wing span wider, body heftier.

His mate floated to a landing on the rim of a nest, presumably their home.

Tsola's drum *tum*-tummed, *tum*-tummed, holding him in this strange world yet connecting him to Earth.

He knew something but he didn't know. He glided to a half-awkward landing on the nest, a bed made of thick limbs and soft, yellow grasses, waist-high to a man and further across than a man was tall.

Suddenly Aku's mate was on his back. Aku had a wild thought that he was under attack. He turned his head directly backward, but his mate's head was too far away to peck. And she didn't look mad. In fact, her eyes had a look that seemed familiar—and he felt it! He was about to get . . . !

He writhed free, clawing.

What the hell are you doing? He hurled the words at Tsola.

Tsola cackled. *Don't give me that, just don't. You knew it. You're bigger—you're the girl.*

Damn it!

Actually, you know, it feels good.

Aku and her mate—Aku was the "her" now—bounced around the edges of their nest, trying to figure each other out.

Did Bola see that?

He can't see you. Only I can.

Good. Don't tell me sex is a learning experience.

Suit yourself.

Aku's mate sailed away. Aku didn't think he was mad.

Why don't you take a nap? said Tsola.

❖

Aku, She Eagle, nestled comfortably on two black eggs. She was content. Grandmother Sun was hot for a spring day, and the rock walls squared around the nest radiated warmth. She wanted to nod off.

Oh, Grandson, said Tsola, *you think this is being a mother?*
Aku didn't answer.

He Eagle let out a little yawp, caught Aku's eye, and pointed down with his beak. A red fox slinked along the hillside, hunting. Its handsome coat was silky, its belly white, the tips of its ears black. Aku liked the nimble way it moved.

Her heart beat a little faster. A fox was a lot of meat, and this time of year, when trees were budding but not leafed out, one fox probably meant two.

She admired the elegance of the fox's strut for a moment, a fellow hunter.

She looked around the nest and saw no threats to her eggs. The two eagles stayed close to the nest while the eaglets were growing inside their shells, but for a prize like this . . . Once they hatched, mother or father would sit on the nest all the time.

Caution or daring? said Tsola.

Aku looked down. The fox was poised, paw in the air, searching for something. Aku made eye contact with her mate. He swooped off to the side, away from the nest. Yes, the fox was worth a little risk.

The game of life and death began. He eagle drifted down toward the fox, further and further down, until he saw he'd caught the fox's eye. The wily one pranced up the hill, toward the jumble of rocks. When He Eagle turned off toward the river, the fox started hunting again.

Aku stepped to the edge of the nest and looked back at her shiny black eggs.

Now He Eagle wheeled and made a fake dive toward the fox. The sly one skittered sideways about fifty steps, an extraordinarily graceful maneuver. Now it was at the base of the rocky slope, and could slip into a crevice.

He Eagle turned away and hovered over the river. The

fox watched the eagle with sharp eyes, wary. As He Eagle drifted downriver, the fox's gaze followed it intently.

This was the moment. Aku launched off the nest and hurtled downward at a speed that made her blood pump. She hit the fox from behind with both talons, and in an instant had it high in the air, legs flailing. She squeezed its neck and felt the body go limp.

She laid the carcass on a flat stone near the nest. She ripped open the belly, and again felt a hollow clang in her chest. She took several pecks into the liver. Something in her felt odd and glorious at once.

Her mate lighted beside her. After a few more sharp strikes with her beak, Aku scooted onto her eggs and watched He Eagle feed. The clang still resonated in her chest.

Something must die? said Tsola.

Someone must be born, Aku answered.

❖

A week later two white eaglets were eating hungrily. Aku could hardly believe how much they consumed. She and her mate no longer spent any time perched in the tops of pines watching the world turn. One of them hunted every moment, and the little eagles screeched for more morsels. Sometimes, when the sun told her to sleep, Aku's belly howled for more food. The mother and father took turns, one hunting while the other fed and guarded infants, and then switching jobs.

Her own offspring dazed Aku. Soft and downy as they were, the babies weren't a bit dainty or innocent. They ate voraciously. The older chick, the girl, often twisted around to get her gaping mouth under the meat as Aku brought it down to her brother, guzzling the drops of blood. In his previous life Aku the human being had thought animals should be more like plants, and not devour each other in crimson gore. Aku the eagle knew better.

❖

The male eaglet, the small one that hatched second, lay scrawny and lifeless on the sticks. The big female chick yawped for the mouse innards Aku dangled from her beak. She dropped them, and the chick pecked at them avidly. The reason the smaller eaglet was dead, in fact, was that the bigger one fought harder for food. Aku looked at her dead child and ached. This ache—agony—had been her entire existence since daybreak, when she woke up and found her dead boy. She hurt until she wished she wasn't alive.

Why?

Tsola's drum tapped out the sound of a heartbeat in the back of Aku's mind. The she eagle whispered, "This is not my true world."

It is true, but not earthly, said Tsola in his mind.

"I want it not to be true."

Where you are, birth and death rule. On Earth, birth and death rule.

"Why aren't we immortal, like the Powers who live above, beyond the Sky Arch?"

You know.

Her mate hovered overhead and dropped the carcass of a badger next to Aku. She slit open its belly and picked out innards with her beak to feed her daughter.

Tsola chuckled.

Aku did, too.

Her mate gave her a look that might have been empathy, picked up the dead eaglet in his beak, and dropped it over the side. Then he launched off the nest to hunt.

Aku looked at her remaining child. The eaglet finished the scrap of food and looked at her mother for more.

Tsola said, *What do you need to live here? And on Earth?*

Aku fed her daughter the badger's heart.

"More courage than I have."

The nest itself constricted subtly, but Aku didn't see it, and Tsola saw only through eagle eyes.

Tsola said, *Say it in its full truth.*

Aku stalled. "In one moon, we will teach this chick to fly. It will follow us and learn to hunt. Then we will never see it again. But we will produce two more eggs late next winter, and the race of war eagles will go on."

The nest constricted again, unnoticed.

Say it in its full truth, repeated Tsola. Both the voice and the drum sharpened.

The nest coiled tight. Aku didn't see that her home of sticks and grasses had become a serpent. Tsola was absorbed in the mind and emotions of the adventurer.

Aku wanted to look her grandmother, her teacher, in the eye. She said, "The courage to be mortal."

Directly behind Aku, the dragon head rose from the serpent body.

Aku turned her head and saw too late.

Tsola flashed herself into the Land Beyond.

Maloch the Uktena struck.

Aku screamed at the penetration of its fangs.

Tsola began to chant the words.

The entire nest wrapped itself tight around Aku. As the serpent squeezed, Tsola shouted the last phrase of the ancient formula.

Maloch the Uktena and Aku fell limp, dazed, numb.

Tsola swept Aku up . . .

21

Aku lay tumbled next to Tsola in the cave of the paintings, exactly where he had downed the tea, bleeding and unconscious.

Tsola cursed. "Get your son and a hide," she snapped. Bola jumped to his feet and ran.

She set to work to stanch the flow of blood on his arms. Then she realized that the fang wounds were too wide. She got her bone awl and some thread made of buffalo sinew and stitched. "Good thing you don't know what's happening," she murmured. It was a crude piece of work, but without it the patient might bleed to death. She felt his arms and chest and decided a rib was broken, with luck nothing worse.

She cursed again. She was a healer—the Wounded Healer of the tribe—but her skill was to heal the spirit, not the body.

With difficulty she lifted Aku's trunk into the air, slid close behind him, and wrapped her arms around him. Then she breathed with him. She believed that breathing along with a patient helped keep his body and life-fire together.

In a few minutes Bola and Bota cat-scampered in, carrying a hide. Quickly, they transformed themselves into human beings so that they could use their hands. They put Aku on the elk hide and lifted it as a litter.

Bola said, "He'll be all right, Mother," and they were gone.

❖

As twilight faded to darkness, from inside the entrance to the Emerald Cavern, Tsola watched her son and grandson help Aku out of the Healing Pond. Tsola could watch him only at night—sunlight was more than her cave-shaded eyes could bear. He had had two full days in the cold waters, and they reported that he was better. "Stubborn," she muttered.

They helped him walk across the stone in the darkness to the entrance of the cavern and set him down next to his great-grandmother.

"You're better," Tsola said.

"They won't tell me what happened."

"They didn't see it." She paused. "Maloch the Uktena followed you into the Land Beyond the Sky Arch—he has powers in both worlds. While you were sleeping, he transformed himself into your nest, a very clever disguise, sticks and grasses. Remember, he can make himself into any shape—he once made himself into your sister.

"Then he started constricting, getting closer and closer to you, there in the center of the nest. He likes to toy with his victims, not just kill them. I was hoping you would see beyond appearance to reality. I almost underestimated him.

"When he bit you and coiled himself around you, I invoked an old power that confuses everyone. Maloch let go, you fell, and I grabbed you."

"Why didn't you kill him?"

"I don't have that power."

"How can he be killed?"

Tsola shook her head. That wasn't a question she wanted to get into.

Aku stared into space and said nothing.

"You weren't ready. I should have been quicker. I told you all this is dangerous. What did you learn?"

But her grandson was asleep. She eased him to the floor.

❖

When Aku woke up groggy, Bola and Bota carried him and dropped him into the cold, healing waters.

Aku exclaimed something like, "A-a-guppff!"

The father and son laughed, changed themselves back into panthers, and walked back to sit with Tsola.

Soon Aku climbed out of the pond and joined them. He walked with a hand supporting his rib, which clearly hurt. His cuts were healing. Bola backed into a shadowed corner. Bota went to help pilgrims who'd come for healing.

Tsola brewed tea and talked gently to her great-grandson. She gave him cakes of chestnuts mashed with blueberries. The tea was a draft that made people more alert. She talked to him about her memories of Meli as a child. As she talked, she could sense Aku putting parts of himself together emotionally, becoming himself.

"I have to move somewhere darker," she said. First light was on the world. After they sat down in a side room, she asked again, "What did you learn on your adventure?"

He seemed to think. Finally, he said, "I am really me. I'm me when I'm an eagle. I'm me when I'm female. I *feel* like me."

Tsola waited.

"I loved my children. Loved them totally. I had no idea . . ." His eyes turned far away. "How I will love my child from Iona."

Tsola waited and watched him sort through things. Finally she said, "And . . . ?"

Aku said thoughtfully, "A Galayi knows his family, he knows his family is the same as him, you can't think of yourself or any one member without thinking of all. But it seems to me that all of us animals, people and other animals, must be much more closely related, more knit together, than I realized. We're . . . the same thing."

Tsola smiled hugely. She was delighted with Aku. And the longer he lived, the more he would experience this connectedness, know it in his heart, where it mattered.

She waited.

"I have lots of thoughts, but I think you're looking for something in particular."

She said, "What did you learn from being a war eagle? Of all birds of prey, he is the great hunter. What did you learn about living and dying?"

He paused. "It's hard to be mortal. Things die. Your children die. Your mate dies. You die. It's hard."

Tsola pitched in. "Also you have to *get* food. You have to build a nest, sew clothes, make a fire, teach your children how to live. And what you need for all that is . . . ?"

Aku nodded several times. "Courage. You need courage." He shrugged. "It's a struggle to live."

"For where you are now, as you are now, courage is the first virtue you need."

Aku looked into the darkness of the cavern for a long time. Then he smiled crookedly at her. "Okay. And you want me to go back to the cave of paintings and learn something like that from each of the animals?"

"Over the course of your life, as much as you can." She hesitated. "Right now I want you to learn something more from War Eagle."

Aku cocked an eyebrow at her.

"The owl was your mother's bird. If your father was a bird—or if he had a bird spirit in his heart—what would it be?"

No hesitation. "The war eagle."

"You have been a war eagle in the spirit realm. Can you become one here on Earth?"

"You mean . . . ?"

"One of your gifts is to be a shape-shifter. Just as you turn yourself into an owl, make yourself a war eagle. Here. Now."

Aku immersed himself. Feet into yellow toes, toenails into black claws. Legs into feathery stumps. Skin of torso into feathers. Arms stretched out into long, long wings. Neck skin into feathers of red-gold. Head small and feathery, mouth a beak, eyes amber, the world taking on a crystalline sharpness.

"Yes," said Tsola warmly. "And here on Earth it is not enough to borrow the form of the war eagle. You must feel its spirit. You must taste its desire to hunt. You must feel its love of riding the air high, high, high, even above the mountain-tops. You must know you're in the purity of its courage—"

"Hello!"

❖

It was a shout from outside. Tsola stiffened. Aku recognized the voice. His eagle heart felt a stab of panic. Feathers to flesh, beak to mouth, wings to arms . . .

Bola padded toward the cavern entrance, muscles aquiver.

"Hello? Aku?"

"Ada?" It was first time Aku had used that name out loud. Tsola smiled at Aku.

He said, "Give me a moment."

When he was ready, Aku jumped up and ran. His father and Yah-Su stood at the cavern entrance, next to Bota, in panther form and on guard. At the far end from Bota was Tagu, wagging his tail and wriggling his whole body. Behind was someone half-blocked from sight.

Aku leaped into his father's arms. Then he stepped back in embarrassment. Shonan grinned at him.

"Yah-Su," Aku said, bewildered.

"Aku," said the buffalo man shyly.

Tagu came forward to be petted.

The smaller figure came around from behind the buffalo man.

"And Oghi? What are you fellows . . . ? What . . . ?"

Shonan said, "You're hurt."

Aku's eyes shadowed. "Maloch the Uktena. I'll be okay. Tell you in a minute."

He looked back into Shonan's eyes. "We're both alive!"

Father stepped forward and hugged son again.

"Have you come to see the Wounded Healer?" Aku asked hopefully, doubtfully.

"Hell, no," said Shonan. "We've come to find you and go get your sister."

"That's what I want." But his tone was drab. "Oghi, I'm glad to see you."

"Iona says to tell you she's well, she's missing you, and your child is growing fine in her belly."

Tsola's voice from within was surprisingly strong. "Bola, Bota, bring our visitors in."

She came partway to meet them, tying a loose-woven mask over her eyes. Aku knew that she could see through it a little.

Aku introduced Shonan and Yah-Su. The Wounded Healer said to Oghi, "Hello, my friend," and greeted them all in a kind way. Bola and Bota flanked her closely. Aku wondered how she knew Oghi.

"I'm sorry, the light hurts my eyes. Will you . . . ?"

The panthers led everyone to a shadowy side chamber. Their hostess unmasked and said, "I think you all have stories to trade." Both panthers hovered close to her.

Aku begged his father to tell first how he'd escaped from Maloch the Uktena and the Brown Leaves. Shonan told the tale enthusiastically, without a hint of exaggeration, and giving Yah-Su plenty of credit. Though invited, the buffalo man had nothing to say.

While they talked, Tsola herself built a small fire and started some tea. When Shonan told about the attack on Maloch, he ended with, "The bastard is really something, getting away from us."

"You were really something," said Aku, "getting away from him. But how did you get here?"

Tsola served the tea in horns and put out bowls of berries in sweetened water.

"We ran like hell from the Brown Leaves. You'd be amazed by how Yah-Su can cover ground, and how he knows the country between the Brown Leaf village and ours, every nook and cranny." He paused, and father and son just looked at each other. "When Iona told us you'd come here, we followed. Time to get moving. My daughter is lying in the Underworld with no life-fire. Your twin is lying in the Underworld with no life-fire. Let's go."

Oghi said softly, "I want to hear Aku's adventures."

The young man told slowly, diffidently, how he searched for Shonan but couldn't find him, how he flew back to see Iona and then on to visit Tsola. He said nothing about the cave of paintings but mentioned vaguely that Tsola had sent him on a trip to the Land Beyond the Sky Arch, where

Maloch momentarily got him in his coils. He didn't need to add, 'And damn near killed me.'

Shonan didn't want to hear about the spirit world anyway. "I want to get going."

"Pray tell," said Tsola, "where would you go?"

That put a stop to conversation.

Finally, Shonan said, "To the Darkening Land."

"And where is that?"

"I'm sure you know, of all people."

"This is rash," said Tsola. "None of you is prepared for the Darkening Land. All of you will be killed."

"What preparation are we talking about?"

The hard feelings between Shonan and Tsola had started the day he married Meli. Aku felt like he could eat the tension between his father and his great-grandmother.

"Physical skills, ones some of you have and some don't. Emotional strength, for what you will see there. Wisdom, to understand. Strength of spirit, to know what to do and how to get back out."

"I don't think we're weaklings."

"No one has ever gone into the Darkening Land and returned."

Shonan grinned like he'd caught her out. "One of your old stories says the seven men who went for the daughter of Grandmother Sun came back."

"But they failed to bring the girl back."

Besides, it was an unfair comment. Everyone knew things weren't like they were in the days of the oldest stories.

Shonan advanced his case. "Seriously, a warrior who dies in battle goes to the Darkening Land and is immediately reborn on Turtle Island. You yourself teach that. And whatever happens down below *will* be a battle."

"Reborn as an infant, which means failure. You are a

good man, Red Chief Shonan, but you are ignorant. To deal with spiritual worlds, you need to be a spiritual warrior."

Shonan made his voice blunt. "I'm tired of this magic stuff. It killed my wife, his mother. If I let Aku go that way, it will ruin him. I know what he needs, and it's action."

Tsola looked at Aku. " 'If he lets you. He knows what you need.' How do those words sit, Aku?"

Aku held his grandmother's gaze. "I go my own way. I am not a tool of either one of you."

Shonan seemed to wince.

"Shonan," Tsola said, "do you feel ready to go to the Darkening Land, even if that means death?"

"A man gives everything to save his daughter. Or son."

"Yah-Su, are you ready to go?" Isola asked in Amaso.

The buffalo man said only, "Yes."

"Oghi, are you?" This was a key question. Tsola knew the seer in Oghi, and he could make the difference.

"I would like to talk to you in private."

Tsola nodded. "Aku, are you ready?"

"I couldn't live with myself if I didn't go."

"All right." She pondered. "All of you except Oghi and Bola, go outside. Aku, you aren't healed yet. Sit in the waters. The rest of you, I'm sure the waters will take away your fatigue."

❖

"Oghi," she said, "it's good to see you again."

When the Amaso people came to the Planting Moon Ceremony at the Cheowa village, Oghi had made the walk up the mountain to the Emerald Cavern. The Wounded Healer agreed to see him. After all, he was a Galayi now, and his village was a risky experiment, the uniting of peoples with different languages and different customs. Immediately, they felt the power of the seer in each other. And at his request she drummed him across into the Land Beyond the Sky Arch.

Nothing bound minds together like a joint trip to the world above, living in each others' heads.

"Oghi, why are you involved in this madness?"

"It's my fault Salya was kidnapped, or partly mine. I should have warned them. I knew I should, and I didn't."

"That's not the reason."

"Have any seers gone down there? Might I have the wisdom they need?"

"No, I don't think any seer has attempted it. We know too much. Do you see clearly enough? Maybe. It's a slender reed to stake four lives on."

Oghi heard the feeling in her voice, and when he peered through the shadows closely, he saw the tear on her cheek.

"I'm just fighting myself," she said. "I hate this. I know my great-grandson has to go. He has been called. But I don't want to say yes. I don't want to send him. I don't want to be the one who kills him."

She clasped herself hard, closed her eyes, and did something within herself. "All right, I have a gift for you. You know it, *u-tsa-le-ta*. The Underworld . . . it's agony to see. It's almost impossible to believe. With this you can go into the minds of the wretches who live there."

She scooped a handful of the red lichens out of a pouch, poured them into a small leather bag, and gave it to Oghi.

"Are you sure?" said Tsola.

"Absolutely." He looked at the pouch of *u-tsa-le-ta.* "Thank you, Healer." Out of respect, he waited before he spoke again. "I want to make a special request."

"Speak."

"You have traveled in the minds of many seers to the world above. Have you ever taken a mind journey into the world below?"

Tsola gasped. "No."

"Our party has two seers. You can go along, inside us."

He glimpsed the changes in her face and wished he could truly see them.

"Incredible." She thought for a long while. "Thank you, Oghi the sea turtle. Thank you. I will be with you every step."

❖

She said to all four of them, "I will do what I can to help you go."

Shonan seemed about to congratulate everyone but stopped himself.

Aku said, "Should we send word to Kumu and take him along? They're promised to each other in marriage."

"No," said Shonan. "It would take half a moon to send a messenger to Kumu and for him to get here. My daughter, your sister, is dying. Salya is our responsibility, not his, not yet."

Aku nodded.

"Let's eat," Tsola said, "and we'll talk about how to begin."

Bola had roasted the hind quarter of an elk on a spit over the fire, first consuming his own portion raw.

Tsola served tea, and they made small talk until she was ready.

"The entrance to the Darkening Land," she told them, "is at the foot of the Tree of Life. Its other name is seldom spoken, for it is also the Tree of Death. Its crown reaches higher than any other tree in the world. Its roots open the way to the Underworld. It is the sacred tree of the Galayi people, the cedar. We burn it during ceremonies and draw in its lovely fragrance because it is the emblem of fertility, the ever-renewed mother of life itself. And, underground, as they are inevitably mated, the great cedar leads to the abode of death. The tree is the home of Tsi-Li, Great Dusky Owl, master of the knowledge of life and death."

Aku's mind perked up—that was his species.

"Tsi-Li has two supremely important jobs. He guards the tree. And he decides who passes through the portal from life to death, and from death to life. Customarily, only the dead may descend. Because I will ask him, he will let you pass into the Underworld."

She hesitated. "Aku, he is your great-grandfather. He . . . came to me once. You are a blossom of that seed." Her eyes overflowed. "You know I have always loved you especially, and feared for you."

She wiped her face openly with her hands and then addressed the whole group again. "Everything you need to know, Tsi-Li will tell you."

Quickly, she spoke into the minds of Aku and Oghi. *I will be with you from the moment you enter the Underworld. Tsi-Li will know that, but say nothing of this to Shonan or Yah-Su.*

"Grandmother," Aku said out loud. "Will you . . . ?"

Not now! she commanded him.

She looked one by one into the eyes of Shonan, Yah-Su, Aku, and Oghi. "Do you all understand? Let me hear each one of you say yes."

Each said it.

"You all understand the risk? No one has ever made this journey and survived. Tell me one by one that you understand."

They did.

"Aku, you have crossed into the Land Beyond and acquired the first of all virtues, courage. Why don't you make one more journey and acquire another strength you'll need? I feel as if you're half naked."

Aku answered immediately. "No," he said. "I'm ready."

Tsola opened her mouth to protest, but Shonan spoke first. "Salya is perishing."

Tsola looked at them for a long moment, took a deep breath, let it out, and said, "Follow me."

❖

She led them to the cave of paintings. The four adventurers, Aku, Shonan, Oghi, and Yah-Su, sat quietly in front of the Great Dusky Owl with their eyes down. Tsola had asked them not to study the paintings. She herself sat brewing tea. From her brisk movements Aku understood that she wanted to get this parting over with as soon as possible, be done quickly with the pain of loss.

"Drink this," she said. She handed each man a horn. Shonan and Yah-Su quaffed theirs immediately. Aku watched nervously, thinking they knew not what they did. Oghi hesitated. He'd seen her put the *u-tsa-le-ta* in it. They would leave the world of Time and go to the Underworld. He and Aku looked at each other. They were scared. Holding each other's eyes, they downed the tea slowly.

Tsola sat beside her great-grandson, kissed his cheek, and held him. She pulled back and looked into his eyes. "I fear I will never see any of you again."

She added, in his mind and Oghi's, *Except with the eye of the spirit.*

"Now," she said, "gaze into the eyes of the Great Dusky Owl. Look, and look, and look, until you are there."

Each man entered into the suns of the great eyes, painted burning gold, with tinges of orange and black portals in their centers—the doors to life and death.

22

The eyes blinked.

Aku jumped and nearly fell. Then he realized he was squatted on a low, thick branch of a cedar. On the next branch, directly in front them all, perched a great dusky owl the size of a man. Earthly great dusky owls hunted and killed birds twice their size, but there were no mortal birds as big as Tsi-Li.

Oghi spoke formally. "Greetings, guardian of the pathway to death."

"To death and to life," answered Tsi-Li, "and bearer of the knowledge of life and death." He had a voice like the roar of distant river rapids.

He clicked his head so that his eyes pierced Aku directly. "I am told you are my great-grandson. I am glad to see you. I would say welcome, but it is painful to welcome a young man to the house of death."

Aku said, "I am honored to meet you, Grandfather." He looked around nervously. The Tree of Life and Death was enormous. An entire village could have nestled in its shade. Aku wondered how many creatures lived in it, not only birds but crawling things. Or did none live here, because it was the portal to death?

Oghi addressed Tsi-Li formally again. "Great Owl, Master

of Life and Death, we seek to enter the Darkening Land to rescue someone we love."

Tsi-Li nodded his great head. "I know your mission, and I see what is in your hearts." His head snapped from Oghi to Aku to Shonan to Yah-Su. "Oghi the sea turtle, you are worthy to enter. I say nothing of your fate." He sized up the other three. "Grandson, Yah-Su the buffalo man, Red Chief Shonan, I give you permission to enter, and along with the permission comes a warning. No one who enters returns alive.

"I can tell you that the world of darkness is as vast as the world lighted by the sun and moon. You live on Turtle Island, and Earth has seven such islands of land, some larger than this one. The Darkening Land extends under every island, and under all the seas. In a hundred human life spans, you could never walk all of its halls. If you find the person you seek, it will be through wisdom."

Tsi-Li waited, clicking his head from man to man, as if to see whether he was being understood.

"Your challenge, what you must do to pass back onto the earth, is to understand life and death. No seeker has yet understood. You have very little chance to come back to the land of sunlight. I am sorry even to let you attempt such a mission."

Tsi-Li looked at each man. Aku wanted to see compassion in his eyes, but what was really there? He couldn't tell. Something beyond mortal understanding.

"Questions?"

Aku made himself bold and said, "Who guards the other six entrances to the Darkening Land?"

"I do." Perhaps amusement flicked in his owl eyes. "We Immortals have powers denied to mortals." He barged on. "You have lamps?"

"Yes, Great Owl," said Oghi, "scores of them." Tsola

had told them to fill horns with animal fat and carry fire-starting materials.

"You know that this land will be a darkness you cannot fathom?"

"Yes," said Aku. It must be a cave.

"The most immense cave you can imagine," said Tsi-Li. "All the seas of the world could pour into the caves of the Darkening Land and not fill them."

Aku hated it when someone read his mind.

"I have a gift for you," said Tsi-Li. "I have never made a gift to a seeker until now, but you are the progeny of a woman who aroused passion in me, in fact love."

To Aku, the Great Owl's eyes looked incapable of any feeling, let alone tender ones.

With his beak he dropped four small bags to the ground. "These are chestnuts, roasted, ground, and mixed with honey, one for each of you. They will help you live longer."

The Great Owl spread his wings, floated a few feet to the ground without a flutter, and stood among the huge, knobby roots of the Tree of Life and Death. The four climbed down beside him.

"We begin then."

He put his beak to a hole in the ground no bigger than a thumb and called, "*Hoo hoodoo hoo hoo, hoo hoodoo hoo hoo, hoo hoodoo hoo hoo.*"

Aku wondered whether the number of calls, three, was significant.

The Great Owl turned his sun eyes to Aku. "Grandson, I'm glad to have made your acquaintance, even briefly." And he flapped upward.

Downward, a voice squeaked. "Come on," it said. They looked that direction. A pink nose poked out of a tiny hole. "Come on."

Four human beings looked at the hole and asked themselves, *How?*

"Just come!" squealed the creature below. The sound was as far as anything could get from the big, sonorous voice of Tsi-Li.

"*How?*" shouted Shonan.

"Just come!" squawked the voice.

Aku hurried to convert himself into an owl. He wanted to be able to see below the surface of the earth.

As a joke, Shonan went to the thumb hole and stuck a moccasined toe in. Even with the gear packed on his back he disappeared like the ground had slurped him up.

Like a child, Yah-Su hopped over and jumped on the hole with both feet. He and the hides lashed to his hump disappeared.

Oghi lit a horn lamp, grinned, shrugged at Aku, and followed.

Aku stuck his head in first and peered around. The hole didn't wait but gobbled him up.

Shonan and the buffalo giant looked at their empty palms. The clubs and spears they carried had evaporated into thin air. They checked and discovered that they still had their knives. Aku still had his flutes in his claws.

"You can't stick a spear into the dangers of the Underworld," said the mole before them. Coppery fur, four feet like paddles, a short tail sprouting out the back end. Eyes overgrown with fur. "Call me Mouldywarp," it said, "and follow me."

Thick roots twisted and tangled in every direction, and from them little strings of roots tentacled through the soil. Mouldywarp crooked his way down through a mole-sized tunnel. Somehow, though they were much too large, the others slithered down behind him. The single lamp showed nothing but big roots, little roots, and finger-like tunnels branching off in every direction. Mouldywarp four-footed downward without hesitation.

"Can you see the route?" asked Aku.

"I have no need of eyes," said Mouldywarp, "and yours won't save you."

Crook and crawl, crook and crawl, down and down they went. Dust fell on them like rain, and all except Mouldywarp sneezed it out. After a long time—Aku guessed that the roots plunged further into the earth than the branches of the tall tree in the world reached into the sky—Mouldywarp stopped on a stone ledge.

"This is where I leave you. Below is a cave with passages leading in every direction. There's running water, so you won't die of thirst.

"There's no way to explain to you how vast it is. By the way, you'll have to swim sometimes. I do." He held up his paddle paws.

"Let's remember," said Aku, remembering his experiences with Tsola, "nothing grows in caves, nothing at all. There's no light."

"It is the land of the dead," said Mouldywarp. He *ahemmed.* "If you're going into it, go. I'm just a conductor, and I don't spend time on good-byes to people I'm not going to see again."

The four stepped down into the stone cavern, and were greeted. It was a cacophony of misery like none other ever heard, a subterranean chorus of howls, wails, shrieks, sobs, moans, and ululations echoing through canyons and tunnels of stone that circled the earth, a symphony of human woe.

They were stunned by it, paralyzed in mind, emotion, and body.

After a long time Shonan put his mouth to Aku's ear to talk. "What do you see?"

"Not much, and nothing dangerous."

Nearly unable to hear, Aku led the way across a stone floor with his owl eyes. He pinch-footed his way forward until he felt water with a claw. "This is running, it's a stream." It seemed like a good idea to stop next to water. He wanted to tell them what he saw with his owl eyes, but knew he wouldn't be heard. He decided to put his claws in the light of the horn lamp and use a crude version of the sign language. "The darkness is scary. Even to me everything is shadowy. We're standing near where we came in, and it's a huge room. Little passages lead in every direction—we could never check them all."

"What dangers do you see?" signed Shonan.

Aku saw in his father's eyes that the Red Chief was struggling with the thought of invisible threats.

"Nothing. Aside from the walls and the odd formations of caves, I see almost nothing. I expected enemies, monsters, every sort of fell creature, and all manner of evil. I don't see any of that."

"Don't be foolish," signed Shonan. "Evil beings could be anywhere." He gestured toward the passages and alleyways that led to infinite nowheres.

"Why don't we plug our ears?" signed Oghi. "This is hard to take." Each man clipped a small piece of hide off his clothing, cut it in half, wadded the pieces, stuck them in their ears.

"Damn well better," said Shonan.

Aku looked around. "As far as I can tell," he went on, "there are no people at all, no skeletons, no rotting flesh, no hair, none of what you might guess. What I see—well, just follow me. And why don't we save our lamp fat? It isn't doing any good." He grasped Yah-Su's hand with his claws.

Shonan grabbed hands front and back and blew the lamp out.

Aku led them several hundred paces, to a wall that looked like it was flowing stone. Now the cacophony of misery was fainter, and they could talk.

"Right in front of me is—light the lamp."

Shonan did.

"Do you see it? It's incredible—what you might call a wraith. It's like . . . like the heat waves you see above a fire. There's no substance to it, but it's in the shape of a person. It's . . ." He hesitated, unable to believe what he was seeing, what he was saying. "Do you see it?"

They all murmured yes.

"Maybe that's what a spirit is. And listen to that wail. The thing's mouth is open, and I'd say it's pointing at things that are invisible and turning its head and trying to get away. Look, there, now, it's backing away, crawling on its feet and elbows. It's cowering. It's terrified."

"Terrified of what?" said Shonan.

"Nothing," said Aku. "Nothing that I can see."

Shonan made a grunt of disgust.

Aku said, "There, there, it's flipped over and is pressing its face into the rock floor and covering its head with its hands."

"Let's keep our minds on our mission. There's nothing for us here," said Shonan. "Let's move on."

Aku saw Oghi start to speak and stop.

They wandered around. Aku, Shonan, and Oghi couldn't think of anything else to do, and Yah-Su seemed content to do whatever the others wanted. They came on twenty or thirty other wraiths, all far separated from the others. Some of them were crawling away from unseen threats. A number were rocking back and forth, weeping. Some were rolling around, beating their hands and feet and even heads on the floor. Except for the wounds they inflicted on themselves by scratching, biting, hitting, and banging their heads on the stone, none of them was being attacked or hurt in any way. All were howling, yowling, crying, yelling, bellowing, screaming, wailing, shrieking, screeching, squealing, sobbing, blubbering, sniveling, whimpering, snuffling, puling, moaning, mewling, keening, or caterwauling—a monstrous mural of cries of human suffering.

"I'm tired," said Aku.

"I'm tired of all this pain," said Oghi.

"I can't stand these horrible sounds in my head," complained Shonan.

"Let's go to the stream," said Aku. He led everyone there, perched, and opened Tsi-Li's gift bag. They ate.

Aku said, "Have you noticed? Whenever you eat Tsi-Li's chestnuts, the bag refills itself."

"Give me the ordinary world," said Shonan. "Does this racket ever let up?"

"I don't think so," said Oghi. "That's why this is called the Darkening Land and no one wants to come here."

"But people get to go back," said Aku.

"Yes," said Oghi. "I don't know how that works."

"How long are they down there? Who decides when they get to go back?"

"The right way to come here," said Shonan, "is by death in battle."

"Or giving birth, or trying to be born and failing," said Oghi.

"Whatever," said Shonan. "Let's just get Salya and get out of here."

"If we can get out," said Yah-Su.

"Tsi-Li said we can't get out unless we gain the knowledge of death."

"He's talking about that old story about how mortality came to Earth," Shonan said.

"I don't think so," said Oghi. "I think what we have to learn is right in front of us. I think we have to figure out what's going on with these poor, terror-stricken people."

"I'd rather find a way to shut them up," said Shonan.

Oghi ignored him. "I've got some ideas," he said. "I'm going to try something."

He pulled some red lichen out of his bag and mixed it with water in a horn.

"Tea!" said Shonan. "That's just going to use up our lamp fat."

"It works cold," said Oghi.

He stirred the brew thoroughly and downed it.

23

The world glowed faintly, even the Underworld. A thought floated idly through Oghi's mind—the glow of the Land Beyond was partly due to the *u-tsa-le-ta*. But he didn't want to spend his journey time on idle thoughts.

Greetings, pilgrim, said Tsola.

The brew slanted his thinking oddly, and he was startled—he'd forgotten momentarily. *Greetings, Grandmother. I'm glad you're with me.* He could hear the tap of her drum, as on his journey to the Land Beyond, the steady thump of a heartbeat.

I've never been to the Underworld, either. We're both innocents.

Oghi started wandering around. The cries of agony came from every direction, bouncing off the stone walls, so that he couldn't guess where a spirit in pain might be. He drifted this way and that, and within fifty paces he saw one. They were much easier to see with the help of the *u-tsa-le-ta*—this spirit actually glowed a pale pink.

He approached the whirl of energy gingerly, uncertain. It was yowling, screaming, and bellowing by turns. It cringed. It tried to bury its face in the stone.

What is it so terrified of? said Oghi. *There's nothing here. It's safe.*

Go into its consciousness, said Tsola.

Which probably meant Tsola was already there. *How does that work?*

If he were in the world, you could see what he sees. As it is, you can see what he's thinking about and what he feels, whatever is in his mind. Remember, you have no control. All the choices are his. You just see.

Oghi floated in, just as Tsola did into his mind, or the other travelers she accompanied. The spirit was confronting a woman, clearly his wife. She was yelling at him, throwing him out of the house. She said he was lazy and didn't bring home any meat. She said he spent all his time lifting skirts, or trying to. She said he didn't care about her or the children. In back of her the whole family chanted the same chorus. He was out. He left whimpering, raging with frustration.

Let's check with each other on what we're seeing, said Tsola.

He told her the pictures he saw, the words he heard. *It feels like I'm rocking on waves of awful emotion,* said Oghi. *It's . . . a sense of absolute helplessness.*

Yes, said Tsola. *You are a talented seer.*

But it's all imaginary. Why does he fret and make himself suffer?

Yes, said Tsola, *why do we?* Her drum underlined her words.

Oghi said, *Now I see something else. He's remembering how his father beat him when he was a child. He feels completely under his father's thumb, and he hates that worse than the beating.* Oghi waited, watching. It was a bizarre sensation, being inside someone else's consciousness.

He's replaying that memory over and over. His screams are furious, and that's why. Helplessness. Terrible fear.

Oghi watched. This was a horrific punishment.

He keeps going through the same memory over and over. What a horrible pain. This is really hell.

Do you feel the pain yourself? asked Tsola.

Yes, but I have some distance from it. For him it's his whole existence. For me it's not even close. He watched a little more. *If this is what death is, reliving everything hateful in your life, no wonder everyone dreads it.*

Tsola said, *Maybe it's not going back through the bad things that happened. Maybe it's the things you dwelled on, the things that might or might not have happened that you were obsessed about, always scared of.*

Whatever, it's his version of hell, not mine.

The man moaned and moaned. He rolled around the ground and flailed his arms. Then he lay still, whimpering.

Wait, he's shifting to a different memory. Now the man was a toddler. His older brother snatched his gourd rattle out of his little hand, threw it in the creek, and laughed as it floated off. The toddler bawled, helpless to do anything about it.

Over and over this string of memory replayed itself in his mind. All the while the wraith rolled around on the ground, alternating between shouting in protest, whining, and sobbing.

Why does he punish himself with the same memory? said Oghi.

There's an old story, said Tsola. *The Galayi actually got it from the Amaso people, about a man who rebuilt a sand dune. Every day of his life, every moment of the day, he would pick up sand in two buffalo horns and walk up the dune and pour out the sand on top. Of course, his footsteps sent more sand to the bottom on every step going up and every step coming down. When he got back to the bottom, he would pick up two more horns' worth and trek back up. This was his entire life, making a sand dune that would always fall down, by his own actions, faster than he could build it up.*

Her drum ended the tale with a rat-a-tat-tat.

Some story, said Oghi. He watched, enthralled and horrified, as the wraith repeatedly became a toddler watching his rattle float away, unable to save it.

This is about all I can stand of this . . . this mind. Let's move on, said Oghi.

Yes. Her drum sang a segue.

❖

The energy of the next wraith was darkest purple. The figure appeared to be squirming around on its back, grunting and breathing heavily.

The drum insisted, and Oghi entered its consciousness.

A woman was giving birth. The pain in her lower back was excruciating. From time to time contractions came in her belly—then her agony and her screams wiped out all thought, all consciousness except for the anguish.

Between contractions came fantasies Oghi participated in unwillingly. She saw a child holding up its own bloody arm and waving it. Blood gushed from the stump. From his expression the child appeared to be seeing too much, more than he could stand.

A contraction swept the imaginary child away.

In the next fantasy the woman inspected a series of her children, spoke to each of them gently, patted each one, and sent it on its way. Somehow she knew, and Oghi knew with her, that each way was some awful, unmentionable fate. Every child had something woefully wrong with it. One had an ear shaped like a hickory shell. Another was missing a hand. Another had a black, alluring hole where its nose should have been. The next had only one leg, and that one grew straight down from the center of its pelvis. It hopped straight toward her and cackled.

Another contraction, a sweep through agony.

The woman was circled by a half dozen children, all with the sunken cheeks and bloated bellies of starvation. In the center of the circle she was rapidly pulling grass and feeding it to them. Without expression, they munched on it. Some swallowed, and some let it dribble back out of their mouths. All awaited the next handful hopelessly.

A contraction racked the woman. With a monstrous effort she gave birth. The child was a beautiful pink creature—but an infant boar, not a human being. It climbed up her belly and began to root in her nose.

The second child was blue in the face. The mother slapped the boar away and grabbed the child. Quickly, she cut the cord and unwrapped it from the baby's neck. She put a finger to the child's nose and felt that it wasn't breathing. She slapped its back. She thumbed the eyes open and saw that they were still and lifeless. She pumped the baby's lungs with her hands. She held the child close against her breasts.

She might never have set the dead child aside, except that a third child came out between her legs. It already had the gray pallor of death. She checked for a heartbeat and found none.

A fourth child came out dead, a fifth, a sixth . . .

I can't stand this any more, said Oghi.

Tsola's drum sounded punctuation, and he withdrew from the wraith's horror-mangled mind.

Too much suffering, said Oghi.

All of it imagined, said Tsola.

Women do lose babies in childbirth, said Oghi, *and that is a big fear.*

Tsola answered, *What's going on with that poor woman is not real loss. It's self-torment.*

Regardless, this is all I can take for now. Let's go back.

Good.

I know this makes sense somewhere, Oghi said. *I need some sleep.*

❖

All of the adventurers munched on something for supper, cakes of roasted chestnuts and honey, dried meat, acorn mush, or balls made from corn flour. They talked offhandedly. The truth was that they were all too discouraged to enjoy company. How on earth—below earth!—were they ever going to find Salya? Wander aimlessly? Around the whole world? What was the point in that?

Yet they knew they couldn't leave. They looked at each other with the knowledge in their eyes. *We're a long way from having whatever knowledge of death Tsi-Li demands to let us out of here.*

Only Oghi felt chipper at all. He had a hint of that understanding, but planned to say nothing, not yet. He said to Aku, "Why don't you drink some *u-tsa-le-ta* with me tomorrow and we'll both go journeying?"

Shonan snapped, "You two traveling around in your heads isn't going to help us find Salya."

Actually, a different possibility had occurred to Oghi. Maybe they could go anywhere in the Darkening Land on the *u-tsa-le-ta,* journey by mind, not body. Maybe a traveling *mind* could find Salya. But he said only, "Why don't we sleep?"

"Since we can't tell day or night," grumped Shonan, "we might as well have night whenever we feel like it."

But Shonan's dreams were disturbed. He dreamt of redeeming himself against Maloch. He, Aku, Yah-Su, and a dozen select men sprang traps on the dragon. But every time Shonan made a fatal mistake. Once he directed all the men to attack Maloch from behind, where the diamond eye wouldn't blind them. Aku's job was to distract the monster with a feint, pretending to try to hurl a spear-thrower's dart down Maloch's throat. Part of Shonan's mind yelled at him, "That's insane, it won't work, and Aku will get eaten." The warriors got nowhere. They tried to climb onto the scales, but the thick body thrashed and threw them off. Then Maloch bit Aku in half.

The dreaming Shonan cried, "*No*," and decided to dream it again and make it turn out differently. This time Shonan was the bait, but Maloch whirled around, blinded all the other attackers with his diamond eye, and with a roar of pleasure ate them as they stumbled around, helpless.

Shonan started the dream over and over. He was determined to find a different ending, an ending where he and Aku would triumph. In the next scenario things went wrong because Shonan turned into a coward and ran, which he had never done his life. Humiliated, he forced the attack on Maloch again. It always went wrong, and always because Shonan himself fouled things up.

When he finally woke up, he saw that others were stirring. Aku was lighting a lamp. "May I have some tea, please?" Shonan said.

"Sure," said Aku. He poured it and handed it to his father. "What was wrong last night?"

"What do you mean?"

Oghi and Yah-Su looked at him oddly, too.

"You kept calling out and groaning, like you were having terrible dreams."

"We don't need to talk about that."

"Shonan," said Oghi gently, "I think we should . . ."

"I said we don't need to talk about that." Shonan fished out one of his honey and chestnut cakes. They were everyone's favorites.

Oghi tried again. "Red Chief, we honor you. We know that you may be our protection against many possibilities in the Underworld. Right now, though, we seem to be in a place where nothing is happening except inside people's heads. Uh, the consciousness of creatures." He paused. "When something unusual happens in our minds, I think we need to know about it."

Shonan snapped, "I had bad dreams about fights. Things went wrong. That's all you need to know."

"More than one? Repeated bad dreams?"

Shonan nodded.

"You failed."

He nodded again.

"You've hardly ever had dreams like this before?"

"Every warrior has night thoughts about what might go wrong. You should worry about the day thoughts I have. Worry about how I am when we're head to head with trouble."

These words came out so harshly that everyone shut up.

❖

"I see something to the left," said Oghi. Aku saw it, too, now.

The wraith was a twisting, contorting heat wave, barely visible because it was purplish black in the darkness. It whined and puled softly, making a song of suffering.

The picture in the wraith's mind was a handsome, fit-looking young man hiding behind a tree in a thick forest. Beyond him fog cuddled up against a slow-moving stream. Two women walked down a trail leading from the village to the stream, carrying gourds. At the waterline they knelt, scooped water from the stream, stood up, and came back along the trail, chatting merrily. As they passed him, they called out, "Hi, Funai," and giggled.

Funai climbed up the tree and into the foliage.

Funai has no interest in those two, said Oghi.

Aku and Tsola said at the same time, *No.*

A roly-poly woman, middle-aged and by herself, headed for the creek to get water for the family breakfast.

The wraith mewled like an injured kitten.

The woman hurried back toward her home.

Who's Funai waiting for? said Aku.

That one, said Oghi.

A slender, very beautiful woman skipped along the path alone, hardly more than a girl. She whirled, so that her walk became a dance.

The observers could all feel the watcher's heart pound.

The pretty girl stooped gracefully on the bank, dipped up water, and trod back toward the village.

Funai followed her through the woods, parallel to the trail, where he could keep an eye on her. Twenty paces into the village clearing a stocky, virile-looking man came up to her and said something. She stopped, they traded some words and smiles, and she went on.

He was flirting, said Oghi, *but she wasn't.*

Not yet, said Aku.

Feel Funai's fear, said Tsola.

They all did. It skittered up and down the young man's nerves as he watched the girl. When Funai's eyes flicked over to the virile man, also walking away, rage played an obbligato over dread.

The girl ducked into her house. Funai slipped out of the woods and walked quickly to the same house with the grace of the natural athlete. When he slid in, the observers could see the whole family gathered there, four generations. Funai gave the girl a quick kiss and her eyes sparkled. She set the gourds down next to an older woman, and the woman gave her a baby.

They're married, said Aku, *with a child.*

And he has a horror of betrayal, said Oghi. Sadness flecked his voice.

If he keeps that up, said Tsola, *she'll give him what he's afraid of.*

The memory circled through the wraith's mind again, unvarying in detail. This time the observers gave fuller attention to his feelings.

Ugly, said Aku, *nasty.*

What a way to make yourself miserable.

Tortured by what hasn't happened.

The wraith curled into a fetal position and moaned, moaned, moaned.

In a moment another memory materialized in his consciousness. He walked after a short, beefy man a generation older. Both of them carried the rackets used in the ball game, long sticks with small nets on the ends. Funai grabbed the older man hard by the shoulder. "Uncle," he said, challenge seething in his voice, "who did you vote for as captain?"

The uncle patiently lifted the gripping hand off his shoulder. "The other man," he said.

"My rival? I'm your nephew," said the young man. "You owe me."

"I owe the team. You are the best player, but you are not the best leader."

"You betrayed me." Funai's eyes flashed fury.

"My duty is to the team."

"What about your duty to me?" Here a hint of whine slipped into his voice.

"It is to help you become a man," said the uncle. "I've always done that, and I'm doing it now." He walked away.

The young man whirled in rage. He raised his racket, slammed it down, and broke it over his knee. He turned toward his uncle and shouted, "Traitor!"

Immediately, the memory started its rerun.

Fear of betrayal, said Oghi.

I wonder how many other fears torment him, said Tsola.

Are they all like this? asked Aku.

They are all consumed with fear, said Oghi. *Fear is the flame that inflicts all their suffering.*

Tsola said, *Everything we're seeing down here is what they're afraid of. None of this happened in real life. None.*

Aku and Oghi had nothing to say.

❖

The wraith was a lurid red. Her terror was loud. She screamed, she shrieked, she caterwauled. Aku and Oghi stood well back, intimidated by the grand display of her agony.

Slowly, half step by half step, they crept close enough to see. A child was running, holding her mother's hand. Lightning struck like a dozen blades of light all around them. Thunder banged louder than any human being had ever heard it on Earth. A deluge of rain whipped at them. The little girl screeched in terror, but her screech was the call of a songbird compared to yowling of the wraith, which was like a thousand horns braying at once, in a horrific clash of keys.

Mother and daughter made it to their hut and scrambled inside. Now the rain was gone, and the lightning was only a flicker through the smoke hole at the top. But the explosions of thunder were immense, overwhelming, soul-shaking.

The mother stripped the child's dress off and wrapped her in a soft elk hide with the fur against her skin. Then mother and father lay down by the fire, both holding the child tightly.

Her screams nearly shattered their ears. They kept holding her. "Rana, Rana," cooed the mother, "everything is okay. It can't get us here. Rana, Rana, it's okay."

When the child switched from screaming to blubbering, the wraith restarted the memory. Booms of thunder like a hundred cymbals struck at once in the head, lightning forks like a thousand fingers of the devil.

Eaten alive by her own imagination, said Oghi.

Abruptly—stunningly—the wraith silenced itself. They felt a hint of calm ease through it.

The scene changed. Rana poked her head out of the family hut. Dark clouds clumped around the peaks to the west. Occasionally, she could see the glare of sheets of lightning, and afterwards the growl of thunder.

"Come in," said her mother, "it's going to storm."

Rana stayed with her head out. The claps of thunder were what she imagined a bear's growl sounded like. She had never seen a bear, but she'd heard her father and uncles describe bears that seemed to jump out from nowhere and roar angrily, or even attack. Usually, the men backed away slowly, leaving the bear to its territory and slipping toward their own.

She'd also heard stories sometimes of men who had visions that the bear was their spirit animal, and who believed that they should kill a bear and wear its claws in a necklace, or wear even its head in battle. In the stories, at least, none of these men got killed. They had to fight fiercely, and some got bad wounds, but they killed the bear, ate its heart to take its courage, and wore a part of it as a sign of their brave spirits.

Rana wanted to be brave.

"Rana," said her mother more sharply, "come on back, a storm is coming. You hate storms."

Rana stepped outside. She took a full look to the west. Flickers of lightning here, forks there, the rumbles of thunder from every direction.

Right then a few raindrops flicked her face. Unsure, she stepped toward the middle of the village common and faced to the west. She told herself it was all right, that everything was going to be all right. Though old men and women told stories about people getting hit by lightning, no one could remember such a person. Lots of people were caught out in storms, and they came home okay.

Rana wanted to have courage.

"Rana," her mother called from the door, "get in here."

The rain sliced down harder, but Rana held her place.

Her mother strode out to the child and grabbed her hand.

Rana jerked it away. "Mama," she said, eyes fixed on the storm closing in, "I don't want to live afraid."

Her mother stiffened in surprise.

"How do I feel brave?"

Her mother thought. She said, "It's not what you feel, it's what you do."

After a few very long moments, she took Rana's hand. They both stood right out in the open through the entire storm. Though lightning bolts appeared to strike the tops of nearby hills, none hit Rana or her mother, or anything in the village.

Wow! said Aku.

She just played it in her mind in a different way, said Oghi. *Nothing hard.*

Tsola said, *The choice was always hers.*

Grandmother, said Aku, *is that why you sent me flying as a war eagle?*

The first of the great virtues—not the only one—is courage. Come to the cave of paintings and learn the others.

If we get out of here alive, said Aku.

❖

Oghi and Aku walked for what seemed like a long time before they saw another wraith, this one glowing an ugly, muddy, mustard-like green. It barely moved, as though barely capable of stirring, but it moaned continually. It was a very old man lying on a pad of elk hides. Being inside his head was unspeakable. He had vertigo all the time—the world spun continually.

This is awful, said Aku.

I'm drawing back, said Oghi. Quickly, he transformed himself into a sea turtle. *In my flat-bottomed shell, with my wide base on the ground, I might not feel so crazy in the head.*

Does it work? said Aku.

Oghi rejoined Aku in the old man's mind. *No,* Oghi said.

He's creating it, said Aku. *If we're in him, we're in it.*

The world is still doing flip-flops.

Every few minutes the old man threw up. Fortunately, they were dry retches. Oghi and Aku hated being there.

His wife stooped down and offered him a horn of broth. "Sip some of this, Mynu."

Mynu flung out a hand to brush away the offer and accidentally hit the cup. The hot broth spilled all over his wife, who jumped back and dunked her hands and arms in cold water.

Mynu's going through a bad illness, said Oghi.

I think it's something more, said Tsola.

Oghi studied Mynu's belly. He hadn't eaten much in days. Oghi let his eyes explore the entire body. It was weak. Mynu was undernourished. Maybe he didn't feel like eating, or couldn't keep food down. Maybe his lack of teeth made eating hard. Maybe the family didn't have enough to eat. Regardless, this old man had been hungry for weeks.

Oghi said, *I can feel the failure of his limbs, the difficulty of his breaths, the weakness of his heart.*

Aku said, *He won't get through the winter.*

Now the spinning of the world slowed in Mynu's mind. He began to think of other things. He remembered his other wife, the left side of her face sagging, even the eyelid, her left arm hanging useless. She lay in her blankets, unable to get to her feet or even to crawl, fouling herself. Mynu's present wife, her sister, had to change the hide blankets, clean her sister, and wash the hides in the cold creek. The old woman lay in a stupor, caring about nothing, acknowledging no one.

As Oghi, Aku, and Tsola watched, all the while Mynu remembered or imagined innumerable times when he'd felt helpless. He remembered when the boys chose teams for the kick-the-ball game and he got chosen last. Instead of playing all out, he shuffled around aimlessly. When he wanted to practice flint-knapping with his own brothers but was too shy to ask for flints, they worked and he watched. He remembered when he wanted to join the circle of men flirting with a girl he fancied. She'd recently had her becoming-a-woman ceremony. But he was afraid to intrude. When they gave her to another man in marriage, her parents never even knew Mynu had been interested in her.

He ran such scenes through his mind one by one, repeated some, leapt forward to others. Helpless, helpless, he was forever helpless.

Oghi said, *Life doesn't have to be that way.*

Tsola said, *It was for Mynu.*

What is all this, said Aku, *fear of old age and death?*

They should worry about hell, said Oghi, *not death.*

It's none of the above, said Tsola.

Suddenly, Mynu's fantasy jumped forward. Oghi and Aku could feel his will take hold, his control over his thoughts, tenuous and weak but real.

He's sick of rubbing this wound raw, said Aku.

Perhaps, said Tsola.

The hut was dark, the fire out, everyone asleep. For the moment Mynu had no vertigo. He sat up and looked around. The three observers saw the opportunity occur to him. Mynu wrapped two hides around himself. He stood up and wobbled.

As the old man in the fantasy wobbled, so did the wraith's imagination. Fear tramped around in the wraith's heart, a monster.

Aku, Oghi, and Tsola felt the wraith ward it off a little. The wraith thought, *To hell with being helpless.*

Mynu wove his unsteady way from the back of the hut around the dead fire to the door flap. Careful to be quiet, he got down on his hands and knees and crawled out the door.

The night air was bitter. Mynu breathed it in and out, his breath pluming, then back in. He smiled. It felt fresh, and it was cold enough.

He hoped the vertigo would stay away long enough for him to get outside the village into the forest, into a snowbank. Something about the idea of snow as a third blanket appealed to him. Snow was soft, the thought of it comforting.

He set out away from the village common into the trees. He didn't have many steps left in his old legs, and he could lose his balance at any time, so he staggered toward the hillside, not the creek. He didn't want the women to find him when they made the trip for water in the morning.

Soon he fell, but crawled on. He got barely to the edge

of the brush. There he fell forward into the snow. He shook the white stuff off his face and head. When his nose was in it, it didn't seem so damn comforting. He got to his knees but couldn't get up. He took thought and smiled. *Why not?* He rolled up in the hides. *Pointless, but . . .* He lay back and smiled. He didn't want to shiver. He would go to sleep and not wake up. *I am not helpless.*

The wraith disappeared.

Simultaneously, Aku, Oghi, and Tsola gasped. They stared at the spot where the energy had lain in misery, howling, moaning, and whining. It was empty air.

What happened? said Aku.

He's gone, said Oghi, feeling foolish for saying the obvious.

Where can they go? said Aku.

The three observers waited, stunned.

Back to Earth? said Oghi.

❖

They sat in a circle and told Shonan and Yah-Su the story of what they'd just seen.

"Reborn?" said Aku. "You think that's what happened?"

Shonan said, "That's just speculation. All of this is what you think you see."

Aku and Oghi looked at each other. The Red Chief hadn't seen, he had no way to know.

Oghi tapped his fingers on the stone floor. Finally he said tentatively, "If you master your fear, I mean, if you don't let your mind panic, maybe you go back and start a new life."

"Maybe if you do it enough times," said Aku.

"We don't know," said Oghi.

Tsola said in their minds, *Only Tsi-Li has the mastery of the knowledge of life and death.*

"But there's nothing here to be afraid of," said Aku aloud. *They're already dead.*

Shonan said something. Oghi said something back. They traded more words. Yah-Su watched, apparently relaxed. Aku heard none of it because he was listening to Tsola in his mind.

None of the above, she said again.

What do you mean?

You always have a choice whether to be afraid, or take a chance and go after what you want. It's the eternal struggle. Which is stronger, your desire to kiss the girl or your fear that she will turn away? Which is stronger, your desire to have a child, or your fear that the child will die or turn into a whirlwind of troubles? Your desire to sing a song beautifully? Or your fear of sounding bad?

Aku mulled on that and decided to throw something into the conversation. "Once Tsola told me, 'It's not death people are afraid of. It's life.'"

"Talk, talk, talk," said Shonan.

From behind them a voice said loudly, "I think you clowns need some help."

It was an alligator.

24

C all me Koz," he said.
      He was as long as three men were tall. The mouth looked big enough to swallow a deer whole, and the teeth sharp enough to shred it for stew. He appeared to be grinning. Luckily, he was a dozen steps away.

Koz said, "I'm the boss down here. The top-dog predator of all Earth in charge of hell, whaddya think of that?"

All four of them were tongue-tied.

"Don't have the gift of gab, I see. Okay, I've come to make you an offer—with, natch, the permission of the big owl himself."

He grinned, showing his teeth horribly. He seemed tickled at himself.

Shonan decided to deflate him. "Why do you talk funny?"

"I'm jiving in from a different time, which we Immortals can always do." He looked into their uncomprehending faces.

"Never mind, back to business. You are looking for Salya, your daughter"—he pointed his snout at Shonan—"and your sister." He indicated Aku. "Here are the words you've been hoping to hear. I know where she is, I can take you to her. And I'm glad to do it." He waggled his tail like a monstrous puppy enjoying himself. "For a price."

Shonan found his tongue. "What do you want?"

"One of you. You want to take someone out of the Underworld? No problem. All you got to do, aside from satisfying Tsi-Li, is to leave someone behind. Any one of the four of you stays down here with me, I don't care which."

"You're a monster," said Shonan.

"An alligator," corrected Koz. "And the boss of the Underworld."

Shonan raised a knife.

"What are you, a jerk?" Koz flicked his tail sideways and knocked Shonan's legs out from under him. The Red Chief splatted to the stone. "Pay attention. I told you the big owl sent me to help you."

Raising onto his elbows, Shonan said, "I don't know if we need a helper like you."

"Whatcha gonna do without me? You gonna walk this whole place? If you stayed down here long enough to breed a hundred generations, which it don't look like you got the broads to do, all of you and your descendants couldn't walk enough of the Underworld to find one this person."

"Why should we trust you?" said Shonan, getting up.

"Hey, *don't* trust me. But here's the news of the day. I know where your daughter is, and you don't."

The four adventurers stared at the alligator.

"We'll talk it over," said Shonan.

"Be my guests," said Koz.

They huddled and talked softly, with the incessant din of the condemned to cover their discussion.

"We don't have any choice," said Shonan.

The other three nodded.

"I am willing to make this sacrifice," the war chief went on.

"I am not willing to lose my father," said Aku. He was surprised at the heat of his own voice.

Yah-Su and Oghi started to say something, too, but Shonan held up a hand.

"Why don't we talk about this later, quietly, when we have time?"

"Talk about who's going to sacrifice his life?" said Aku.

"Yes." Shonan regarded his son. "Dying isn't the worst thing. Living like a coward is."

He turned to Koz. "Offer accepted," he said, "on the condition that you actually find her for us."

"Then off we go," said the alligator in a perky voice. "The short way or the easy way?"

"The short way," said Shonan.

"Every hundred years we get a visitor here, and he always says, 'the short way.'" He shook his head as if to say, *Oh, brother.* "Regardless, down here, any company from outside is a bit of fun. Follow me."

He started off. "You know, this place, vast as it is, tunnels in every directions, cracks in twice as many directions, lakes, rivers, everything you can imagine and a thousand times bigger, it's not as complicated as your brains. All these people in here, or the lost spirits of people, they're lost in their own heads. Have you ever seen the inside of a brain, all those little tiny blood pathways everywhere, more trails than there are on Earth, unbelievably complicated? No, you're mortals, so you wouldn't. Take my word for it, your brain is much bigger than the entire Underworld, and much worse to be lost inside of."

"Enough," said Shonan.

"Let's go. It's your asses."

❖

Koz told them to keep the lamps out, save them for when they really needed them. Shonan, Oghi, and Yah-Su followed Koz by his chatter. Above, Aku winged from perch to perch and watched with his owl eyes. It was an eerie and uncanny scene. A dark brown alligator led human beings and an owl through an environment as hostile as anyone could imagine. It was totally dark, the kind of dark that disoriented you and made you think everything was an illusion, invited you to populate the darkness with all your worst imaginings. Dark as madness.

Aside from the fears engendered by the darkness, there were actual drop-offs, slides, climbs, rivers, and lakes. By far the worst of all was the inconceivable pandemonium of human misery, wraiths yowling, yelling, wailing, shrieking, sobbing, moaning without end.

It seemed to Aku it must be the greatest affliction he would ever face, wading through this testimony of woe. No, second greatest, he reminded himself. He couldn't allow himself to think consciously, *The sacrifice of your father.*

Koz's jibber-jabber was a godsend. Not only "Watch your head there" and "a bit slippery here" but chitchat about the amazing things he'd seen people do. "People, to me, are the most curious creatures ever invented. I know what goes on up there, you know. All us Immortals know without even having to look in your direction.

"When Thunderbird sent you to a different world and slipped mortality in with you—now *there's* a nasty bit—he must have temporarily lost his mind. The mischief? It boggles the imagination.

"So there's death, it's waiting. Rebirth, yes, you know that, and it takes some sting out of death. So you carry on through your days on Earth frozen stiff by another fear, living. The one big gift, your chance to jump over the moon, and you're boo-hoo scared of it. Whatever you're doing, the song in your mind, it's, 'Be careful now, you might get hurt. You might mess up right in front of everybody.'

"Well, as you see, you pay for playing scaredy cat. Listen to your comrades, oh, ain't they sufferin', same in death as in life—ain't that a hotsy paradox for you?

"Oh, the chorus of suffering." He started dancing while he walked and got a chant going—"Illness, old age, hunger, thirst, war, drowning, lightning, sea storms, childbirth, attack by bears or panthers, floods, fire, cold, and the worst bugaboo of all—embarrassment. Oh, what a multitude awaits you, every part of it a little reminder—*things might go wrong!*

"And the way you obsess. You remember the quarter moon you were sick, or limped from a cut in your foot, not the twelve and a half moons you felt fine. You remember the baby that died, not the six brothers and sisters you've got. You dwell on the great-grandparents who died, not the ones still ticking, or the four grandparents and two parents you still got. Brother, you human beings, you are something to watch."

He let a moment of silence hum, and all four of his followers got nervous.

"I tell you what, though, there's a favor mortality does you guys that is really something. Sometimes you sneak around some way and get past your fear. I don't just mean warriors going into a fight—"

"About time you mentioned that," said Shonan.

"Hey, who's the guide here? Yeah, fighting for your family and tribe," he went on to Shonan, "that's good. Hunting animals for meat that might turn around and hunt you, that's good. But what I mean is, there are some people who stand more on the foot of what they like than what they're afraid of. Like people playing with kids in a totally carefree way. Like a woman making up a song to sing a child to sleep, and feeling something warm for that child. Like a guy who loves his wife so much he gathers shells and makes a necklace for her. I'm talking about people liking the world they're in— it's a beauty, you know, and nothing more beautiful than the way it comes back to life every spring." He stopped chattering for a moment, and they could hear his tail scraping along the stones. "I'm talking about people really liking each other. That's when they rise out of their fear for the moment and enjoy. We Immortals, we gave you life, too, you know. And we gave you Mother Earth—oh, don't she bring forth life! We gave her to you. Some of you appreciate instead of being afraid.

"Well, mouthy as I am"—he clacked his awsome teeth— "I must say that human beings, while being the nuttiest and most disgusting things on Earth, they still make me marvel. I've seen it over and over, they come down here to retrieve the ones they love. They never get out—they know they'll never manage it, though they always hope they will, and I hope so, too. I even hope you boys might. Never seen anybody learn what you have learned, but I don't know if it'll be enough for the big owl, no way of figuring that.

"Anyway, they come down here out of love. Nothing else, love, pure and simple. They surround someone with such special feelings that they . . . There's no explaining it, no understanding it, I just have to stand back and admire it, I do. They fill the world with ill will above and come down here bearin' love. That's human beings for you."

"It's better than the boss of the Underworld does," said Aku. Everyone held his breath. Aku was surprised at himself. "Why should you make us give up a life to get one? Is that love?"

Koz sat up on his tail, whirled his awesome head, and snapped the air in front of Aku's beak. The owl fluttered back a few feet. Then Koz laughed, a fine belly-rumble from the gut. "A boy oughtn'ta get in the face of the boss. Even a boy who's out of reach."

Koz turned casually, slithered for a moment, and said, "Okay, pay attention, this is a rock slide. I get down it easy, but not you, not in the dark. Light a lamp and see where to put your hands and feet."

He started down and looked back. "Yeah, that's good. Now when we get to the bottom, you're gonna fall a ways, maybe as far as I am tall. You're gonna land in a river up to your chests. So your stuff, hold it tight and keep it high."

But Aku flew above the water clutching his flutes.

❖

They took a rest and some food. Before their sleep, away from Koz, Aku forced the issue. "I cannot sacrifice my father to get my sister back."

Shonan looked impatient. "I'm the one. It's obvious. Our two friends here are only friends. They're generous beyond bounds to take these risks with us at all. It would be appalling to ask either of them to take one further step."

Aku opened his mouth to speak, but Shonan stayed him with a hand on the knee.

"And you? What are you going to do, abandon your child before he's born? Abandon your wife?"

"You're abandoning me!" Aku sounded immature even to himself.

Shonan spoke peaceably. "You are a man. You are a father. You can take care of yourself, and in fact take care of a wife and children. No one depends on me anymore." He paused. "No, not even you."

"Ada . . ."

"Enough," said Shonan. "We are in a great battle here. I

will die a warrior's death and return to Earth immediately."
He made a downward motion with both hands, meaning,
"No more."

❖

After their sleep, and the next sleep, and the next, the rock
slide and the river were only a start on their troubles. Aku
had a much easier time, able to fly where the others had to
climb and able to see when they couldn't. Shonan and Oghi
wore themselves to a frazzle and got considerably scratched
up on the arms and legs. Yah-Su seemed tireless, and was too
hairy to get scratched much.

Aku was cruising along until he got really scared.

"Nothing to do but swim it," Koz said. "Bit of underground river, not too awful."

Aku studied it. The entry made the stream look like a
tube, and that seemed terrible.

Immediately, Oghi started changing into a sea turtle, nose
to beak, arms to legs, fingers to claws, back to carapace. Aku
was just as busy changing into his human shape.

"Water's high sometimes, low sometimes, occasionally
there's a bit of air along the middle stretch, you can get a big
breath and go back down. Looks high today, though.

"What you do is, breathe in and out two or three times,
suck up the biggest bit of air you can, and go, go, go. Current's
with you, there's a break. Keep kicking and you'll make it.

"The one rule is, do *not* try to turn around and go back.
The current will flush you out backwards, but it will take a
lot longer, and you'll get the long lease here. Meaning get
killed, understand?"

"Let's go."

Aku slipped in last and hesitated a long while. He breathed
in and out until he began to feel dizzy, waited a moment,

filled every speck of space in his lungs with precious air, and dove.

Right away he was totally disoriented. He had no sense of what direction was up, down, or sideways. A couple of times he scraped his fingertips on the sides, and once he bumped his head.

After a while he began to see colors, a lot of colors, pure, like the ones you see in a rainbow, floating across his mind in bars, very beautiful, perfectly lovely, everything was lovely, he was very well, he was . . .

Rough hands grabbed him and heaved him forward.

When his head came out of the water, he heaved in a canyon full of air, eased it out slowly, and did the same again.

Yah-Su was holding Aku in his arms, and he said a whole lot of words in a row. "What did you do, stop kicking? When I grabbed you, you were drifting."

Shonan explained to Aku that Yah-Su got worried, dunked down in, and walked a few steps up the river before he bumped into the limp Aku.

"I got fascinated by the lights."

"They shine your way to being dead, guy," said Koz. "But, hey, you're welcome here."

After they followed the stream a while, they had to jump. Koz insisted that Aku not change into owl shape and fly down. "No place to light," he said. "It's all been slicked smooth as bat dung by hundreds of winters of runoff. If you try, you'll just wing it back up here and have to jump anyway."

Aku believed him. He went last, hearing splash after splash of body into water. Then he was sorry because he was left alone at the top in the dark, about to hurtle into absolute darkness. "Hello, down there," he called. They all called back. "Will someone please come back up here and push me off?"

They all laughed, and Koz hollered, "Jump, you coward!"

He did. Judging from the infinity in the air, it was about as high as a mountaintop reaches above a valley. Flying would have been glorious. Plummeting into darkness was . . . The water saved him. Air, water, back to air.

The rest of the day they swam two more underground rivers, and the party made Aku go first, so they could shove him if he slowed down. But he didn't. Scared into good sense.

❖

When they woke up, Koz said, "It's not far now."

The group walked in a hush. They had come so far to see Salya. What would she be like? Fear jiggled in their minds.

They climbed a short hill. Koz stopped beside an alcove, "Aku, Shonan—your sister, your daughter."

Shonan barged forward, and Aku peered around his father at his twin. She was a dead thing. Salya, face up, naked, arms and legs akimbo, head dropped back. The stillness in her felt like something hard and immovable, a boulder.

Shonan knelt and put a hand on her heart. "Still pumping," he said.

"Body alive, spirit gone," confirmed Ohgi.

"Every once in a while we get one of these," said Koz. "After a long time, what I guess you would call many winters up on the surface, the body quits, and there's nothing. Until then we just leave them be."

Aku felt like he had been hit by a flash flood. For the first time the enormity of what Maloch had done crashed into his mind, into his emotions. The dragon had eaten Salya's *life*. Even the wraiths down here, however miserable, were alive. They felt, they moved—even pain was a kind of energy. Salya was dead, her spirit-fire gone. The wraiths would return to Earth and walk and jump and see and smell and laugh. Salya was *dead*.

He sat down and looked at her. For a long time he didn't hear whatever his father and Koz were talking about, didn't notice what Oghi and Yah-Su were doing. Waves of awareness swept over him. Salya's dead face. *My dead face. That's what I'll look like when I'm dead.* For a long time he was struck immobile.

Slowly, tentatively, he got out his red flute. He touched his father's elbow and got his attention. "Now I have to do something." He held up the flute. He swallowed with difficulty. "This is the song the Little People taught me that brings people back to life."

Shonan started to speak, but Aku's glance cut him off.

He launched into the sound. His fingers and ears took over the song, and his mind sailed away. He saw pictures floating on the stream of notes. He saw the first leaves on oak trees unfurl, the ones with their green still silvered by fuzz. He saw the wildflowers of spring—gaywings, the dwarf iris, Salya's favorite, in royal purple, the scarlet trillium, his own favorite, with its three points, the suns of marsh marigolds. He saw flocks of blackbirds swimming through the sky, whirling together beautifully, a single creature dancing.

The next drifting picture shocked him, a glimpse of the future. He saw Iona, legs split wide and a tiny head with a tinsel of hair emerging. He wanted to cry out, "My child." He nearly spoiled the melody he was playing, but his devotion saved the song for Salya.

Now he saw the elusive denizen of the deep woods, the brown wood thrush with its spotted belly. When he listened for its haunting song, he heard instead the song of healing he was playing for Salya. And that song was coming to an end.

She didn't stir. She didn't blink. Her mouth didn't move, or her fingers twitch. She didn't breathe.

He looked into his father's face and tried to speak but couldn't.

"Notice," said Koz, "she don't even breathe. Air feeds the fire of spirit, and she's got no spirit. She's, like, frozen."

"Let's get going," Shonan said. "Let's get her out of here."

He got a buffalo hide, stretched it out, and rolled Salya onto it. Aku started to help, but one touch of Salya's arm made him jump back. Somehow he hadn't expected her to be cold.

"It ain't the heart, boy, it's the spirit-fire. Life ain't physical."

Incomprehensible. Not breathing yet heart beating. Dead but potentially alive. Impossible, but this was a different world. He looked into her face, his face, her death, his death.

Shonan's tone was gentle. "You yourself said that your song only works when the person has just died." They both wondered whether that meant when the spirit was still in or near the body.

Shonan and Yah-Su hoisted the dead weight. "Where to?" said Shonan, looking at Koz.

"Well, boys, we can't go back the way we came, against the river current and up long drops and through the squeezed alleys. There's a way, and it's not as hard, but it's long. Very long."

The alligator looked at Salya and her bearers. "Carrying her is gonna get old," he said, "real old. You big ones can't do it all the time, and you two can't pair up. We'll put a big one with a little one."

They accepted.

They marched, marched, marched. They switched off carrying Salya and marched.

"By the way," said Koz, "you're going to run out of candles soon. Then we get to walk in the dark. And you"—he pointed his snout at Aku—"Put out your candle." Koz said to Oghi, "I said put out your candle."

Oghi did.

The darkness was appalling.

"That's just right," said Koz, "that's just right." His voice was eerie. "Now, when we're walking in the absolute darkness, you'll know where I am. I'll jabber, I'll keep the words coming straight out." Silence and darkness. "If I fall silent, watch out."

"Why?" said Aku.

"Because this is coming!"

Koz clacked his teeth what seemed a dozen times. The sound was like an avalanche of stones hurtling out of the darkness. Aku fell down and barely kept himself from crying out.

"Now that you're all proper scared," said Koz, "light the candle."

Oghi did.

Aku breathed again.

"Stick it up to my mouth." He gaped his jaws wide.

Oghi thrust the candle near.

"Come on," said Koz, his voice completely normal even with his jaws open, "stick it right in."

Oghi did. The teeth gleamed like knives in the full moon.

"Teeth are handy, you see."

Koz started off again, and the four adventurers followed, Shonan and Aku carrying Salya in the litter.

"Need a break," said Aku. They set her down. Aku shook out his aching fingers. "Lucky alligator," he said, "born with no hands."

"Teeth are better," Koz agreed merrily. "This way I don't have to help the fools who come to the Underworld."

❖

That night they camped beside a small stream of clear water. While everyone else slept, Aku lit one of the horns for a moment, sat close to Salya, and blew it out. She was wrapped in one of his robes, but she needed no decency in the darkness.

He changed into owl form and just sat. He didn't know what to do, what to think, what to feel. He looked at his own face on her bones, a dull face, inert. He searched for words. *Not animated by life.* That phrase didn't do it either.

He wondered whether she slept. He didn't think so. When you slept, your awareness went from outside to inside, world to dream. Salya had no awareness, nothing inside there that could sleep.

She wasn't dead, either. Dead was something that happened to the body, and her body was whole. The catastrophe, what befell her, happened to her spirit.

He looked at her and again saw his own face deprived of its spirit-fire. He felt himself teeter on the edge of something unimaginably awful. He felt hollow, empty, a hole.

He closed his owl eyes, looked where he knew she was, and pictured the presence of his sister, of his twin, his companion through the years of his life. The sassy girl who played with him, shared his feelings, endured the death of their mother, even defied their father when necessary. He thought of the time she stayed out all night with Kumu. They weren't a bit apologetic, either, not Salya, not Kumu, and not his father Zinna, who declared himself glad that she was full of Kumu's juice. No, they were full of fire and dare. Salya

backed Shonan down. Aku loved her. He missed her. He
wanted to save her. For himself.

He thought again of his two flutes. They were also empty
holes, but if a man blew into them, if he poured his spirit-
breath through them in that way, they made beautiful songs.
Hollow as he felt, he could use his breath to make a story for
Salya.

She used to like for Crani to tell her stories, the stories
that came down from the oldest times, when all the animals,
including people, were first on Turtle Island and were dis-
covering who they were and how life on Earth might work.
He remembered that she liked the one about how the people
lost tobacco and got it back, so he told it now to her limp
form.

"In the beginning," he said, "the people had plenty of
tobacco, and we smoked it at all the dances and ceremonies
and whenever we wanted to pray and have our breath carry
our prayers to the sky. Before long, though, we used up all
the tobacco, and everyone started suffering. People felt list-
less and lackadaisical. Some felt ill. And one old man was
dying.

"This man's son, Walelu, knew that his father had been
surviving for some time on smoke alone, and he loved his
father very much. So he decided to make the long journey
to tobacco country and get some more.

"It was a hard journey. Tobacco grew in a place far to the
south, over high mountains, and the mountain passes were
guarded.

"Walelu, though, was a shaman and a shape-shifter. When
he got near the passes, he opened his medicine pouch, took
out the skin of a hummingbird, and slipped it on. Up he flew
over the mountains, as hard to see as a whirlwind. The guards

at the tobacco patches didn't see him either. He took a whole plant, tucked it into his medicine pouch, and sailed back over the mountains."

Aku looked at his twin, or rather the husk that was not his sister. He wished he could tell her that he had done what she wanted, and what their mother wanted, and become a shape-shifter. *I am owl.* But the husk had no way to feel glad.

He went on, "When Walelu changed back into a man and was walking home, he saw a very beautiful woman looking out of a hole next to the lowest branches of a tree. Immediately, he wanted her. He tried to climb the tree but slipped back. Walelu wasn't stumped by that. He took medicine moccasins out of his pouch and scooted right up the tree.

"When he got to the hole, it wasn't there. He looked up and saw that it was higher. Up he climbed, and the hole was still higher. No matter how high he climbed, the hole was always higher.

"Walelu had no choice. He put his lust away and climbed back down. As he walked, he pondered. Walelu was a shaman and knew that he had seen the beautiful woman and the hole in the tree with his spirit eye, not his physical eye. The spirits don't appear to human beings idly—they always have a purpose. So Walelu thought about what that purpose might be.

"When he got home, he immediately gave his father some tobacco to smoke, and the old man perked right back up.

"Then Walelu thought about that beautiful spirit woman and how he wanted to plant his seed in her, and suddenly he understood about tobacco. He took the tobacco seeds and planted them. The people knew what seeds were, but no one had ever tried to grow a plant from a seed on purpose. The people have been planting it ever since."

Aku waited, but his audience didn't respond to the story. His voice just rattled off the walls of the cave and echoed down the long passages.

He transformed himself into his human shape, took a deep breath, blew it out through his hollow self, and rolled up and went to sleep.

25

This is the easy way?" Aku tried to make the words sound light, but everyone heard the undertone. At the moment Aku was in human form, helping his father carry his sister.

"Bitch, bitch, bitch," said Koz.

"We have been walking for days," said Shonan.

"There are no days or nights in the Underworld," said their alligator guide. "No time. Well, time as you know it. All times forever are here, past to future. *If* you get back, it'll be the same day you left, ain't that handy?"

"You are our torturer," said Aku. Quick as a snake Koz turned his head as far to the side as he could, straight toward Aku. "And guide and executioner," the alligator said with a smile.

This "easy way" out of the caverns of the Darkening Land seemed four times the length of the long walk they took to find Salya. They ran out of lamps, which slowed them down painfully, Koz and Aku directing every step of the three blind men. They ran out of all food but Tsi-Li's chestnuts, which they got sick of eating. At one point they traveled two and a half days without water.

"I may as well toss you a bone," said Koz. "Before we sleep, you'll be in the big owl's house."

"All but one of us," said Aku.

"Exactly," said Koz.

❖

Mouldywarp said, "Aren't you the ones? To make it back when the others didn't." His pink nose twitched.

"Don't do that thing with your nose, okay, Mouldywarp?" said Koz. "Just make a path for us, would you?"

Mouldywarp had a kind of magic. He was only the size of Aku's hand, but when he nosed through a dusty, root-crossed passage his own size, human beings and alligators could follow him. So could men bearing a litter.

Tsi-Li, Great Dusky Owl, materialized as from nowhere and looked the adventurers over. "Thank you, Mouldywarp." The mole disappeared. "Well, behold. I see you pilgrims have damn near killed yourselves. Mean to save me the trouble?"

Aku was feeling drained and mopey. He didn't need his great-grandfather's grim idea of humor.

Suddenly Tsi-Li's owl visage was huge, looming. Aku didn't expect any leniency from him. Probably in Tsi-Li's mind justice worked in the world the way a rock fell, impersonal and inevitable. Between the Great Dusky Owl and the Boss of the Underworld, none of them would get out of here alive.

Inside their heads Aku and Oghi heard Tsola whisper, *You don't need me for a while now. Good-bye.* Aku flinched at these ominous words.

Tsi-Li said in a soft boom, "Let's see the prize you brought forth." He regarded Salya's limp, gangling body for a long moment. "What it inevitably must be." Though the master of life and death probably intended to sound neutral, Aku heard the sorrow in his voice. Salya was his grandchild, too.

The great owl put his head closer to her, his attention acute. Aku wondered if he was trying to enter her mind. Surely the immortal owl had that power.

"Truly dead," he said.

Tsi-Li opened a portal that hadn't been there a moment ago.

"Come into my home." Suddenly, magically, they all saw the house, there in the thicket of roots. It looked magnificent.

"You'll need to leave the young lady," said Koz. "If I have her, one of you will come back for her. Our little bargain."

"Well and good," said Shonan.

"This way," said Tsi-Li, still holding his door open.

"You go ahead," Yah-Su said to the others. "I want to stay with Salya. I don't trust this alligator."

"As you wish," said Tsi-Li.

Aku thought, *That's odd*. He said, "You should be with your friends."

The buffalo man looked sheepish. "It's wonderful to have friends."

"This way," the owl repeated, nodding Aku, his father, and Oghi into a large room with a smaller one on each side.

Aku went ahead. He suspected that Yah-Su felt uncomfortable about going into such a fancy place.

"Have you ever been in a house with three chambers?" said Tsi-Li, knowing perfectly well that none of his guests had. He invited them to look into one of the side rooms. "For sleeping," he said. It had a perch with plenty of head room for a bird the size of a man, and something bowl-shaped straight below.

He led them back into the large room and across to the door of the other small chamber. It had a fire in the center, a spit with a roast, and various cooking utensils. "I cook here, on the rare occasions that I cook. We owls like our meat as nature makes it. We have our feathers to keep us warm, and we don't take to flames." He shuddered, as though at the thought of fire brushing at his feathers.

"Thank you, then," said Shonan, "for making something for us."

"Oh, yes, we'll have food and drink. It is a special occasion. Afterward, we'll have some questions. Perhaps even some answers."

Aku was in a complete muddle. He didn't know whether to be more afraid that he'd lose his father or afraid they'd all be examined and sent back to the land of the dead.

Tsi-Li turned back to the main chamber and spread his wings wide. "So do you like my home?" The huge abode was directly beneath the Tree of Life and Death, the big roots themselves acting as beams to support the walls. These walls were not dust that got up everybody's nose or mud that fell on them. They were plastered into a hard shell and buffed to a shine. It occurred to Aku that having a large home among the roots was physically impossible, but then Immortals didn't play by the rules of Earth.

Aku kept sneaking looks at his father. *No. Impossible. I can't lose him.*

The large central room they stood inside seemed to be for Tsi-Li's pleasure. In the center sat a large flat rock, though Aku couldn't imagine why. The walls were decorated with feathers of every possible color, tied to suggest avian bodies and wings dangling from the walls.

"I'm proud of my little collection," said Tsi-Li. "Not every bird on Earth is represented here, far from it, but I've gathered my favorites. The ones with bright plumage appeal to me especially." Aku wondered if that was because Tsi-Li's feathers were a gray-brown that could serve as camouflage. "These feathers are from peacocks—you'll notice I have quite a few. Spectacular, aren't they? A bounteous bouquet of blues and greens."

He pointed with one wing to an entire side of the room in different colors. "These are the feathers of parrots and cockatoos. Those dazzling whites you see, ornamented with gold, yellow, and reds, are the cockatoos. I revel in the purity of that white, rarely matched on Earth." Now he pointed to the largest panel in the room. "Parrots are among my favorite members of our avian family. Notice how this background of green feathers shows off the other colors, which are deliciously flamboyant. I'd wager you've never even seen some of these bright shades. Fuchsia, who would not relish such a bold hue? Rose, doesn't it seduce the eye? Peach, azure, aquamarine, amethyst, which is one of my favorites, carmine—isn't that fabulous?—cinnabar, I love that name, coral, magenta, I could go on and on."

Aku was afraid his great-grandfather would. Dread was coiling tighter and tighter in his guts. *Which of us is going to die?*

"It's time. Be seated, please." Tsi-Li gestured at some contraptions none of them had even seen. "Sit!" Tsi-Li said with a smile, and planted himself on one of the contraptions. "They're called 'chairs.'" The three human beings tested them out. Their host slapped the big flat rock. "This is called a table." The guests eyed each other oddly.

Tsi-Li jumped up and went to the cooking room. "First, we have something special to drink." He passed out horns of liquid. "This is a drink called champagne. Like your corn juice, it is fermented, but from grapes. In fact, it's fermented twice, so that it bubbles. See if you like it." He sipped from the horn with his bird beak.

The guests copied their host and exclaimed, "How wonderful!" "Terrific!"

Shonan said, "Why haven't we ever heard of this drink?"

Aku thought, *My father is damned cheerful, considering.*

"Well," said Tsi-Li, "it's known as the nectar of the Immortals. We keep the secret of making it to ourselves."

The great owl served roasted acorns, then corn mush, then long, green onions sizzled half dark, and last the buffalo roast. Before each course they quaffed a horn of champagne.

Shonan said, "I've never had such a marvelous meal."

Oghi chimed in with his own compliment.

"I'm glad you like it," said Tsi-Li, an eyebrow arching.

Aku couldn't enjoy a thing. His eyes, his thoughts, his feelings—all were on Shonan.

When they finished the slices of roast, they downed another horn of champagne. Tsi-Li said, "My friends, are you feeling strange at all?"

"Woozy," said Shonan. He seemed happy about it.

"I like it," said Oghi.

"Champagne does make your mind tilt a little. One day we will give human beings the secret of making it. Consumed in small quantities, it's enjoyable. It can even make people sing and dance better. And romance better. I wonder if I've given you a little more than is ideal. Tell me, Shonan, are you able to answer questions?"

"Always," said the Red Chief.

Ada, thought Aku, *why are you pretending?*

Tsi-Li nodded to Shonan. "I think I'll start on another tack. Aku, Ohgi," he said, "you saw what hell is."

The two looked at each other.

"You saw and then showed me," Aku told Oghi.

"Both of you saw fully," said Tsi-Li. "I joined Tsola and traveled along with the two of you."

Aku was taken aback. Someone else was in his mind. He felt a low flame of anger.

We Immortals do as we please, said Tsi-Li in Aku's head.

Aku flinched.

"It's all right, Grandson," said Tsi-Li out loud.

Aku gave him a wan smile.

"As I say, both of you saw what the punishment of the Darkening Land is."

"Yes," said Aku, "endlessly reliving whatever scared you in life."

"Not the bad things that did happen," said Ohgi.

"Clever, isn't it?" said their host. "Even demonic."

He turned the yellow globes of his eyes on Shonan. "You saw none of this."

"What? The screaming and whining were horrible. Beyond horrible. Disgusting, too."

"Yes, but you didn't actually see what the spirits were afraid of."

"I don't know anything about that."

"Ada," said Aku painfully. Shonan didn't seem to notice.

Tsi-Li regarded the Red Chief. "I want you at your best. Let's take a few minutes of sight-seeing to help you toward sobriety."

Aku wondered what the fancy word meant.

The great owl got up, stood on the table, and said, "Follow me. Just jump." He flapped upward, a swirl of a hole opened in the solid ceiling, and Tsi-Li disappeared through it.

The three people gaped at each other. Shonan stood up

with a what-the-hell attitude, stepped onto the table, held
his arms high, jumped, and disappeared. He dived upward
into solid earth.

Oghi did the same.

Hesitating, then wobbling, Aku followed along.

They found themselves high in the branches of the giant
cedar, the biggest tree in the world, the Tree of Life and
Death.

"Don't worry if your stomachs are queasy," said Tsi-Li.
"You're way up in the air and you're tipsy. But you can't fall
from here, I promise.

"So," said the Great Owl, "look around at the world." To
the west, which lay in half shadow, rolling hills gave way to
prairies, which stretched away forever. A liquid sunrise
lolled on the bald summits of the mountains to the east,
leaving their steep, timbered sides dark in shadow. The sky
above them, horizon to horizon, was the innocent color of a
robin's egg.

"Exquisite, isn't it, that hue?" said Tsi-Li. He lowered his
eyes to the earth that rolled away in all directions. "Exquisite world, in fact. I've always been impressed with Thunderbird, that he gave such a beautiful world to the creatures of
mortality. But then he's the master of the world above, and
I only of the world below.

"Never mind all that, though," the great owl chippered
on. "What do you see on the branches of this magnificent
cedar tree? Do you see our company?"

They all looked hard.

"I don't see a damn thing," said Shonan, "except cedar
leaves."

Tsi-Li waited.

"Ada, don't you see?" ventured Aku. "There's energy on
the branches here and there."

Tsi-Li's sun-yellow eyes brightened. He waited.

Oghi added, "The same energy we saw down below. These branches are full of wraiths."

"Spirits," said Tsi-Li. "Here reside the spirits of the dead, those who have earned their emergence back to the world. They are waiting for venues of birth, women's bellies to swim into and then out of. They are people waiting for their corporeal forms."

Aku was amazed. It seemed to him, now that the sun was above the mountains and the Tree of Life fully lit, that the branches were spinning with energy, human potential.

"What do they do," said Aku, "to earn this . . . rebirth?"

"You already know."

"Learn not to let fear trample them."

"Close enough. They've learned *some* of what you say."

"How much?"

Tsi-Li shrugged with his wings. "It's my call. Let's just say that I am the master of the knowledge of life and death." He waited. "Have you seen enough?"

Aku breathed in and out. "I'd just like to sit here a few minutes and look and . . . absorb it all."

Tsi-Li nodded. They all sat in silence. Finally, Tsi-Li said, "Ready?"

Aku nodded.

Tsi-Li said, "This bit is scary, but just jump. Dive, straight down." He did it himself, wings folded back. In an instant he disappeared among the branches.

"Okay for a bird," said Shonan.

In his human form Aku dived. His body disappeared just before the branches hid him from view.

Oghi and the Red Chief leaped head down. Abruptly, they sat at the table in Tsi-Li's central room.

Amazingly, Salya lay by the fire, wrapped in robes.

Aku leapt and opened the door. Outside was no Koz, no Yah-Su, nothing but roots and dust.

"Where is my friend?" said Aku, his voice trembling.

"He went with Koz," said Tsi-Li.

"*Why?*"

"He made the choice he thought was right. He is the sacrifice. He *chose* it."

"I don't understand."

"His life was hard. He looked like a monster. People treated him like a monster. He felt like a monster. Now he wants to come back as a man who can have a family, friends, and a place in a community."

"*We* were his friends," wailed Aku.

"He was very grateful for that. He told me to thank you for being the only friends he ever had, and very fine ones."

Aku started to protest again, but he felt overwhelmed. Shonan put a hand on his shoulder.

"Don't wail for Yah-Su," said Tsi-Li. "He is doing well. You see, though he said nothing, he also learned something down below, something very great. He lost his fear of death. He crossed over to seek life.

"As he has gone down out of wisdom, he will come back in grace. Very soon."

Aku held to the spinning world, determined not to fall off.

"Now," the Great Owl said, "you have been very good guests, exceptional guests. This is a historic occasion, for I'm about to say words I have never said before. Aku, Grandson, you have gone into the Underworld and returned with knowledge of life and death. You are free to go back to the world." He repeated the same words for Oghi. "I salute the two of you," he said. "Who else can say he entered the Underworld and came back alive? You have the reward of great understanding. Use it well."

Aku felt a spike of elation.

Then Tsi-Li regarded Shonan with the yellow globes at eyes for a long time. "Red Chief, you are a more difficult case."

Aku cringed. *No. Don't let it be.*

"Tell me, what do you think of what you saw—or rather heard—down below? And what do you think of what you saw, if you saw them, up high in the tree?"

"I'll tell you what I told these two," Shonan said. "All this stuff about how awful fear is, it's just a lot of blather about what every good warrior already knows. Before a fight, or before you ever get near any fight, you can cripple yourself in your head. You can imagine your arms being hacked off. You can see a spear ramming straight through your gullet and writhe in agony. You can feel your head being yanked back and your throat slit."

He clapped his hands on his knees. "I don't want any men like that at my side. They're useless. They're cowards. They get wounded in the mind twenty times for every wound they might get in a lifetime as a warrior. They get killed a thousand times for the one time they'll actually have to die. And what they do is, they cut their own balls off. They terrify themselves so they can't fight. And then they *do* get hurt or killed, because they've taken the weapons out of their own hands. Their hands quiver, their legs shake, and they can't do a thing. Believe me, I've fought next to men like that, and doubled the risk to myself to save their tails."

He huffed breath in and out. "A real warrior bans such pictures from his mind. He pictures himself killing the enemy, never himself getting killed. He feels the thrill of the charge, the bright gleam of the danger, the pleasure of the use of his skills, the exhilaration of danger. Live? Die? He is beyond caring. Because for those moments he is truly alive, he is all he can be as a man."

He shrugged. "And if fate should be against him, or luck, and the enemy defeats him, he makes a short trip to this place and is immediately reborn on Earth. We're promised that."

He fixed each listener in turn with his eyes. "So what is this fine wisdom we supposedly got in the Underworld? Old stuff. True, fear of death is trivial. That's not what undoes a man. What steals away a man's days in this world? Fear of life, yes, life. No warrior needs to go the Darkening Land to learn that." He spoke directly to Aku and Oghi. "But you know nothing, because your so-called understanding is words and thoughts. If you followed me into war, into the roar of life and death, I would teach it to you where it matters, teach you so you feel it in your blood!"

In the wake of Shonan's big speech everyone held his tongue. Aku was flat scared. *Ada, after all this, will I leave here without you?* He thought of his life-saving flute song. No chance, he thought. The Great Dusky Owl would never let him use it.

Shonan kept his eyes on the owl. They said without words, *And I mean it.*

Finally, Tsi-Li broke the silence. "You dare to speak to the master of the knowledge of life and death in such a way." His words had a sting.

Then Aku thought he saw a laugh in the Great Owl's eyes. "Actually, what you just did is a fine example. Faced with death by my judgment, you are not afraid."

Aku breathed. Then, immediately, he jerked. The tap of Tsola's drum put him on alert. He saw the same tug in Oghi's eyes.

"As for the rest, your understanding is admirable. Like your companions, you might understand more. You might see that a man needs courage not only to fight but to do the right things to make a good marriage, and to teach his children to be good human beings."

His eyes clicked from one listener to another. "Still, each of you has some genuine understanding of life and death. You have triumphed in the Underworld. You are free to go."

The drum spoke powerfully. *Bang*-bang! Bang-*bang*!

The Great Owl flapped his wings wildly. A dust storm seemed to rise up, and they were blinded.

26

Shonan blinked over and over. "Where in hell am I?"

Tsola said, "I think you know, Red Chief."

The three travelers were flopped on the cave floor around Tsola's low fire.

From a corner, the black panther, Bola, said, "Welcome back to the Emerald Cavern." A rich irony lined his gruff voice.

Aku reached out and took Salya's limp hand. Still cold, still dead.

"What happened?" said Shonan.

"I know you didn't quite realize how unique it was, but you traveled to the world of the Immortals, the Tree of Life and Death. I can whisk any mortals away from there."

"And you just did," said Bola.

"Yes." She met the eyes of each man. "I'm sorry about Yah-Su."

"It wasn't right," said Shonan. Aku heard unexpected emotion in his father's voice.

"I speak to the living. Red Chief. Grandson. Seer Oghi. You are splendid. Many mortals before you have gone to the Darkening Land, always hoping to bring back someone beloved. Except in the ancient stories, no one returned until now. Until you. Congratulations."

Aku gestured with an open palm to his dead sister.

Tsola turned to business. "Let's examine her."

Bola licked his paws. Aku thought he was impatient.

The Wounded Healer put her fingers below Salya's left breast. "Yes," Tsola murmured.

She placed a palm on Salya's forehead. "Mmmm." She rolled the body over and inspected all of it for injuries. She thumbed back one eye, then the other. "Just what we thought, body whole and well, spirit-fire missing. Gone."

"Stolen," said Shonan.

"Eaten," said Aku. His heart twisted as he looked into his grandmother's eyes. "Can you do anything for her?"

Bola growled, but the growl might have been taken for a chuckle.

"This far exceeds my powers. I have never seen anything like it."

"There's got to be something," said Shonan.

Tsola shrugged.

"Grandmother, I . . . Grandmother, we could take her to the Land Beyond. Surely there . . ."

Now Bola's growl was menacing.

"Aku, I know that the worlds above and below, the Immortals, all that seems like magic to you. But it isn't, they're just different realities. And like Earth, they have a particular nature, a way they work. Mortality only exists here. Life can only be restored here."

"So what do we do?" said Shonan. "Because I'm damn well going to do something."

Tsola's eyes glinted. "Perhaps this will please you, Red Chief. It's really very simple." She waggled her eyes crazily. "You kill Maloch and take Salya's fire back."

Shonan ignored her attitude. "How do we kill Maloch the Uktena?"

Aku focused on his father in amazement. In effect, he treated it simply as a practical problem.

"Maloch has thick fish scales," Tsola said. "Bola, come here." The panther padded to her. "The dragon is four-legged, more or less like Bola. Here"—she touched her feline son on the left side—"just behind and below his shoulder, that's where his heart is. It's covered by the seventh scale, counting down from the spine." She touched Bola's spine. "A fighting man must lift that scale and strike hard underneath. That blow will be fatal. No other wound will faze him."

"When I know my enemy's weakness," said Shonan, "he is dead."

"Is he?" said Bola. "Will you attack in sunlight? His diamond eye will blind you, and he will kill you."

Tsola said evenly, "Yes, he will kill you. To Maloch you are no virgin whose spirit must be taken ceremonially. You are an enemy."

"Who damn well needs killing." Bola held Aku's eyes with his mysterious cat globes. "Both of you." Challenge gleamed from the panther's eyes. "Why would you attempt it?"

Aku said, "I have to."

Shonan said, "She is my daughter."

Tsola hung her head in what could only be sorrow.

Oghi said, "If we don't kill him, he will never leave us alone. Every year or two we will sacrifice another sister, another daughter, another Salya."

"A man may fail," said Shonan, "but he may not surrender his children one by one to a murderer."

Tsola lifted her face to Aku's. For the first time she looked worn out to him. "Go, then. If life calls you to a hopeless mission, so be it." She looked at her son. "Help them get started."

❖

Each of them pointed his mind toward home, toward Amaso. Aku was impatient to get there and see Iona and touch her belly full of child. Oghi was eager to get back to his town by the sea, the only home he had ever known. Shonan wanted his fight.

They scooted Salya onto a hide.

"I want to recruit some soldiers on the way," Shonan said. "Not a lot. As many as I have fingers."

"Father," said Aku, "we have fifty or sixty warriors at Amaso." That counted men from both Galayi and Amaso heritage together.

"Not like the ones I'm thinking of," said Shonan.

They hoisted the hide bearing Salya, and Bola led them through the night-dark passages of the Emerald Cavern, arguing as they went. Since he needed his cat eyes to see the way, Bola stayed in feline form and held his corner of her litter between his teeth.

The four came out of the Emerald Cavern into a night with a half moon, a dazzle of brightness after the absolute darkness of the cave. Bola said, "Tsola told me to help you down to the village."

Bola changed into human form, paws to hands and feet, fur to flesh, feline head to an elderly man's face. The four trod the trail to the Cheowa village, carrying Salya through the moonlight. They slept in Bola's son's house, and when they woke up, Shonan said, "Let's leave Salya in here and say nothing about her. There's no need to cause talk."

The others agreed, and then joined the other men walking down to the river to wash themselves. It was the way the community of Galayi men greeted the dawn.

Shonan looked back at the main village. Three other

clusters of houses huddled by the river upstream and down. The main village was marked by the big council lodge in its center. This was where all Galayi villages gathered for council three times a year, when they held their great ceremonies.

"A peace village," said Shonan. He painted the word "peace" with disgust. Two Galayi villages were peace villages, which had no Red Chief, where men did not train seriously as fighters, and haven was offered to anyone who sought it, even an enemy. Shonan had told Aku many times that there were two peace villages only because the five war villages protected them against other tribes.

Still in human form, Bola said, "Red Chief, there's a man here who could be valuable to you. Tol may be the finest flint-knapper in the tribe. I will introduce you."

As they walked toward Tol's home, Aku said to his father quietly, "Why would a peace village have the best knapper?"

"Everyone needs points for knives," said Shonan, "even women."

"But your men will already have sharp spear points."

Shonan said, "You can never have too many points, or ones too sharp."

In fact, Tol had a number of obsidian points. Bola said, "Will you sharpen the points of Shonan's men, or replace them?"

"Of course," said the knapper.

Bola also asked three of his male relatives to go along with Shonan's party to help carry Salya's litter. That way half the men would have their hands free at all times.

Before noon they took the trail south and east toward the Tusca village, where the warriors Shonan knew well lived. He told Aku, "I want men I can count on."

"What good will that do us against Maloch?" said Aku.

Shonan smiled at his son, ever innocent about war. "Who

knows who will be with Maloch? There may a gang of Brown Leaves to take care of."

Shonan bent to scoop water out of the creek and sip it.

"I want one man who throws a club well. I'm thinking about the dragon's diamond eye, that thing might be vulnerable. Maybe it can be knocked out of its socket."

"Grandmother said only a strike to the heart can kill Maloch."

"What are you going to do to help?" said Shonan.

Aku flushed. "Watch." He and Shonan were leading the way, so Aku did it in the middle of the trail, where everyone would see. Flesh to feathers, arms to wings, mouth to beak, head brown, neck red-gold, and eyes the amber of the war eagle.

Shonan watched every change, even the tiniest. His face gave away nothing.

"I will be the eyes of this small party," said Aku. His eagle voice was identical to his human voice. "And search for enemies."

He launched into the air. When he changed into bird form, he felt a sudden revulsion toward being on the ground. He did what he had done in the Land Beyond the Sky Arch, flapped up the sides of the mountains until he began to feel the air lifting him. He rode it high, high, high. From the tops of the mountains he could see each blade of grass. No enemy would elude his eyes.

❖

At the Tusca village Shonan immediately took Salya to the relatives of his dead wife. Before letting them see the body, he said, "Do not cry out," meaning the traditional wailing of grief. "She seems dead, but she can be saved. We will restore her life."

Shonan and Aku lifted the buffalo hide covering Salya. People began to cry softly.

Meli's brother touched her first. When he felt Salya's cold cheek, he recoiled and yelped. One by one everyone—Salya's aunts and uncles, her cousins, everyone but the children—put a hand on her flesh.

"It is a terrible story," said Shonan, "but it will end in triumph. Until then we cannot tell it. I ask every one of you not to talk about what you've seen." He turned to Aku. "We'll leave her here for now. Let's go."

"Some will talk," said Aku.

"All we can do is slow the talk down," said Shonan. "It's going to get to Maloch sooner or later."

"That we rescued her from the Darkening Land."

"Yes. He'll know what we're going to do next." Shonan paused. "Now we're going to have to face Kumu and tell him what happened to his fiance."

It was Kumu's father they faced first.

"Red Chief?" said the club thrower. His voice was wary.

"Zinna, I'm sorry for the things I said last time we saw each other. I was wrong."

"I was drunk," said Zinna.

"We have something to show your whole family, especially Kumu."

Kumu came out of the hut looking like an animal hunted to exhaustion. His mother Monu followed him, and the family walked across the common to the hut where Salya lay.

When he saw her, Kumu fell on her and wrapped her in his arms—he screamed. He looked wildly at Shonan and Aku.

"She's cold," said Aku, "but she's not dead." They explained, but Kumu kept wailing. The words meant nothing to him.

"Zinna," said Shonan, "I—*we*—need both of you. We intend to bring Salya back to life. That means we have to kill Maloch."

Zinna said, "Where do we go? When?"

"To Amaso," said Shonan, "which is Galayi now. Maloch will come for us there. If he doesn't, we'll go after him."

"Count me in," Zinna said. He looked at his bereft son. "Him, too."

"Good man. We leave in the morning."

The Red Chief led the way to the home of Fuyl.

"Her other suitor?" said Aku.

"No," said Shonan, "the best spear thrower in the village." Yim, Fuyl's father.

Yim invited them in and his wife gave them tea. Most of the family seemed to be out and about.

Shonan gave Yim his story.

"Sorry, I'm out," said Yim. "My medicine has led me another direction. Let me show you."

"I don't have much time," said Shonan. His mind was scrambling to think of someone to replace Yim.

"This will be worth it."

He walked to the back of the house and came back with an elk antler in each hand. Rather, they'd once been elk antlers. The branches had been cut away. The thick ends of the remaining stems were polished to a high gleam and— Aku had trouble crediting his eyes—carved into graceful images of bounding elk. Though the Galayi liked to carve, Aku had never seen anything finer. On the other ends were . . .

Shonan knew immediately. "What spear throwers!" He grabbed one and swung it overhead. "Balanced, strong, beautiful."

"They are made with strong materials and strong medicine," said Yim.

Yim knew few villagers were as skeptical as Shonan. "And I have something even better for you," he said. "Tell me, Red Chief, who is a better spear thrower than me?"

"No one," said Shonan, "not even me."

"Wrong. I have taught my son slowly and carefully. Since you left he's proved his mettle in a buffalo hunt. *Truly* proved it. He is the best in the entire Galayi nation."

Yim wanted to show his boast was good, and Shonan was willing. They found Fuyl practicing for an upcoming ball game. The handsome youth was probably the village's best ball player.

Fuyl got his darts and one of Yim's beautiful elk spear throwers. "With these throwers," said Yim, "and my strong boy, you can throw thicker and heavier spears."

The three went hunting and rousted out a buck. Fuyl hurled a spear through it so hard that the point sank deep into the ground beyond.

"That's power," said Shonan.

"Let me show you power and accuracy," said Fuyl. He drove a dart all the way through the trunk of a sapling.

As they walked back, Shonan told the young fellow, "You're the best with your weapon."

Fuyl said, "That's good, Red Chief, but I'm tired of throwing at animals—I want men."

"I can give you all the challenge you want," said Shonan.

"I'll hold you to your promise."

As he strode off, Aku said, "Spears won't hurt Maloch, Father."

Shonan huffed out a laugh. "Do you believe all the gossip you hear? Anyway, think about Maloch trying to bite someone when he has six or eight spears down his throat, each one tall as me." Now Shonan laughed out loud. "Or think about him trying to eat supper that way."

Shonan led Aku around the village, deciding on the best men. Shonan picked three or four husky ones and told them to cut the shafts of their spears short. "I want you to be able to stab with them," he explained, illustrating with a gesture. They looked doubtful. "Listen, that's what I'm going to carry for my own main weapon. A short spear. Also the heaviest club I can swing."

The men set to work.

As the Red Chief and his son walked away, Aku asked, "How will you get close enough for a stab?"

Shonan turned to Aku, his eyes aflame. "I'm going to ride the dragon. One way or another, I'm going to get on the bastard's back. Then, if the heart is in that place, I'm going to slide down and . . ."

He lifted his short spear and pantomimed driving it home. "The one to kill Maloch is me."

For a few steps he enjoyed the picture. Then he said seriously, "You get your flute and your song ready to bring your sister back to life."

Aku said gravely, "Yes."

"That's the most important part."

"Yes."

They walked.

"And what will you do, Father, when you possess the diamond eye that reveals the future?"

"Well, if I see anything in it, I might start believing old women's stories." He nudged his son with an elbow. "Let's get a good meal and rest. We've got a ten-day march to Equani. We'll get some more men there. Then a long way to Amaso. Carrying Salya, we'll be slow."

27

Aku looked down at the tops of the low hills, across the forest, and beyond to the sea. Its horizon cradled the last of the sunlight, fire fading into water. He turned into the wind and dipped and looked down at his father, their dozen men, and their pack dogs trudging along the trail, within steps of the tops of the foothills. There the trail to the other Galayi villages met the trail to the Brown Leaf village. The place was simply called the Junction.

At the Junction Aku's Galayi companions from Tusca and Equani would see the ocean for the first time, most of them, and they would stop at the good campsite there, and get their first look at Amaso, where they would fight for their lives.

Aku wished he could stay up here, in his eagle form, riding the winds. But eagles didn't have night vision, and he had a duty that was worse than painful. Once he spoke the words, he certainly would not sleep.

He could see the rest of his life with perfect clarity.

Tomorrow he would carry the body of his sister Salya into the village, rescued from the Underworld but still dead. Then he would fold his arms around his beloved, Iona, and around the child in her belly. He would breathe in Iona's warmth.

And the next day he would die. All the men of the village would die. The lucky might live an extra day, as they were hunted down one by one.

Aku's woman and child would be taken as slaves. Iona would share robes with some Brown Leaf man. That man would raise Aku's child in a world he didn't know, speaking a tongue not his own, or hers.

He would fail his sister forever. She would never get her life energy back, never return to walk the good Earth. Worse than dead, far worse.

He looked up into the sky for other eagles, as though he might search out an alternative life there. But almost everything he loved on Earth was below, within sight, and doomed.

The wind from the sea was rough—it buffeted his big wings. The world buffeted his feelings, knocked them topsy-turvy.

There was nothing left but to do his duty. It made him want to scream. Not an eagle *scritch,* a human scream.

He glided down through the cooling air. As his little fighting outfit trudged up to the campsite, he cruised over their heads, out of reach, as he did every day. This time they didn't lift a hand, didn't even look up. They didn't look at the ocean, either. They were in a sullen mood. Shonan had pushed everyone so hard that even the pack dogs were worn out.

Aku lit on a low branch well away from the dogs, changed into human form, dropped to the ground, and walked into camp. He didn't know how to tell his father and their friends that they were about to die.

Four men lowered Salya to the ground on her litter. Then they walked away quickly, not even glancing at her, shaking the ache out of their fingers. They were weary of shifting off and on, off and on, bearing the never-ending burden of the dead woman. Their eyes said, though their lips would not, *This is pointless.*

Oghi sat down with Salya, like he was keeping her company. He did that a lot. Everyone else was setting up.

"What's the news?" said his father. Every day the same words, every day the same expectation. Shonan didn't really think avian eyes in the sky would bring back any intelligence the men could use to fight.

Only pain ran through the words Aku had to say. "The Brown Leaves are marching toward our village." He addressed his father, but all the men could hear. Oghi rose and came close.

"How many?"

"About two hundred," Aku said.

Every man of them figured out what Shonan now said. "Outnumbered three to one."

"Maloch is out in front. He might make it four to one." Aku felt a need to be blunt.

"Where?"

"They were setting up camp on Squirrel Creek." They both knew the place, had walked the trail. Shonan asked himself whether Aku in his inexperience could make a mistake. *No, as high as he flies, he can see the whole country.*

Aku said, "They'll stand right here tomorrow, in the middle of the afternoon, looking down at our village."

"Then they won't want to make a move until the next day at dawn," said Shonan, thinking out loud.

Every man was considering what the move would be. No reason for a siege. No reason for a negotiation of any kind. Surely an all-out blitz. Kill the men and adolescent boys, take the women and children as your own. Why else come in such force?

Eyes traded emotions.

Finally Shonan said, "At least they won't surprise us."

"In fact," said Oghi, "we may be the ones springing a surprise."

"My idea," said Shonan, "is for a surprise that comes sooner. In fact, I say, right now."

Oghi started to go on, but Shonan held up a hand. "Is this something you can show me tomorrow afternoon?"

Oghi thought and said, "Yes."

"Good. Zinna, you're in command until I get back." Zinna was the most experienced hand, and sneak attacks weren't his style.

"Fuyl and Kumu, come with me."

Fuyl reached for his spears and spear thrower.

Shonan said, "Bring them, but we won't waste the spears." He hadn't told them about Maloch, and wouldn't until the day of the fight. "This is a job for knives, throwing knives." Kumu was the man for that. Shonan was glad to give the young man a job. Every day, all day, he had carried Salya or marched alongside her. The clown in him was squelched, and his pain was hard to witness.

"I want to go," said Aku.

"Your job is to be the eyes of the men who defend our village tomorrow."

Shonan, Kumu, and Fuyl tucked away a little dried meat. "We'll be there tomorrow about the same time you will, midafternoon."

Aku felt drop-jawed. He said to his father quietly, "I admire the way you lead."

"Decisive," said the Red Chief without turning back to his son. He nodded to Fuyl and Kumu, and they were off.

❖

Shonan and his two young men ran through the twilight. Armies were slow. Whatever distance they could march in a day, determined runners could cover in less than half the time.

The last lingering light faded, and Shonan walked along by starlight. When they came to the bottom of a little valley, he stepped into the small stream, scooped water up and drank. He said to his two companions, "When will the Sun that Dwells in the Night rise?"

"Less than a quarter through the night," said Fuyl. The young man was exact and intense.

"And Kumu, which quarter will it be in?"

"Gibbous," said Kumu. The three-quarter moon.

Shonan smiled. Kumu was bucking up.

"Good fellows." They were observant, as Shonan taught them to be when he was Red Chief of their village. A fighting man needed to know what part of the night would invite him to move and what would not.

They sat in comfortable silence. Soon the sounds of the night came back. The insects, the birds, the four-footed animals accepted these men as part of the scene. An enemy venturing along this little creek would find nothing to make him suspicious.

When the Sun that Dwells in the Night rose out of the sea, Shonan simply started running again, followed by the two novices. They ran, ran, ran. They stopped for nothing but quick mouthfuls of water. Shonan could feel the excitement of the two friends. He used it as a pulse to drive him. He ticked off the creeks they crossed. He didn't want to walk into the middle of an enemy camp by accident, especially not these enemies. He'd flung mud in their faces once already.

Well before the middle of the night they came to Any

Chance River and made an awkward crossing in the moonlight. Rivers were always mysterious, and in the dark they
were spooky. His companions followed Shonan without a
word, and he felt proud of them. When they stood on the
far bank, dripping, he whispered, "This is the last hill. From
the top we see the drainage of Squirrel Creek."

They walked slowly to the crest and stopped before they
could make silhouettes. They crept forward, raised their heads,
and looked toward the bottomland along the stream. Shonan
couldn't see the camp, but he knew it stretched along the
creek, more than a thousand paces away. He nodded to the
left side, and they eased off the trail.

He pulled Fuyl and Kumu close. "The sentries will be near
the camp, not up here. We will move in absolute silence."
He put a flattened hand on the chest of each. "When we get
there, we'll watch. Then we'll put fear into their hearts."

He could feel it all now. The cool night air. The danger.
Blood, enemy blood.

He also smelled the anxiety of Fuyl and Kumu. They had
hunted, but they had never hunted men. They had reason to
be afraid, far more reason than in an ordinary battle. If you
died at night, your spirit might get lost, or bad spirits might
confuse it and keep it from the road to the Darkening Land.
By leading them into this skirmish, Shonan was making a
rare guarantee: we will kill with no risk to ourselves, none.

"Do exactly as I do," he said.

He padded along a grassy verge beside the well-worn trail.
After several hundred slow paces he turned into the woods.
Now he placed each step slowly and shifted his weight carefully. His companions imitated him well. Shonan didn't care
how long it took to get near the camp. Concentration and
care—nothing else mattered.

Finally he pointed. They saw the glow of embers of many campfires, and humped shadows near them. Two hundred men made a lot of humps.

They crept cautiously, slow step by slow step into the forest and toward the camp. After what felt like a long time Shonan led them onto a low boulder. Shonan pointed to his eyes—*Watch!* They fanned out slightly, lay down, and looked for movement, or any clue at all.

Shonan could watch in utter stillness forever. His two young warriors were fidgety—their version of stillness was restless. If they stood guard, an enemy with silent eyes would see them. Shonan ignored them and put all his energy into his eyes.

He would have liked to spot all four sentries. Not that he knew there were four. Galayi outfits customarily posted outlooks to the east, south, west, and north. He himself had often thought he should break this routine to confound enemies. The Brown Leaves might have any number of sentries, placed anywhere. On the other hand, their experience with the Amaso people, who never fought back, might make them careless.

Eventually, he saw two of them, across the trail from each other. The near one was alarmingly close. Had the man been good, he would have spotted them and raised the alarm. But he lounged against the trunk of a tree, unwary. Apparently, he was being annoyed by mosquitos. He made a lot of itching and scratching motions. Shonan felt the same insects but never slapped or scratched.

The man across the trail was more subtle. He stood between boulders so close they formed a slot. His body was concealed by the deep shadow. But he turned his head every once in a while, up the trail, down the trail. Maybe he felt an obligation to look in several directions. Maybe his neck just got stiff. Either way, he moved his head, not his eyes. Too bad—that choice might get his throat cut.

Shonan put his lips against the ear of the young man who loved his dead daughter and said, "Come with me." He motioned Fuyl to stay put.

As Shonan led Kumu the short distance, he was aware of the spirit of the young man behind him. Kumu was nothing but intensity and excitement. He had a true warrior spirit. He grinned, and his crooked tooth caught the moonlight.

Shonan brought them to about ten paces behind the sentry, undetected. The enemy leaned on the trunk with his left shoulder, exposing his entire back. Shonan indulged in a smile inside. It really shouldn't be this easy, but for Kumu's sake he was glad.

The sentry cursed and slapped a shoulder. What a fool, making noise while on guard.

This was an easy throw. He nodded the go-ahead.

Kumu cocked the knife well back. As he hurled it, the sentry said, "Damn it!" and jerked down.

The knife sliced across his back and bounced into the night air.

The sentry screamed and reeled.

Shonan sprang forward and thunked a knife into the idiot's back. As the fellow arched backward and fell, Shonan hefted his throwing knife out. Then they started running.

The man across the trail hollered the Brown Leaf war cry. So did the other sentries.

Sprinting by, Shonan waved to Fuyl to get going. They hit the trail and ran like hell.

Shonan knew. *We're tired, and they're fresh.*

❖

Sprinting was not long-distance running, but they had a new elixir of energy. Fear charged up and down their bodies, driven by their blood. It raised their legs, pumped their arms. Three men against a dozen, three against a score—that would fan the flames of any man's fear.

Shonan chortled as he ran.

Up the trail to the crest, down the hill to Any Chance River. Shonan sorted things out while he ran—hell, he thought best when he was running.

Before long they crouched in the darkness next to the Any Chance, no more than a man's height from the whoosh of the river. To avoid showing any tracks leading into these woods, they'd waded into the river, slipped downstream a score of steps, climbed out, and crept back to this good position.

Shonan liked their spot fine. The pine trees were open enough for Fuyl to hurl one of his darts. They were also open enough for the enemies to see the three Galayis, if they looked. With luck they would inspect the riverbank first, their backs to the Galayis in the shadows, and . . .

Shonan nudged each of the young men with an elbow. He could feel Fuyl's intensity like a bed of coals.

Then the Brown Leaves came in silence. The *whisker-whisker* of the river covered the noise of their running footsteps, but the moon showed their shapes. Speed as a weapon, silence as a defense against ambush. Shonan knew that the Brown Leaf leader would be thinking about ambush, but what could he do about it?

The five enemies took a brief look at the riverbank. Fuyl was waiting, as Shonan had instructed, until two of them were lined up behind each other. Four of the enemies knelt or sat down on the bank for the short drop into the water. The most observant turned toward the three shadowed Galayis.

Before Shonan could urge him, Fuyl let the dart fly. It

pierced the observant man's belly, stuck out beyond, and hit another enemy in the ear.

Shouts, moans, and wails.

Shonan, Fuyl, and Kumu used the racket to run half a dozen steps and slip into the water. In a moment they were swimming downstream as quietly as possible. Shonan didn't know whether the Brown Leaves had seen them. He didn't care. They had struck a blow. The Brown Leaves might think the Galayis had followed the trail back toward their village and search in that direction. They might figure out the trick of going downriver and come that way. Regardless, they would come slowly and carefully—too slowly.

Shonan arched his back as he swam, stretching. Everything was right. His young companions were good men. They would get to the ocean at about dawn, sleep briefly, and run back to the village. Shonan looked forward to the run—he always felt good *doing* something. Time enough to rest at the village. And the story of their two attacks on the enemies would boost the courage of the fighting men there.

28

Eagle Aku took a predawn cruise. He saw the Brown Leaf army getting itself ready to march. He looked for Maloch, who could turn himself into the Uktena. For some reason even eagle eyes couldn't pick out the dragon this time. He couldn't quite think of Maloch as human, doing as Aku's marching companions were doing, taking a morning piss, lashing gear onto their dogs, stretching stiff muscles. The Uktena wasn't human.

Tonight the Brown Leaves will be at our last camp, tomorrow in our village.

He winged back along the trail to his own camp but didn't see his father, Fuyl, or Kumu. Probably they were catching some sleep, well hidden.

His own outfit was just now ready to move out on their final leg to the village. For them this would be the last, long day of carrying Salya.

Aku turned toward the sea and flapped into the wind toward home. Yes, Amaso felt like home, because Iona was there.

He wanted to see her alone, and as he came to the village, he got an idea. He lit on top of an oak snag and watched her hut. One of her sisters came out and walked toward the river carrying gourds. So the whole family was inside. This was his chance.

He flapped to the village circle and landed atop the family hut. He put his beak to the smoke hole and said in his own voice, "Iona."

"Aku?"

He pictured her looking around wildly.

"Iona," he said in his crude Amaso speech, "meet me below the pine tree."

It was the phrase they'd used dozens of times for the same place.

"Aku?" she cried out. "Are you up there?"

Before she could see his eagle face, he flew to the trees lining the river. He made the transformation to the Aku shape she knew. Soon he crept up the sand dune, jumped, grabbed her, and rolled over and over. She kept herself from shrieking. They spent a long time kissing.

❖

As the sun reached its height, Shonan, Fuyl, and Kumu trotted into Amaso. The Galayi members of the village came running to the common to greet them. Shonan had been gone so long that many thought the Red Chief must be dead, and his strange son with him. Amaso members of the village hung back, looking for the seer, Oghi, and not seeing him.

Quickly, the stories spread. A Brown Leaf army was on the march toward Amaso. Shonan and the two young men had struck at the Brown Leaves last night and killed two or three. Some Amaso people thought that would only make the beast more angry, and they wanted to flee. By now everyone had learned to communicate, and the Galayi members told them that Shonan would do everything that could be done. But even they looked worried.

Shonan looked around for his bird-man son and didn't see him. *Damn, just when I could use his eagle eyes.* The Red Chief looked around the crowd. "You, Cyz, and you, Amar, pick two Amaso men you know. Go back along the trail until you meet our party coming in. If they have seen the enemy, two of you run back and tell me, the other two watch them and come back just ahead of them. If not, all four of you follow the trail until you see the Brown Leaves. They'll probably camp at the Junction tonight. Run back and let me know for sure."

The scouts went. Shonan, Fuyl, and Kumu lay down for naps.

Later a hand rocked the Red Chief's shoulder. Shonan opened his eyes abruptly and looked into Oghi's face.

Shonan sat up. "Is our party in already?" He meant the Galayi bearing Salya's body.

"I ran ahead," said Oghi. Shonan could see he was sweaty.

"What's up?"

"I said I'd show you a surprise."

"Okay. Is Aku here?"

"I know where he and Iona are."

❖

The sea turtle man waded ahead of Iona, Aku, and Shonan across the river. On the far side they were all soaked to the waist.

"Are we going to the cave?" said Iona.

"Yes."

"I like the cave," said Iona, "but it will be underwater now."

Oghi started up the hillside. "When the tide's out," Oghi

told the others, "there's a beach to walk. For now we use the cliff."

The sea splashed against the foot of the palisade. Aku couldn't tell how deep the water was. They walked several hundred paces along the top. Then Oghi led them on a path that angled down and around the corner.

"Pretty special, huh?" said Iona, grinning.

The cave entrance was shaped like an axe, wide at the bottom and pointed at the top. The base was about ten big steps wide, and sloshing with seawater.

"It's our hideaway," said Iona.

"Not exactly," Oghi said, "but there's a surprise."

"How deep is the water?" said Shonan.

"At low tide the bottom is sand."

"You can walk it," said Iona.

"High tide?"

"Usually a little over a man's knees." He met Shonan's skeptical gaze. "I know the tides. So did my father and grandfather."

"How far back does it go?"

"More than a hundred steps."

"That's not much room for a couple of hundred people, and the mouth is too wide to defend." Shonan looked around. "Worst of all, it's a trap. No water, no food, no way out except into the arms of your enemies."

"That's the surprise. Iona, take the Red Chief you-know-where but don't show him you-know-what."

"Let's go," the girl said, tapping her feet. She had a touch of the hoyden.

"Be serious," said Shonan.

"Oh, we are serious," said Oghi, "and we're also having fun. Go."

Iona led the way, scrambling up the rocks. Shonan cast a

suspicious eye back and disappeared over the rim of the cliff.

Oghi said, "Aku, become Owl."

Aku transformed himself, mouth to beak, arms to wings, flesh to feathers.

Oghi gave a little whoop and jumped feet first into the water. An unruly wave sluiced up onto his privates, and both of them laughed.

"Come on, Aku."

Aku fluttered down and watched Oghi transform himself, covered by his carapace. When he stuck his turtle head out, his eyes were merry. "Let's see this place where the sea spumes into the earth," he said. "I'll swim, you fly."

Aku winged his way slowly, from outcropping to outcropping. The angled walls were rough and bumpy, with lots of places to light. Oghi swam with only the top of his back touching the surface, red-brown against the green sea.

The cave was lit in a way that seemed mystical. Near the seaward entrance, light glowed off the emerald water. In the middle was a web of shadows and reflections. Toward the back was something strange. Aku didn't make it out until they were most of the way there. The rear of the cave was lit somehow. Oghi pulled himself with his front flippers onto a big rock there, and Aku perched beside him.

A crooked shaft gave an eerie light. Aku peered up through the curving, jagged hole but couldn't see the sky that must be the source of the light.

"Here's what you really need to notice," said Oghi. He crawled across and flipper-tapped a vertical corner of rock. Aku fluttered, landed on Oghi's carapace, and took a look. Oghi stuck his flipper straight through the corner.

Aku craned his head. It wasn't a corner. Two walls of

rock overlapped. When you looked at them from the side, the slit was easy to spot.

"Kind of looks like the place where you came out, being born, doesn't it?" said Oghi. "That's our story about it. That the Amaso people emerged from the earth through this hole to the ocean, and that's why we've always lived at the shore. Amaso means 'sea.' "

Aku took a short flap through the opening, which was a weird sensation, considering Oghi's story. He landed on an outthrust rock and looked around with his owl eyesight, excellent in the darkness.

Immediately beyond the slit, the ground level rose and was dry. After a few steps it made a hard left turn.

"We need to show the Red Chief this part," said Oghi. "Let's change back to human."

They both did.

Oghi scrambled easily up some rocks and stuck his head into the open air. He picked up a pebble, tossed it, and a half dozen steps away hit Shonan in the neck.

"Hey!"

"Hello to you, too."

"Hah," said Iona, "you sat right by the entrance and didn't even spot it."

Shonan surveyed the lay of the land from the sea to the narrow hole in the rock. "I don't know what good this is going to do."

"Come see."

When all four had clambered down, Oghi climbed through the slit above the sloshing sea and his voice sounded from the other side of a solid wall. "Come on! Follow!"

They did, and stood up into utter darkness. Aku felt a bolt of panic.

They heard some scraping noises and knew what Oghi was doing. In a moment he lit a torch.

Here was a completely different kind of cave. This one had the limestone walls and muddy bottom Shonan and Aku knew from their home mountains. They didn't recognize the rock the sea cave was made of.

"It's a complicated cave," Oghi said. "We don't know how vast it might be. We have food and fresh water stored further back, enough for about one quarter moon."

"So you hide until your enemies go away." The edge in his voice was contempt.

"Unfortunately," said Oghi, "we stay inside until they take everything we own and leave."

"Yeah." Shonan pondered. "Why don't they come in here after you?"

"They don't see the little entrance we just used. That's why my great-grandfather chose this spot. Now, I have one more little surprise." With the torch blazing, he led the way down the left-hand passage for about twenty paces. "This leads a long way and opens into much larger rooms. If you go far enough, you come to an underground river. Except for the darkness, a whole village could live here."

"Maybe your ancestors did," said Aku.

Oghi said, "We came onto Earth from this cave. Anyway, our enemies have never come in here. They look into the sea cave. If the tide is out, they walk up here and give up. If they didn't, we'd kill them one by one as they squeezed through the slit."

Iona said, "See, my father has it all worked out."

"My great-grandfather, actually," said Oghi.

"You're a lot better prepared than I thought," said Shonan. Still, there was reserve in his voice.

Aku thought, *He can't stand the idea of hiding from his enemies.*

"And we know ways out, far up above. We can always escape."

Shonan gave him a long look. "I guess it works." He looked back into the passage but showed no inclination to explore it. "Let's go."

Oghi led the way out of the slit and up the crooked hole.

When Shonan stood in the open air, he looked all around, took in the sea, the tidal plains, and the hills. Finally he said, "When's the next low tide?"

"It's going out now. It will be low tomorrow afternoon."

"In the morning, get the women and children to walk the beach and come through the sea cave into the other cave. The sooner the better."

"All right." Oghi spoke uncertainly.

"The men, all the men of both peoples of Amaso, will stay aboveground and fight."

Iona flinched. Aku spoke like a man slapped in the face. "You intend to go to war against Maloch the Uktena and two hundred men?"

"You said you went to the Land Beyond the Sky Arch to learn courage." Shonan gave him what might be called a smile. "Now's the time to use it."

"We may need more than you think," said Oghi, studying the sky. They followed his gaze to sea. "That looks big."

"I don't understand," said Shonan.

Oghi's voice wavered. "Looks like a hurricane."

29

R ed and yellow, kill a fellow. Red and black, poison lack."

Maloch chanted this little ditty over and over. He adored it. He lolled it on his snake tongue before he hissed it out. "Red and yellow, kill a fellow. Red and black, poison lack." A common rhyme for the least common of beasts, himself. He hiss-laughed.

Maloch was supremely satisfied. He had transformed himself into one of his favorite creatures, the coral snake banded red, yellow, and black, definitely the "kill the fellow" variety, where the red and yellow bands touched. Unlike the ordinary earthly examples, which he scorned, Maloch the Uktena was huge in his coral snake form. Like theirs, his venom worked by stopping the breathing of his prey. While theirs took hours to start working, his was instantaneous. He loved watching his victim's eyes grow huge as the breath wouldn't come, and wouldn't and wouldn't come—*A sky full of air, and none at all for me?* He liked to slither back and forth across the victim's body as the lips turned blue, the body writhed, and finally went into convulsions. At this sovereign moment Maloch crawled to the face and went nose to nose with his victim, glaring directly into the poor creature's eyes, so that the dying man could peer deeply into the black iris, into the abyss of evil as his own vision clouded into death.

Now Maloch arrived at the top of the last hill and raised his head into a stiff breeze. Good—exhilarating. He liked it. High winds felt right. He would descend upon the village like a scourge and cleanse it. Let the winds blow away the debris.

He looked across the plains at the Amaso village. He was surveying a great banquet, and he could already taste his greatest triumph. He raised his head high. He was privileged as leader to ride coiled around a pole held overhead by one of the war leaders of the Brown Leaf army, his head swaying above its top like an emblem or a flag. But Maloch was no symbolic threat. He would crawl down from the pole and enter the fray. If women and children were foolish enough to face him, he would bite every one of them he could reach and would terrify the rest. When he faced warriors, he would return to his dragon magnificence, protected by scales of slate, and work havoc. He chuckled—*hisss!*—at his mental pictures of the warriors turning tail and running. He did not need this army to defeat these poor villagers. He could do it by himself.

Eventually, of course, he would kill Aku, the one with the seeing gift, the greatest threat in the village, though he was too childish to know it. Then he would kill Shonan, the man who had dared to attack the great Maloch. He would add their life-fires to his own. Since they were powerful men, he would make a great gain in strength. Then, like an afterthought, he would consume the body of their precious sister and daughter, destroying all trace of her anywhere in the universe. Very satisfying, *yesss*, very satisfying.

He turned his snake head slowly from southern horizon to northern horizon and back, lingering on where he knew the village was. Whether in his snake form or as a dragon, he did not have the gift of superb eyesight, and from this distance Amaso was nothing but a smudge. But he had excellent intelligence from his scouts. The village was another quarter day's march away, and he had overwhelmingly superior forces.

Out to sea he noticed some dirty clouds of an odd olive color. They didn't matter. Today and perhaps tomorrow Maloch would administer a gory triumph. The flowing blood would belong to the Amaso soldiers, not his.

"Maloch?"

The speaker, Mor, was the tall man with the crooked nose who held Maloch's staff high. This man was the son of the grand old chief whose throat Shonan had cut. Now Mor was the chief in name only. Maloch had taken all leadership for himself. He was finished with living alone in the high mountains. He liked ruling people. He liked making them bow, watching them cringe. The man who wanted his attention was no worse than most human beings, but then it was a species barely to be noticed.

"Yessss?"

Mor said, "Those clouds out there might be a storm."

"Yessss?"

"The wind is stiff, sir. This could be a hurricane. They can be rough."

"How rough?"

"I haven't seen one myself, sir, but there are stories."

Stories, nothing could be sillier than the stories of human beings. Maloch himself had spread stories among them. The creatures were easily frightened.

"What are wind and rain? We will make them help us." Maloch had heard of big storms but had never seen one that impressed him. Until a few winters ago he had been a mountain dweller. Human beings were afraid of the silliest things.

"Let us march," said Maloch.

"Yes, sir," said Mor. He had seen how quickly Maloch killed men who disagreed with him.

"We will march straight into the village," Maloch said. "No running. We are not assailants, we are conquerors."

❖

The wind was rising. Strangely, it came not from the east, where the the storm prowled closer and closer, but from the north.

Shonan had to shout to explain the battle plan to the men squatting around him. The Galayis just nodded their acceptance. The Amaso men murmured among themselves, unable to believe that they were going to fight back. It would have been rude to speak up, but the winds whipped their mutterings out to sea anyway.

Chalu, their venerable chief, rose and stood next to Shonan. He cupped his hands and called into the gale, "Pay attention. Get ready. This man is our war chief now. It's a good plan." He brandished a fist. "It's about time we fought."

A few men chorused under their breath to their neighbors, "About time."

Many more men whispered to each other, "Why?" Since the time of Oghi's great-grandfather, when enemies threatened, all the Amaso people, men included, had simply taken refuge in the limestone cave, up behind the sea cave, and waited until their foes left. True, they had losses. No family ever got all its belongings into the cave, and the marauders walked away with whatever they could grab. Stomping around, unable to find their prey, they got frustrated and even took children's toys and threw them into the river. And they destroyed the huts. But since the dwellings were only made of brush, who cared? So these men were thinking, *Why are we going to fight now?*

Chalu raised his fist again. "We have good news. Our spies say that Maloch is not with their army."

Some of the men cheered lustily, some sardonically. Shonan smiled to himself at this foolishness.

"What next?" came a voice from the rear.

Shonan gave them all a hard look and summed things up in a commanding tone. "My job is to think and then lead. Yours is to join in and fight. So let's get ready."

Getting up, the men looked at their women and children trekking toward the entrance to the sea cave, carrying all the belongings they could. Then most of the men retired to their huts to make medicine to get psychic strength for this afternoon's fight. They said prayers and sang songs. They tied feathers into their hair. They fixed headresses onto their heads or shoulders, carcasses of small animals like ravens and foxes, the entire heads of bears and buffalo, emblems of their animal guides. The preparations were meticulous and time-consuming. When they were ready, they would finish helping everyone and carrying everything into the cave.

Shonan said to Aku, "Take care of Salya." Fuyl and Kumu volunteered to help him, and Iona insisted on carrying one corner of the hide.

Aku looked at the dead body—*body* was the awful reality. Somehow Salya had become the center point that his life circled around. *What I am doing is right, but will it ever end?*

The four of them hoisted the hide bearing his sister. Aku looked at Iona holding a front corner. *I have a woman and child. I want a life.* Yet he could not picture a life without his twin, Salya.

They trundled out of the village and across the flats, then

staggered through the knee-deep braids of the stream. With Oghi's help the move had been planned while the tide was ebbing, halfway out. As they approached the corner of the cliffs on the far side, Aku looked up and saw the sea turtle man standing on the rim, leaning forward into the wind and wrapped in a hide, looking out to sea. Aku followed Oghi's gaze and saw dark, sick-looking clouds pushing across gray ocean, ever closer.

The four got better grips on the hide bearing Salya and made their way along the beach below the cliffs. At this tide the strip of sand beach was narrow, and occasional run-ups of seawater sloshed at their ankles.

Cave mouth. Into the mystic half-light. A hundred strides—it took the hide-bearers two hundred footsteps—along the sand to the emergence slit. They walked awkwardly up the steep, narrow uphill passage and then along a flat that seemed to go forever. "I like this place," said Aku. That was a relief, because his fingers were at their bitter end.

"You'll like this even better," Iona. "Most of the people will camp here," she said, indicating a great hall just ahead. She led them across the room, past a spot where Aku heard water trickling, and into a kind of alcove with a low ceiling. A small forest of slender stone pillars, like the trunks of birch trees, separated this space from the large space, as though holding the floor and ceiling apart. "Beautiful," said Aku. Here Salya could rest deep in the cave, safe, and in a way honored.

After they set his twin down, Aku lifted her hand and kissed it. He'd gotten used to the awful coolness of her flesh.

Then the four of them set in to helping the refugees as much as they could. They carried frightened children through the river. Though most could have waded at this low tide, the children were terrified by the howling winds. Babies bawled, children wept, even adolescents quailed. Aku could barely hear their plaints above the gale, even when they were right in his ear.

Aku didn't try to understand anything, he just labored, carrying kids, calling comforting words over the gale, putting them in the arms of their relatives on the far side. This was his assignment from his father, and he was glad of it. A few men joined him and Iona, but most were still in their huts, making medicine. Aku wondered how many of the Amaso men had ever been in a fight. Not that he had much experience himself.

Finally, after too long a time, all the women and children had crossed the river. For some reason scores of them huddled on the far bank, beneath the cliffs, partly out of the wind. Aku herded them on toward the sea cave. People stumbled up the narrow beach, struggling to balance against the wind. Occasionally a gust knocked some of them down, or they splashed into the lapping sea. Most of them wandered slowly, in mute passivity. Children whimpered and wept, mothers carried them or shooed them along. Men and young women made ferries of belongings across the river. *Walk, walk,* thought Aku, *hurry, hurry.* "Not far!" he yelled over the wind. Five hundred paces along the narrow beach to the cave, a hundred steps penetrating the innards of the earth, and through the emergence slit to safety.

Though the cliffs protected the beach in part, Aku thought the winds would drive him mad. He and Iona made countless trips herding people, then carrying possessions. Finally Aku thought Iona had had enough. When they turned into the cave and out of the wind, he said to her, "It's time. Take a load through the slit and don't come back."

"I can still help."

"You are carrying our child!" He pointed toward the

emergence opening. "If I have to go back there and hold you down, I will."

Iona went.

As Aku pushed back out into the wind, the rains hit— and *hit* was what they did. They pelted all the men packing the belongings to shelter. Aku bit his lip and shouldered goods across the braids of the stream, over and over and over. Stagger across the river, stagger along the sand, keep going somehow to the entrance of the sea cave and then the slit, and hand the goods into arms waiting in the limestone cave. Aku had never worked harder in his life.

He made his mind up. The people would have clothes, hides, dried food, cooking utensils, cloth, knives, awls, and other possessions to resume their lives when the troubles passed. If they passed.

All the adult women remembered well what it was like, having your town pillaged by an attacking army. The older ones remembered having Amaso torn to pieces by the rage of a hurricane. With both threatening, they were all a-babble. Aku heard tatters of their conversation when he handed goods through, but he paid no attention, just turned around and packed over another load. Every time he got back to the village and ducked into a hut to get belongings, he wondered whether he would find Maloch waiting in the shadows with an evil grin. He wondered if Maloch would transform himself into the shape of a hut. Aku hesitated before going in.

When he came out of the sea cave and across the beach to the river one more time, he saw his father signaling for him to come to the ledge that cut the cliffs halfway up. A quick scramble and Aku stood between his father and Oghi near a dozen fighting men. Another dozen squatted down on top, their backs to the wind.

"The enemy is almost to the village," his father said.

"Father," said Aku, "I want to fight."

"You will," Shonan said with a lopsided smile. He pointed straight up. "Can you fly in these winds?"

Aku felt a spritz of happiness. His father was acknowledging his value as an eagle. "Not a chance," Aku said.

"I'm going to the village to fight now," said Shonan. His voice gleamed with pleasure. Before Aku could protest, he said, "Your turn will come, and it will be the big fight. Stay with Fuyl and Kumu." Aku hadn't seen them on the ledge until now. "They know what to do. Anything you can add, do it."

Aku was relieved that his father didn't say his son was no good with weapons.

"Everybody," called Shonan. Only the dozen men nearby could hear him. "We've caught some luck. You know about Maloch's diamond eye that blinds attackers. In this rain it may not work, or it won't be so bright."

"Hooray!" said Kumu.

"Damn well hooray!" said Fuyl.

"*Still!* We take precautions. See this cloth." He held up a big strip of mulberry fabric dyed red, about enough to make a dress. He tore it in half. "Rip off a piece big enough to tie around your head. If the Uktena shows up, use it as a blindfold. You'll be able to see him through the weave, but the diamond eye won't blind you." He said to himself, *Maybe*. "Do it!"

Shonan handed the cloth to Fuyl, who tore some off and passed it on.

Father stepped up to son, embraced him hard, and turned to the cliffs. To Aku's amazement, he climbed up, even buffeted by the gale. In a moment Aku could hear him giving the same speech to the men hunkered down on top. Shonan stood tall, leaning into the wind, defying it. Aku had never seen his father look so alive.

30

The Brown Leaf army marched down the trail to the edge of Amaso openly, with no attempt at subterfuge. Shonan peered out through the crack at the top of the hide door in the nearest hut. He wanted to size the army up and see how it was standing—in a mob? In a long line? But he couldn't see much except for a long pole carried by a tall man with a crooked nose. He wondered why anyone would carry something so pointless into battle.

The Brown Leaves didn't even pause, but strode between buildings and into the common. Passing between huts, they were forced to walk in a line, which was what Shonan wanted. He shook his head. He couldn't even see the warriors in the middle of the common. Never had he experienced rain so heavy. According to Oghi, the last time they didn't search the village—they just assumed the people had fled. Shonan was counting on that.

He waited until the last warrior had passed, eased out of the hut, and peered through the slashing rain. Since he could hardly see, he'd have to hope the other men had done as instructed. Leaning into the wind for balance, not a bit concerned about making noise, he walked to the back of the last soldier, set his feet, swung his war club, and bashed the man's head in.

One of the Brown Leaves saw Shonan standing over the fallen enemy. The man charged. Shonan got off the best spear throw he could manage. It hit the enemy's hip, ripped a jagged hole, and bounced onto the grass. Shonan sprinted forward. The man was trying to get his balance with one leg. Shonan put all his hips and shoulders into a swing of his club that caught the fellow in the temple. He collapsed.

Shonan sized up the situation—three Brown Leaves were rushing him. He threw a regretful look at his spear and ran. He grinned. He glimpsed others of his hand-picked men making their attacks. Though he couldn't hear over the wind, he could imagine dozens of outcries. He hoped all of them came from Brown Leaf throats, or nearly all. He'd told his men to fight until faced with two enemies, and then to hightail it. They would make their way to the river, letting the enemy see that they were heading for the beach. At the last moment they were to climb up the cliffs instead. For now, if his forty men put forty enemies out of the battle, that would swing the odds a little. And on the cliffs they would have the high ground.

A gust slapped him hard, and he splatted into the mud. Before he got near the river, he was knocked down twice more. Walking in this wind and rain—he'd never done anything harder.

❖

On the ledge, Aku asked Oghi, "Do you think we have a chance?"

Oghi answered, "The hurricane will win."

❖

The Brown Leaves ran into the river. The Amaso men, lying flat on top of the cliffs, chuckled as they watched the warriors wobble as they used their spears for poles to keep them upright, or just pratfalled into the water.

Then the wind decided to show more of its muscle. It unleashed a fury Aku would have thought impossible. The Amasos crawled behind rocks where they could. They held onto their totems, eagle feathers or ermine tails in their hair, whatever they wore for medicine. They lay flat on spears, spear throwers, darts, and especially blow guns, which were made of cane. They prayed that they wouldn't be blown away like mosquitos.

The Brown Leaves were lower and the trees along the river provided some shelter. Still, they went down hard and got up slowly.

On the cliffs only Oghi and Shonan, lying behind the same boulder, occasionally shuttered their eyes with fingers, stuck their heads out, and looked at the enemy. They were watching for Maloch. Both of them had the same thought. *He's around somewhere, and close.*

No one knew how long the gale blasted them. It abraded like a corncob rubbing skin, it hit like a hand slapping hard. As in all such times, it lasted forever. Minds drifted through timelessness. Pain racked each body for an eternity. After two or three eternities, it slacked off, and time clicked back in.

Men looked around, disbelieving. The wind hadn't just eased. Bizarrely, it had quit altogether. Though the sun was behind the hills in the west, the temperature along the river, the beach, and the cliffs tranformed from cold to warm. Amaso men who had been clenching their teeth against the chill blast felt languid, lazy in the balmy stillness. They smiled indolently as they watched the Brown Leaves gather themselves, file lightly and easily across the river, and trot along the beach. The warriors talked, laughed, and held their arms up into the glow of the sun.

Shonan was ready. He ran among his men, now more than three score of them. He touched them, he whispered to them. The warriors crept to the edge of the cliffs but stayed low, out of sight. Those with blow guns, more than half of them, rested their weapons on the lip of the cliffs, pointing downward.

Shonan went to Aku and talked briefly with him. As asked, Aku began making the change into eagle form. "The light is running out. Use what there is. Think of your wife," Shonan said, "think of your child. Be a warrior for them."

With the tide all the way out now, the beach made more than enough room for two hundred Brown Leaves. Shonan sneaked a look down and thought that there weren't two hundred, not anymore. They still advanced behind that high pole. How odd. Shonan saw now that it had a snake carved into its top. He hadn't heard of the Brown Leaves having a snake as a totem.

Before the Brown Leaves in front got near the mouth of the cave, Shonan whirled his hand above his head, the signal to fight. The first assault was to be silent.

The Amaso blow-gunners dipped the points of their darts in their small horns of poison. Their time had come— Shonan had shown them the way. They spat gusts of air through their canes and the feathered darts flew. They could only shoot the closest walkers, those within ten strides or so. Most of the darts hit flesh. The tips made only a small wound, like being hit with a thrown awl, but the attackers roared with victory. The victims wailed, knowing the poison was usually fatal. Their lives would be an hour of feeling okay, a miserable night, and death before dawn.

Kumu and the Amasos flung throwing knives. Some hit

and some did not. A few threw spears and did damage. The Brown Leaves backed away from the cliffs, toward the sea.

Fuyl hurled three darts with his spear thrower—he killed two men and wounded another in the leg. He let out the Galayi war cry—"Woh-WHO-O-O-ey! Woh-WHO-O-O-ey! AI-AI-AI-AI!"

The Brown Leaves threw their spears, but their targets popped up from behind rocks and ducked back down, making elusive targets. Then the Amasos grabbed the Brown Leaf spears and hurled them back. Shonan checked the feel of one and kept it.

Quickly, the man with the crooked nose and the long pole started shouting, and the Brown Leaves retreated further toward the edge of the water, out of range of any weapon. The wounded sat down with stoic faces and began singing their death songs.

Aku could still see, but the light was fading. He hesitated. "Iona," he whispered to himself, "Iona and the baby." He launched into the warm, still air, floated toward the fleeing Brown Leaves. He flew landward from the cliffs, circled out to sea, and turned back unnoticed—just another eagle. He took a deep breath and dropped onto the shoulders of one of the milling warriors. He raked the fellow's neck with talons and lifted back into the air. His next victim flailed, and when he turned his head toward Aku, the eagle man sank his beak into his foe's eyes. Men began to yell and point. Two or three threw spears. Aku screamed his eagle war cry, flapped up, folded his wings, and dropped onto an enemy. When he saw blood running from the big vessels in the neck, he flew up and attacked another one. He surprised himself—he felt exhilarated.

A hand grabbed his right leg. He winged up but couldn't tear loose. A knife raked fire across the bottom of his belly.

He turned and became the aggressor. He ripped the Brown Leaf's face with his left talons. He pecked savagely at the head, the nose, the eyes, whatever he could reach.

In a moment the Brown Leaf let go and ran.

Aku flew after him. He landed on the man's left shoulder and with his right talons ripped a bloody track across his neck.

Aku flew up and screamed. The Brown Leaves screamed back in panic. Some waved their spears, spear throwers, and canes in the air pointlessly. Others crouched below their comrades, cowering.

From the cliffs the Amaso men roared and hoo-hawed. Attacked by an eagle! Whipped by an eagle!

In the near darkness Aku swooped low, screaming. He felt a sharp jab in his left wing. A spear arced beyond him and back to the sand. A couple of his primary feathers fluttered through the still air.

He turned his head and saw a man with a crooked nose shaking his staff and yelling.

Aku whirled and launched himself straight at the man. He and half a dozen comrades scattered like frightened children.

Aku soared up, looked down at the chaos, and laughed in a human voice, a vibrant, raucous laugh.

❖

In the last glimmer of twilight the pole was more shadow than substance. Fifty strides out onto the wide beach the top of the stick seemed to wriggle. The men atop the cliffs thought it must be an illusion, a trick of the light.

The man with the crooked nose knew exactly what it

was because he felt it. The serpent circled down the pole to his hands, from his arms down his chest, down his legs, and onto the sand. The feeling was eerie, it was savage, and it hinted of triumph. Then the coral snake crawled toward the cliffs without a word or a hiss.

The man with the crooked nose walked back as evenly as he walked forward, and with a sense of ceremony.

❖

"They're coming back," said Shonan.

Aku perched on his father's shoulder and ignored the pain in his wing. Sitting there atop his father, alongside Oghi, comrades at war—it was exhilarating.

Yes, by the light of the westering sun the Brown Leaves were traipsing toward the cliffs. The night would be a safeguard, would force a truce until morning.

"They won't camp on the beach," said Shonan. "The tide will come in."

"They don't know the tides here," said Oghi.

Shonan nodded, understanding. "But the water won't get more than knee-deep, right?"

"Right."

"When?"

"After midnight."

Shonan considered. "It might be worth something."

That last word was torn away by a gale. As suddenly as it quieted, the winds hit again with mad fury, and impossibly, they came from the south instead of the north. Men who had been standing dived to the earth. Shonan and Oghi hit the ground and crawled behind rocks. Aku got knocked into the air. He opened his wings, felt like they were going to get torn off, folded them, hit the grass rolling, and did the fastest change into human form he'd ever made.

Even under these circumstances Shonan had a job for Oghi. He shouted into Oghi's ear, "Make yourself a turtle, that way you won't get blown over, and go see whether the enemy finds the cave."

Oghi transformed himself and turtled along the top of the cliffs. At times he wondered whether the terrible winds would get underneath his shell and flip him upside down, but they didn't. He felt good about being able to move around in the storm when no one else could.

On the beach below, the Brown Leaves surrendered to their tormentor. They fell to their knees and crawled toward the base of the cliffs, seeking shelter. It was a pitiful sight, over a hundred men on their hands and knees, inching forward like caterpillars. And the cliffs provided no respite. The wind swept straight along it, like lava rock scraping their skins.

At the far south end of the beach one man blundered into the opening of the sea cave. Since he was loyal to his comrades, he crept on hands and knees to the fellow nearest him, pulled him by the arm, and showed him the cave opening. Before long all the Brown Leaves were wombed within its protection.

It felt amazing. The air of the earth womb was perfectly still. Yet the wind, raging across its mouth, made a roaring whistle. It seemed comical, how the wind howled its threats but could not touch them. Some men laughed. Some yelled back at the wind. They gathered around Mor, their leader, and clapped each other on the back.

Just outside the entrance, seeming to be only a stone, Oghi the sea turtle watched them go back toward the emergence slit, and was afraid.

31

Maloch cared nothing for the wind. He slithered up the cliffs as easily and naturally as water flows around rocks and melds back into the river. Such an advantage, most of the time, not to be a human being. What an advantage, when the time came, to be a dragon. But now was the time to be serpentine.

He oozed onto the top of the cliffs, raised his red and yellow head, and peered around. He slinked between the wretches of the so-called Amaso army—who could call men who'd never stood up for themselves an army? They were huddled behind boulders, clutching their clothing tight against the wind and shivering like cowards.

They meant nothing to Maloch. The son of the war chief, Aku—that was the man he sought. Being prescient, Maloch knew that this man above all others was dangerous to him, the young man who could shape-shift into an owl and an eagle—what damage he'd done on the beach, destroying bodies and morale.

In the darkness of the storm and night Maloch could see almost nothing. But he could sense the warmth of human bodies, and he would smell Aku when he found him. When he did, Maloch would sink the fatal bite home. The Uktena would enjoy watching the young man, the would-be hero,

294 ❖ Caleb Fox

gasp for breath, writhe and thrash and kick his feet in protest of the shortage, and die of parched lungs. Maloch savored his triumphs.

When Aku was dead, and only then, would Maloch permit himself to spread his poison to other Amaso men, including young Aku's upstart father, Shonan. First things first.

At that moment Maloch would have been annoyed— more than annoyed—if he had been curled up on the lee side of a nearby boulder, the tallest on the cliffs. There a man who looked like a turtle was shouting to Aku and Shonan in a human voice, "They *are* going into the cave."

The war chief thought about it. The emergence slit at the back of the cave was narrow and easy to defend. But only women and children were in there. No one would fight out here for hours, not until the sun came up, or even longer, until the winds eased off. Meanwhile, the women and children could be taken hostage. They seemed safe, but . . .

Shonan hated to run for safety. He argued with himself. All his warriors would have a better night in the limestone cave. Everyone would be more ready for the real fight that would come in the morning. Like the Brown Leaves, they would have the advantage of a night's sleep.

It struck him then. He checked with Oghi, each yelling directly into the other's ear. "When the tide comes in, the Brown Leaves will come out?"

"For sure. They don't know how high the tide might get."

"They'll have to go back out into the wind."

"Yes."

"No place to camp there."

Oghi laughed. "Not in knee-deep water."

Shonan looked toward the river. Not only green leaves were being stripped off the trees, but entire limbs. "They might camp in the trees." The winds would make it a miserable night. They might even rip trees out of the ground and drop them on the enemy. The enemy was going to have a bad night.

He decided and hammered each word into the gale. "Tell everyone, and I mean everyone, to go up and use the hidden entrance to the back of the sea cave and slip down and into the limestone cave. Inside the cave they must be *totally* quiet. You and Aku lead the way."

"Don't worry," said Oghi, "the sea cave is like a giant version of one of Aku's whistles. The Brown Leaves can't hear a thing in there, or see a thing."

Shonan nodded. "Fine. But absolute silence, total stealth."

As the men passed the word, they crawled one by one up the hill. They didn't give a damn how uncomfortable it was. The thought of escaping this horrific wind, the thought of shelter, the thought of food and hot tea, the thought of their families . . .

At that moment the wind lashed them with a hard rain, driving them underground.

Shonan almost felt sorry for the Brown Leaves.

He brought up the rear, making sure no one was left behind. When he ducked into the half-hidden entrance, he called to the man right ahead of him. It happened to be Kumu.

"Kumu, take the first watch."

The young man who wanted to marry Shonan's daughter looked at his leader. He shaped his ravaged features into the pretense of a smile and said, "You trust me to take watch." He didn't add, *After I missed the knife throw?*

"Fuyl will be next. I'll tell him to kick you out into the storm if you fall asleep."

"I will do my duty, Red Chief."

Shonan wondered. On this night of madness he'd have been uncertain of any of his men. Even he could barely stand up.

He lowered himself, slipped through the butt end of the sea cave like a ghost, whispered his name at the emergence slit, and stepped into a haven.

Now a stone lamp helped him see. Chalu and three other men were guarding the slit, big clubs in their hands. Oghi came walking down the passage. He said, "Let's get some more hands and block this slit."

Shonan looked at him blankly.

Oghi said, "Don't question me this time. Use that slab."

Shonan said, "We can get in and out above."

"Yes."

"Easily?"

"Easily enough."

Chalu said, "Do it."

The old chief started the lift. Grumbling, everyone helped. Finally, they levered the huge stone into position, Shonan pushing harder than anyone.

Chalu stood back and surveyed the work. "Get big rocks and pile them against the slab. Make them shoulder high."

The soldiers gaped at him.

Shonan lashed words at them.

The men nodded and set to.

Shonan walked up the passage, which was lit by occasional stone lamps, just enough to see by. Families made hide-covered humps. The first hump he came across was Aku and Iona, wrapped in each other's arms.

Shonan felt a sharp pang, a blade to the heart. He stood over the sleeping couple. He knew he must be beyond exhausted, beyond the defenses he always lived behind, to feel such a pang. Before he could think, he reached into a shadow to find Meli's hand, and grasped only emptiness. It had been years since he'd forgotten himself that way, and he was embarrassed. His eyes lingered on his son's face at rest, his peace in Iona's arms.

He climbed further up the passage and found his daughter sprawled in an alcove, but not asleep, or ever able to sleep. He adjusted the hides to cover her better, sat down next to her, leaned back against a rock, and stared into the darkness.

32

Maloch watched in fascination. He followed at a distance, because the rocks were his safety, and on the grasslands he was exposed to being clubbed. Not that anyone would see him. To his eyes his enemies were only black shadows against a gray night.

It didn't make sense. Why would people being pummeled by wind and rain move uphill? Though not worthy rivals for himself, Shonan and Chalu were better leaders than this.

The shadows disappeared into the ground, one after another.

Maloch circled around the opening, for an opening it was, and took a look. He slid to the edge. No light came out, so it was safe. He avoided the big hole the human beings needed and slicked his way through cracks and dirt holes the size of a thumb. No person would look for a dragon master in such a place.

Where the entryway came into the open, at the very back of the sea cave, a guard stood tapping a club against the palm of one hand. He was a young man whose lips didn't quite close, pushed open by a tooth that stood a quarter sideways in his mouth. Maloch felt a spurt of revulsion. It was unnatural. Why did human beings have these faults? The women he chose for the sacrifice, the ones whose life-fire flamed along with his own—they were perfect. Except, of course, for the serious fault that afflicted all human beings. They wanted to be good, and thought others wanted to be good. Maloch himself wanted to be evil, in fact perfectly evil, as well as perfectly strong, perfectly powerful, perfectly dominant. Goodness was a silly choice, entertained by no other species. It was also a fatal ideal, one that made people the weaklings they were. The life-fire should be taken from every one of them. They did not deserve to be its bearers.

Maloch figured out easily how to slip by the sentry. What else were stony crevices and dirt passages for? When he could look up at the soldier, he slithered down the last few feet of the hidey-hole and stopped, puzzled.

He waited a short while and snaked a score of human paces toward some human beings he could smell. They turned out to be his own soldiers, bivouaced this far toward the back of the sea cave. So where were the Amasos going? Strange doings, tricky doings. And if they were slipping down the hidey-hole, they were passing within steps of his soldiers. They got away with it only because of the absolute darkness of the cave and the extraordinary whistling effect the wind made blowing over its mouth.

Maloch peered toward the sea end of the cave and saw nothing. If the tide eventually piddled in, his soldiers would have plenty of time to splash their way out.

He coiled up and waited at the bottom of the hidey-hole. But not much was happening, and Maloch was easily bored. He decided to take a chance. He flicked a pebble with his tail and hit the guard on the leg.

The man whirled.

Maloch said, "Hey!"

It was no risk, really. In the whistle of the wind the sentry probably wouldn't even recognize the sound as a voice, certainly wouldn't recognize the word.

But he did step carefully down the passage. In the dark he almost put a foot on Maloch—*That would have been worth your life, dolt!*—but the serpent oozed out of the way. And the guard disappeared.

Wild with curiosity, Maloch slid after him, taking care to rub along what seemed to be a solid rock wall. And then it wasn't solid. In fact, two walls overlapped here without touching, leaving a slender space wide enough for most people.

Maloch turned along with this wall and eased around two corners.

Immediately in front of him stood the sentry, the old chief, and three men armed with clubs. Beyond them, up a hall, occasional stone lamps lit a soft way among sleeping figures.

I have found their hiding place!

He coiled and slithered back the way he came. Maloch was undoubtedly fast enough to defeat any attacker, but why risk getting bashed by a lucky swing?

I have found their hiding place!

Always good to know people's secrets, even if he didn't yet see how to use them.

Maloch reversed his track along the wall and through the trick opening. The young man with the crooked tooth followed, unknowing. Not that he could see anything in the darkness, including the serpent.

Maloch considered. His bias, in general, was to distribute death and destruction simply for the sake of being evil. That was his nature, and he liked it. He considered for a moment, though he wasn't customarily judicious. If he left this young

fool dead, the next sentry would be alarmed. He might call
Shonan. With the help of a lamp the war chief might find
the bite, or might not. Even if he did, he wouldn't be able to
figure what serpent could kill so quickly, and he would not
suspect Maloch. The Uktena preferred tearing people apart
with the power of his jaws and ripping their flesh with his
huge teeth. He was not a creature to be subtle.

At that moment the old chief, Chalu, suddenly stepped
through the slit and climbed up. "Kumu," he said, "you've
been on duty long enough. I'll take the watch for a while."

"But . . ."

"Kumu, obey orders."

The young man left. The old chief started to raise his
head into the air, realized how violent the storm still was,
and sat down.

How delicious. The enemy's chief, so easy. So the serpent
slithered close, coiled, eyed the tender flesh between Chalu's
ankle and heel, and sank his teeth there.

The chief shouted and swept his club in that direction,
though he was much too slow. He stomped around a little,
cursing, which no one heard over the great whistle of the sea
cave. Then he began to gasp, next to wheeze. He fell down,
clawing the air, as though to stuff it down his gullet.

Maloch stayed to the very end, enjoying the spectacle.

33

It began as wind. It aroused itself far out on the water-everywhere, farther away even than the width of the world, from this very shore to the mountains that held the people's villages, and beyond them to the rolling hills where the Tree of Life and Death marked the western boundary of all the lands the Galayi knew. For all this distance and more, the wind whisked along the surface of the sea and urged the waters toward the shore. The mischief-maker was friction—the rubbing of the wind raised the water into waves, and then into higher swells, and finally into great troughs and summits that frothed with anger.

Imagine a man holding one end of a long rope in his hand. The rest of it, perhaps as long as ten men are tall, stretches away from him on the ground. The man raises his hand high, readying to unleash power, and then he slashes the cord down. It reacts like a whip—the energy runs through it, sending a curling wave from one end to the other.

On a gargantuan scale, a similar energy was gathering itself far out on the ocean, the child of the hurricane. It sailed as the storm winds blew, straight toward the Amaso people and the Brown Leaf warriors. In its magnificence, in its splendid power, it thought of human beings no more than does an earthquake.

Oghi lay awake and wondered whether the great surge of seawater would come. Only his great-grandfather had been caught in the midst of a hurricane, so Oghi had no more than memories of childhood tales as guides. Oghi no longer told the Amaso his stories, because people thought them the waggings of the tongues of foolish old men. He knew the Brown Leaves had no experience of such a monster wave, either. They lived on a well-protected bay and behind a row of barrier islands.

From time to time Oghi trembled. This wave, if it came, would coincide with high tide, and then . . .

In the sea cave the Brown Leaves were beginning to feel the incoming tide. It sloshed up the sandy floor of the cave and made them uncomfortable enough to get up and start trudging outside, grumbling as they went. They were weary of the whistle-roar, and getting soaked made their tempers worse. Outside the winds were stiff, but not as horrific as the ones that followed the period of utter calm, the blasts that chased them into the cave in the first place. The first soldiers outside looked at each other and smiled grimly. Which was worse, that damn racket or these bludgeoning winds? It was a toss-up.

Now back in his dragon form, Maloch positioned himself on top of the cliffs just above the entrance and yelled to his fighters as they emerged. "Go to the end of the beach," he bellowed, "then double back onto the top of the cliffs. Tomorrow we'll hold the high ground." The soldiers staggered forward into the wind, thinking they might pay attention to him and they might not.

Maloch had his battle plan. Surely the Amaso fighters would not try to lift themselves one by one out of the hidey-hole. If they did, his men would accept the invitation to cut them down one at a time. If the Amasos came charging out of the sea cave onto the beach, his men would reverse their luck and show them how it felt to be on the beach in heavy fire from above.

Maloch the Uktena was in high dudgeon.

About half of his army had dragged itself out of the cave when the wave hit.

Its crest smashed the top of the cliffs. Half the army went topsy-turvy back into the cave, churning head over heels in the turbulent waters, with no idea which direction air might be. It didn't matter, because the surging sea filled the tube of the cave completely.

The men already on the beach got slammed into the cliffs, though only spray broke over the lip.

In the cave and among the rocks, rattlesnakes and copperheads eeled out of their dens, desperate for air. Wildly, they fanged everything that moved.

On the beach Mor was lifted like a chip of bark and slammed crooked nose first into the cliffs. His nose, facial bones, and skull all cracked like a hammered nut.

The man next to him flew into the rocks with his other end first. His pelvis shattered, and splinters of the bones cut his guts to pieces.

Maloch was knocked backward by the foamy top of the wave, but managed to scramble away from the rage of tons of seawater.

To the north the waves bashed their way up the river, reversing the flow. It roared across the tidal plains, tearing bushes and all but the biggest trees out of the ground. It whisked away the Amaso huts like leaves, leaving no signs even of where people's homes had stood. The flood charged all the way to the inland hills, deposited every kind of flotsam there, and slowly receded toward its oceanic home.

When the wave smashed against the rear of the sea cave,

it clobbered the emergence slit and pounded the great slab blocking the way. Probably it was the slit itself that stood strongest against the waters, because the wave lost force in turning its corners. It still hit the slab hard enough to knock it half way down. Water slurped around both sides.

Oghi got inundated. He made a quick change to sea turtle form and swam to the surface.

Higher up the passage, Aku and Iona got swamped. They grabbed each other and treaded water.

Above them the passage inclined steeply. Some people got splashed, but no worse.

Oghi, Aku, and Iona swam to high ground.

Shonan walked briskly down to them. "What happened?"

"No idea," said Aku.

"My great-grandfather said that one huge wave comes with a hurricane," said Oghi. "This must have been it. The sea cave is probably full of water, the village knocked flat."

"The Brown Leaves?"

"Very few people out there could have survived." Oghi hesitated. "It's best not to guess. We'll see in the morning."

"Why didn't you warn me?" said Shonan.

"What my great-grandfather told me, well, no one believes it." Now he gained confidence. "I did tell you to block the emergence slit."

"Let's go look."

On the way to the slit, they met Kumu and the other three soldiers with clubs knee-deep in water. Next they almost stepped into a small brigade of snakes escaping the liquid.

Shonan hollered, "Every man come quick! Bring clubs!"

A dozen men whacked away at snakes until their backs hurt, and until the water seeped away.

Shonan rested, leaning on his club. "What are we going to see in the morning?" he asked Oghi.

"I have no idea."

"Except for one thing," said Shonan.

"What's that?" asked Aku.

"Maloch," said Shonan. "He's alive, and he's waiting for us."

Oghi nodded. "Yes."

34

The rays of the morning sun shot into the cave—it was a slaughterhouse. The great wave and the tide had slid back to the infinite water-everywhere, leaving no comment but bodies. Shonan, Aku, Oghi, and a phalanx of soldiers walked through the carnage, nauseated. Brown Leaf bodies were mashed and mangled where they'd been flung against the rough rock walls. Skulls were crushed, legs snapped, arms twisted into impossible shapes, rib cages smashed. Most corpses were snake-bitten. The Amaso had to be careful where they stepped, because some snakes still squirmed among the dead bodies.

"I think they all drowned," said Shonan.

"This cave—this tube," said Oghi, "was full of water for a long time."

"The whole damn ocean tried to jam its way in," said Shonan. "Aku, will you count the bodies?"

But Aku had no heart for it. When they got to the seaward end, Aku told his father, "Fifty-something, I think."

Shonan nodded. "If we meet any enemies out there," he said, "run back in here." He flicked his eyes across their faces and said what didn't need saying. "Damn well do not go down the little hidey-hole and give it away." He paused. "If we see the Uktena, turn your back and run like hell. It's bright out there." As an afterthought, he said, "Everyone got his blindfold?"

Everyone but Oghi did. Shonan gave him another one.

The beach told the story of the cave again, except that the Brown Leaves hadn't drowned—they'd been crushed against the stony cliffs. Maybe a dozen were still half alive. Shonan walked among them, ramming the point of his spear deep into the chest of each one that groaned or stirred or seemed to breathe.

Aku was appalled. He noticed that his father was murmuring something. "What are you saying?"

"The prayer that sends a true warrior to the Darkening Land," Shonan said.

Aku walked in silence.

"Ending their suffering is a kindness," said Shonan.

❖

On top of the cliffs, in his coral serpent form, Maloch lay in a crevice between rocks and watched his enemies walk their triumph. Except that they had accomplished nothing—the sea had done everything.

Maloch regretted that his army had stumbled into the storm at the wrong moment. But that would not stand in the way of his real purpose here. He wanted to gobble up the life-fire of the young hero who knew not his own power, Aku, son of Shonan, and while he was at it the life-fire of the father as well. Strong in spirit, both of them. He looked down on his victims with satisfaction. Their ignorance pleased him. The thought of conquering alone, himself against all the Amaso warriors, pleased him even more. He needed no army to conquer his enemies.

As for the Brown Leaf people back in their village? He did not need them. He had the guile and the dominance to

take over any village and make it his own. He smiled to himself. Even Amaso.

❖

Aku, Shonan, Oghi, and their soldiers picked their way to
the north end of the beach and gaped across the river at
their town. The ocean had turned it to rubble. Their hearts
sank.

"You want to go over and inspect it?" Shonan asked Aku.

"Not right now."

Oghi added gently, "There's nothing to inspect."

They studied the landscape, the tidal flats, the river and its
bottoms, their fields of corn, the plains beyond. All the way
to the foothills in the distance, all was devastation.

Then Oghi voiced it for everyone. "Where's Maloch?"

They stared at each other.

Suddenly Aku said, "I've got to get back to Salya."

❖

Maloch didn't see the Amaso leaders turn and head back to
the sea cave. He was busy taking a new form. In a cave, who
would be suspicious of a bat? Who would worry about a
bat? Who would think a bat might be the most terrible of
enemies?

He extended his new wing–hands and took pleasure in
the feel of the membranes stretching between the bones.
He looked around. Though his vision was somewhat dim, he
would have an amazing sense of every obstacle he flew near.
If he winged his way through a gang of swinging clubs, for
instance, his ability to detect flailing stone heads would guide
him through untouched. He had a sharp sense of smell and
excellent hearing. He could sense the warmth of any living
being nearby. Surely a bat was a perfect adaptation to the

darkness of a cave, and all the people therein who intended him harm?

He flew to the hidey-hole. Carefully, he crawled along the roof above the guard, someone he didn't recognize who'd replaced the chief. Maloch smiled to himself at the memory of the chief's final throes.

He glanced at the sentry's face and saw the fool was asleep. But even awake, why would a sentry get excited about a bat? Or, in the half-darkness, even notice a bat?

Still, Maloch didn't like ineptitude. He decided that, as a favor to Shonan, he would punish this incompetent. He landed delicately on the man's shirt where it covered his shoulder. Then he bit the neck ever so gently. The man felt nothing, probably would have felt nothing even if he'd been awake. But the teeth injected a terrible poison that Maloch had concocted. In a few days the man would develop a raging thirst, go crazy, and suffocate.

Maloch flew back to the ceiling and crawled through the emergence slit. He was less visible, he thought, when he merely crept along. He looked ahead. The passage showed the soft glow of lamps. He winged his way silently for a few paces, crawled, and winged again. Slowly, he made his way past sodden bedding, scattered belongings, and other chaos wrought by the great wave. Maloch reveled in chaos.

Eventually, the passage opened out into a great room with a high ceiling. This was the spot for Maloch. Up he flew and into a large, dark hole where the wall had crumbled away from the ceiling. Here he could see without being seen, and with a little maneuvering recreate himself into dragon form.

He looked around and observed little of interest. The wave had not splashed its way this far into the cave. Women were making tea and breakfast, and everything was orderly. The light from the horn lamps played with the shadows and lent the room a certain beauty. Beauty made Maloch shudder, but he knew how to destroy it.

He looked for Salya. His plan was to attack her, or seem to, and create an uproar. That would bring her brother and father running. A rush to death. To him Salya was no more than a fly to brush away. This foray was to suck in the life-fires of Aku and Shonan and zoom away, boosted in power.

The difficulty was that he didn't yet see Salya. *Damned eyesight.*

Just then Aku, Shonan, Oghi, and some soldiers walked in. In the hole Maloch quivered with excitement.

❖

Aku strode ahead, leaving the others behind. Some soldiers drifted off toward their families, and others walked into the passage beyond the great hall to their own camps, in a passageway that led to the closest of the uphill exits. Aku slipped through the grove of stone trees, past the guard Fuyl, and into the chamber where his twin lay in endless half-death.

Salya was ever unchanged. Aku felt impatient with himself for even noticing that. Since they found her in the Underworld, she hadn't altered a whit, nor would she ever, not until he helped her. Kumu sat next to her, holding her hand. Her lover sat with Salya at every opportunity, always touching her, as though to pass his own warmth into her lifeless form. Kumu's eyes looked hollow and vacant. Aku caught a glimmer, in that look, of how he would feel if Iona lay dead, and their child dead inside her. He blinked at the horror.

Oghi came into the chamber, his sympathetic eyes on the husband and wife to be.

"*Maloch!*"

Aku took a moment to register the voice, his father's, and what it meant. He was a step behind Kumu and Fuyl, sprinting through the stone tree trunks and into—

Maloch the Uktena dominated the great hall. He looked half as tall as the chamber and wide as a huge boulder. Women were scattering in all directions, shooing or carrying their children. Aku was glad to see that the men were padding toward Maloch—uncertain and hesitant but on the advance. They wore their blindfolds, but Maloch's diamond eye sent out only the barest glimmer. The stone lamps offered too little light to feed it.

Maloch's enormous mouth yawned open for a roar that deafened everyone, and reverberated in the chamber a long time, a weapon that itself stunned most of the warriors.

Fuyl stepped forward and hurled a dart from his spear thrower into the monster's maw. Maloch turned his head and it glanced off his teeth.

Shaking his spear, Kumu ran behind the monster and toward the tail, as if he was going to climb the beast. The tail flicked. Kumu skidded screaming toward the nearest wall and hit with a thud.

Aku stepped back among the stone trees, made a lightning change into war eagle shape, and flew out shrieking. He winged his way clockwise, to draw the beast's head away from the side of his heart. The shriek seized Maloch's attention, and the great head followed Aku.

Fuyl hurled a second dart, and it knocked a fang out of the side of Maloch's mouth. The dragon snapped out a bark louder than a tree crashing to earth.

Aku flapped behind Maloch. Not all the motion of his feathers was flight—some was terror.

Aku saw his father circle to the side where Maloch wasn't following Aku with his head. Shonan meant to get at the heart. Kumu was on his feet and circling the opposite way.

Aku screeched and flew straight above the tail and the spine and landed at the base of Maloch's neck, talons gripping the ridge.

Maloch bent his head hard to reach the war eagle but couldn't. He flailed at the eagle with one of his short forearms, then the other—he missed both times. He roared hideously. Aku's nerves and feathers fluttered.

Now the dragon turned the cave into an echo chamber of bellows. Roar crisscrossed roar between the stone walls. Hearts quailed. Minds got confused.

Oghi grabbed someone's spear and ran to Maloch's front. He threw it hard at the monster's neck, but didn't even puncture the scales. Maloch swept his head the other way, and Oghi tumbled across the floor as if he was falling downhill.

Clinging to the dragon's back ridge, Aku saw that the turn of Maloch's head pointed his eyes toward Shonan. The chief charged, his spear aimed at the scale protecting the heart.

Maloch snapped his huge head that way. Shonan flew, butted by the big snout and raked by the teeth. One side of his body drizzled blood from shoulder to hip.

Aku screamed in terror. The monster drowned out his screech with a crow of triumph.

Aku feared that the monster's greatest weapon was his roar. Somehow Fuyl gathered himself and launched his last dart and drove it deep into the soft palate.

Aku clung to the ridge of the monster's neck with one

foot, bent down, and pried up a scale with the other. *Let this be the one!* he cried to himself. He sank his beak into the flesh.

Maloch yowled. For the first time he sounded hurt.

Somehow Shonan got to his feet.

Aku ate.

Fuyl rushed to where Aku had his beak jammed in. At full charge he rammed his spear toward the same exposed flesh, but the dragon whirled, snapped, and bit his foe in half.

Shonan crawled toward Maloch on all fours.

Aku tore flesh as deep and hard as he could.

Kumu ran forward, spear raised. He slipped in the dragon's blood and slid directly beneath the great belly. The dragon mouth stretched toward Kumu but didn't reach. Kumu ran out between a back leg and the tail.

Shonan staggered to his feet and mustered all his waning strength for one running thrust toward Maloch's heart. The spear point skidded along Aku's beak and sank in next to it.

The great beast shuddered. It screeched out a cry greater even than all the wails that had assaulted Aku in the Underworld.

Maloch fell sideways onto Shonan. The spear's shaft hit the ground square, and the monster's bulk drove it deeper.

Crushed by the great weight, Shonan cried out life and death.

Aku hovered in the air for an uncomprehending moment. Then he sailed beyond his father's body and began the transformation. When he looked human again, the red and green flutes were, as always, in his hand.

He ran to his father. From behind he heard Oghi calling loudly but didn't understand the words.

Aku knelt in his father's blood. For a moment he fumbled

with the flutes—he couldn't remember which one raised the dead. Of course, the red one. He put it to his lips.

Oghi, Kumu, and Iona knelt in the same blood. In their arms they bore the body of Salya.

"My wife first," said Kumu.

"Your sister first," said Oghi.

"Your twin first," said Iona.

Aku screamed—what words he didn't know.

"Take care of Salya," someone said.

Aku couldn't figure out who was talking.

A low voice: "Take care of Salya."

Praise be the Immortals! His father's lips were moving.

"You will die," said Aku. "By the time I play the song for Salya, you will bleed to death."

A whisper: "Take care of Sal . . ."

"You are my father."

Less than a whisper: "Take care of Sa . . ."

Aku screamed again. He felt like he was being split in half.

Oghi snatched the flutes out of Aku's hands. The sea turtle man and Kumu took Aku by the arms and led him to the mouth of Maloch, still open, its last breaths gasping out. Then they picked up Salya and laid her where the breath ran over her, warm and moist, bearing the spirit. Oghi handed Aku the green flute.

Aku's soul quaked as the earth sometimes quaked. Half conscious, half transported, he put the green flute to his mouth, looked into Salya's face, and played.

His eyes closed, Aku saw it even as he heard it. The music floated, but it also spun. It drifted, yet it whirled. It spoke of timeless beauty, yet it danced. It changed colors, beginning in the green of the earliest leaf of spring, warming to the yellow of a gentle blossom, deepening to salmon, and twisting itself into every color at once, scarlet, lavender, gold, and the blue of the loveliest twilights. Yet always it seemed frosted with green, a green that brought back to Aku the sense of promise he got from early grasses after a long winter.

He did not see Salya begin to move. Her lips compressed, then opened. Her tongue ran along them.

Aku played.

Salya's eyelids fluttered, opened, shut, opened, shut.

Aku played.

On Salya's hands random fingers waggled. She bent a knee.

Aku breathed the last of his song through the flute. He held the instrument across his legs.

"Look," said Iona.

Aku looked, and saw Salya's eyes gazing at him.

He kissed her lips gently.

Weeping, Kumu took her in his arms.

Aku walked to Shonan, knelt, and saw that his father's eyes were fixed, unmoving. Aku could not bear to look into his father's face again. He took up the red flute and marched into a grave and stately music.

At the end of the song, Aku said, "I have failed him."

"I don't think so," said Oghi.

Aku touched the slack face of his progenitor and shed a tear. "Father, come back to us."

He walked over and started to sit beside Salya. Instead Kumu stepped in front of him. The warrior of the crooked tooth held out a prize to Aku—the eye of the dead Uktena, the diamond that foretold the future.

"You earned it," said Kumu.

Aku cupped it in his hands.

"Wha . . . ?" Salya said. Aku and Kumu sat down next to her. "Who? What? Tell . . ."

It was such a long story. Aku, Oghi, and Iona took turns telling it while Kumu held her. Salya remembered walking down the dune. She remembered one whack on the head, and thought maybe a second whack sent her into the darkness. She remembered nothing else.

They couldn't tell her about the ceremony where her life-fire was stolen—none of them had seen it. They could tell her how she looked when they found her in the Underworld. They told her some of what they saw and heard down there in the Darkening Land—the people writhing in agony, the imaginary causes of their pain.

Here Salya perked up and began to ask some questions. They promised her all the answers tomorrow, when she had rested.

When she protested that she'd had months of rest, Kumu said, "And now I'm going to see that you get some real rest."

Oghi went to check on Shonan.

The others told Salya about the Great Dusky Owl, the Tree of Life and Death, how Yah-Su died, and how the Master of Life and Death determined that the other adventurers had passed the test and could return to life, carrying Salya. How they bore her for many days' walks, from the Emerald Cavern to the Tusca village to this spot.

Then, in considerable detail, with pride stirred into grief, Aku told how they'd fought Maloch the Uktena and killed the monster.

Salya laid her head back against Kumu, took his hand, closed her eyes, and seemed to be at peace.

Footsteps grabbed Aku's attention, and he turned toward Oghi. In front of the sea turtle man, his steps a little tenative, walked Shonan.

Aku jumped up and embraced his father. He trembled in the big arms.

Shonan broke the moment. "All right, I give in." He chuckled and patted his son's back. "I guess maybe magic works."

Aku said, "You know it does."

"Hey, you two," said Salya.

They separated. Shonan squatted and took his daughter's hand. Tears ran down both faces.

"There's one more thing," Salya said.

"Yes," said Aku and Shonan at once.

"I want to know."

"Yes?"

"What took you so long?"

Aku and Shonan laughed and clapped each others' backs.

EPILOGUE

The next moon was momentous—Aku knew he would remember every day separately, an occasion to be honored.

The people of Amaso first elected new leaders. Oghi was named chief and Shonan war chief. Because Aku possessed the diamond eye, they chose him as seer.

Oghi called for the rebuilding of the huts brought down by the storm.

Shonan recommended sending runners to ask the Equanis for help.

Emboldened by his new position, Aku said he had a better idea. Everyone liked it. He led a group of Amaso men and women to the Brown Leaf village and met with the women, children, and elderly people left there. Since they were defenseless with their warriors dead, and facing hungry moons, he proposed that they join the Amaso people.

The Brown Leaves instead offered their own houses to the Amasos, stout houses of wattle and daub, a bay better protected from the ocean, and the security of a joined community.

Aku immediately transformed himself into an eagle, flew back to Amaso, and gave the word to everyone. They applauded the offer.

Shonan said, "I set out to add fifty families to our tribe, and my son has added another hundred and fifty."

Aku was flattered, but more impressed with what had to be done. He, Shonan, and Oghi organized the trek to the Brown Leaf town—every Amaso went.

On the seventh evening they made camp and looked down at the distant village of their onetime enemies. "It's a good place," Oghi said to Aku and Iona, "better protected against storms than our old village, and with more fields to plant."

The three of them rolled up in their elk hides. Aku looked distracted.

"What's on your mind?" said Oghi.

"Two weddings to be held at the ceremony."

Iona squeezed his hand.

"What's really on your mind?" said the sea turtle man.

"My responsibilities," said Aku.

"Which ones?" said Iona. Her mind was on their coming child.

"To be a good seer, I have to go back to the Emerald Cavern many times and learn much more."

Iona sat up and slapped him lightly on the shoulder. "To be a good husband you need to give me lots of loving, raise our kids right, and hunt enough food for all of us. Think you can keep your mind on that?"

Aku kissed her, then caressed her. He said, "I don't think that will be a problem."